THE MAN IN THE SHADOWS

THE MAN IN THE SHADOWS

Alys Clare

SEVERN
HOUSE

First world edition published in Great Britain and the USA in 2022
by Severn House, an imprint of Canongate Books Ltd,
14 High Street, Edinburgh EH1 1TE.

Trade paperback edition first published in Great Britain and the USA in 2022
by Severn House, an imprint of Canongate Books Ltd.

severnhouse.com

British Library Cataloguing-in-Publication Data
A CIP catalogue record for this title is available from the British Library.

ISBN-13: 978-0-7278-2304-5 (cased)
ISBN-13: 978-1-4483-0749-4 (trade paper)
ISBN-13: 978-1-4483-0748-7 (e-book)

All Severn House titles are printed on acid-free paper.

Typeset by Palimpsest Book Production Ltd.,
Falkirk, Stirlingshire, Scotland.
Printed and bound in Great Britain by
TJ Books, Padstow, Cornwall.

For Richard and Ratty, who told me
about the river and the old hop garden.

PROLOGUE

Lewes Gaol, early morning, December 1880

He couldn't stop shivering.

They'd told him he could dress in his own clothes today, and he'd put on a vest and his warm flannel shirt under the shabby old suit he'd worn in court. His mother had sponged and pressed the suit before sending it in to him, and taken such care to put a sharp crease in the trousers. He pictured her hands with the knobbly joints holding the old flatiron. Then he tried to think about something else.

Perhaps she'd thought it would help if he looked spruce and smart. 'You were wrong there, old Ma,' he muttered. He was hit with a sudden, frighteningly undermining rush of emotion. He tried and failed to smile.

He sat on the hard bunk. Waiting.

He heard a clock strike the quarter hour.

He waited.

Suddenly there was the sound of smartly marching feet in the corridor outside. Two, no three pairs. Snap, snap, snap, in perfect unison like soldiers marching, the metal segs on their heels ringing on the stone flags. The door was unlocked and flung open, revealing the warder, his deputy and a small man with a bright, expectant expression. He was clad in brown and he had several leather straps in his hand. Quickly, neatly, the little man in brown had the prisoner pinioned, hands behind him, arms tight to his sides. Then the two warders took up their positions each side of him and, with the little man skipping along behind, briskly they set off on the short walk along the corridor. From somewhere he'd been lurking in wait, the clergyman emerged to join the procession. It was the other one; the one who'd replaced the regular chaplain. This man was young, there were beads of sweat on his upper lip despite the cold, and the voice that quietly murmured the continuous litany of prayer was taut with nerves.

Then they were outside in the chill, clean air of the yard. It was an irregular space with a garden of sorts in the far corner. Someone had told the prisoner that they grew celery there. The prisoner had a sudden memory: pale celery stalks growing inside an earthenware tube. 'Blanching,' said his mother's voice. For a moment he was a small boy again in the sleepy summer countryside, the sun warm on his back and birds singing in the trees.

Then he glanced up and saw the high walls.

Lowering his eyes, he looked across the yard, and there it was, the terrifying edifice he'd heard them building yesterday: two heavy wooden posts joined by a sturdy crosspiece with a heavy staple set in it from which hung a long, thick rope. The prisoner's eyes skittered wildly around, wanting to look at anything but that. The clergyman, noticing this, hurriedly stepped in front of him. Not quite quickly enough: before he blocked the view, the young man had caught a glimpse of the black rectangle dug into the earth over in the deep shadows under the high wall.

He managed to walk up the steps unaided. He had been utterly determined to do that.

Then he was standing on the wooden trapdoor. Beneath it was a brick chamber, another, smaller one beside it. There was a large lever beside the trapdoor.

The clergyman was praying more fervently now.

The little man in brown stepped daintily forward and fastened the last of his three straps around the prisoner's legs. The young man closed his eyes tight shut, his heart beating so fast that he thought it would burst.

Nothing happened.

He was aware of the little man standing right in front of him. He could smell him: soap, and a faint hint of bacon. *He's managed more in the way of breakfast than me then*, the prisoner thought.

Frantic now, wondering what was meant to happen next, the prisoner opened his eyes.

He looked down. He was tall, and the little man only came up to his chin. The little man had a white linen object in his hands. 'Sorry, lad, but you'll have to bend down,' he said. His voice was so kind, so gentle . . .

Obediently the prisoner bent towards him.

The object was a hood, and quickly, almost roughly, the little man pulled it down over the prisoner's head.

A little thought tripped across the young man's mind: *He's not really being rough*, it went. *He's just trying to be quick, for he does not want to prolong this moment.*

The rope was now around his neck.

The clergyman, appreciating perhaps that they were only waiting for him to finish his prayers, speeded up. He was gabbling now.

The prisoner counted. He reached fifteen, sixteen . . . Briefly he felt someone hold his captive hand: the little man in brown, he thought.

A clock began to strike the hour.

It was nine o'clock.

There was a thump as the lever was pulled back. The bolt supporting the trapdoor slipped smoothly back, the trapdoor fell away with a loud crash and the condemned man dropped ten feet down into the dark pit below.

The young man's neck broke instantly and cleanly. The body spun in a lazy half turn and was still. Steam rose from it, and there was the sound of liquid splattering on the brick floor of the pit.

There was still business to conduct, a rigid procedure to follow: there must be an inquest on the body, for which townspeople had been selected as jurymen. Together with those who had witnessed the execution, the officials of the prison and the coroner, they must determine a cause of death. First, though, the jurymen were taken to view the body. Some demonstrated an inappropriate, macabre eagerness, disguising it as firm-jawed determination to do their duty as good citizens whose upstanding, law-abiding character could not have been more different from the dead man. Some, clearly hating these terrible moments in the cold, clammy little room stinking of sweat and urine, kept their distance from the corpse in its cheap coffin on the trestle and barely looked at it. Then they were escorted to the prison's committee room, and after a brief but solemn discussion, the expected verdict was pronounced. The prison governor stated the prisoner's identity in a loud, clear voice. The surgeon pronounced in a quieter voice that death had been by hanging.

Then it was over. Rapidly the committee room emptied as the assembled company hurried out into the weak December sun.

The priest was the last to leave.

He wished he could go back to the body on the trestle, for he desperately needed a few quiet minutes alone with the dead man. He was a replacement for the prison chaplain, who usually performed this grim duty but who was in bed with a fractured femur, and he had got the timing of his prayers wrong. He wanted to say he was very sorry for making the poor man wait. Those seventeen seconds had felt like an eternity to him, so the dear Lord above alone knew what they'd been like for the prisoner.

He'd asked, but the prison governor had said it was impossible.

The priest stood outside in the street, staring at the formidable size and strength of the prison doors, now very firmly closed. Then with a deep sigh he walked hurriedly away.

ONE

August 1881

S ummer is at its height, and the weather is persistently, relentlessly hot. The millions of assorted people who inhabit London in greater or lesser degrees of affluence and comfort are sick of the heat. It was wonderful at first, for the winter had been cold and seemed determined to go on for ever, but now the pattern of day after day of a brilliant white sun in a pale blue sky without a single cloud has become as wearisome as the apparent eternity of bitter wind and icy pavements.

In the office of the World's End Bureau at number 3, Hob's Court, Chelsea, Lily Raynor has propped doors open to provide a breeze, although she is all too aware that this breeze is only a figment of her imagination. As her assistant Felix Wilbraham muttered a short time ago, not quite far enough under his breath for Lily not to hear, it is as hot as the Mississippi delta.

She has no idea if he opines from personal experience, and she certainly isn't going to ask. In any case, the house is probably as cool as anywhere, for it is a couple of centuries old and solidly built, with stout walls and high ceilings. Indeed, Mrs Clapper – inherited by Lily from her grandparents along with the house – has found several jobs to occupy herself some time beyond the hour she usually finishes for the day, and has been heard to remark more than once that she'd rather be here working and relatively comfortable than back home sweltering in her own parlour.

It is now almost half past five, and from the sounds echoing through to the office from the back quarters, Mrs Clapper appears to have embarked on one of her turn-outs. Lily imagines the old stone floor covered in towering stacks of pans, baking trays, sieves, colanders, piles of dinner plates and rows of cups, and Mrs Clapper's bony backside bouncing up and down as she vigorously brushes out the very last speck of dust from right at the back of the last shelf . . .

Somehow the mental picture makes Lily feel even hotter.

With a firm resolve she returns to her account book. This is enough to cheer her up, for the past six months have seen a marked improvement in the fortunes of the World's End Bureau. She reckons that it will not be too long before she is earning enough money from the Bureau to enable her to give notice to her tenant. This will be a joyous day, because the tenant is the Little Ballerina and she has been an ongoing thorn in Lily's side pretty much since she arrived. She pays her rent most of the time, although always grudgingly and invariably late, moaning in her idiosyncratic English that she is only a poor dancer, alone in this cruel world, all the time darting narrow-eyed, accusatory glances at Lily and muttering in Russian. Lily is quite sure these mutterings would translate into something on the lines of *You are a wealthy woman living in this huge house that your grandparents left to you and you ought to take pity on a poor foreigner and not demand this ludicrous amount of rent every month.*

Increasingly, Lily asks herself if she wouldn't rather make some stringent economies and do without both the rent and the Little Ballerina, but since the first of these economies would almost certainly be dispensing with the hard-working, fanatically loyal Mrs Clapper – who probably would not survive without her wages from Lily – she always answers her own question with a firm *no*.

Lily is pretty sure whom to thank for this increase in Bureau custom, for in the course of an investigation[1] at the start of the year, she had occasion to comply with a very delicate request from a man of great importance in the land. He told her that, in return for compromising her principles, he would pass the message among his colleagues and friends that Lily's private investigation business was efficient, trustworthy and highly discreet and had his personal recommendation, and it appears that he has been as good as his word.

While no one running their own organization would

---

[1] See *The Outcast Girls.*

complain of an influx of clients, all the same Lily – and Felix too, she suspects – has become very tired of the sort of cases that have been brought to their door. Rich people, it appears, are just as likely as their poor compatriots to tire of their wife or husband and yearn for the greener grass, although it is only the rich who can do something about it; the poor have to stumble along in claustrophobic misery and the bitter nightly confines of a narrow marriage bed until one spouse dies.

And the rich tire, and yearn, and do something about it in what seems to Lily an unending trail of smartly dressed, attractive, confident men (and sometimes women) who keep turning up on the Bureau's doorstep. And, in the quiet seclusion of Lily's Inner Sanctum with the door to the outer office firmly closed, they tell their tales and make their demands. One of the many eye-opening surprises is that, no matter what they have done, how appallingly they have behaved, what havoc and emotional pain this abandoning of a wife (or husband) is going to cause, almost without exception those who engage the World's End Bureau to obtain their freedom for themselves clearly believe they are entitled to have it.

Even Lily, who has by no means led a sheltered life, is regularly amazed at the depths to which some of her clients have sunk. Sometimes, when recounting the details of the interview to Felix (because the firmly closed door is purely to save the client's blushes), she has to force herself to repeat what she's just been told. Sometimes he is incredulous (the man and his wife's King Charles spaniel); once he actually burst out laughing (the enormously fat minor royal who described a love chair which had been made at his request and which he swore was the same in virtually every detail as the one employed by the Prince of Wales in a Paris brothel).

The power of sex, Lily now reflects as she tots up a last column and inks in the total, can never be underestimated, and she wonders if the husband of the most recent client has yet felt the first stirrings of regret; if not, it can only be a matter of time. He is a titled man in his late sixties, a genial, readily recognizable public figure who fell for his granddaughter's governess. Now his clever wife is bent on divorcing him and she appears to have no notion whatsoever of discretion. Surely he must be wondering if the admittedly beautiful governess was worth it, Lily thinks, for the rather embarrassing evidence of wrongdoing provided by the World's End Bureau has proved his guilt as decisively as if he'd been caught with his trousers round his ankles (he very nearly was). His coldly furious wife took first-class legal advice that robbed her husband of one of his houses, a great deal of his fortune and virtually every last shred of his reputation.

The acquisition and the passing-on of that evidence, however, had dismayed both Lily and Felix. Glancing up at him now as he works at his desk in the outer office, Lily thinks they would both very much welcome a case that did not involve the over-indulged and not terribly moral rich . . .

Felix, she notes, is wearing his new lightweight summer suit. He has removed the jacket, which hangs on the back of his chair, and sits in waistcoat and rolled-up shirtsleeves. She smiles, for the new clothes are an outward symbol of their recent affluence; business has been so good that she has awarded them both a bonus.

With a silent reprimand to herself for daydreaming, she returns to her books.

Half an hour passes. Lily hears a nearby church clock strike six. Then the street door opens, there is a soft tap on the inner door and she hears a man's quiet voice, then Felix replying. From the friendly nature of the exchange, it seems the visitor is familiar, and after only a moment, Lily has identified him.

It is the Reverend Mr James Jellicote, vicar of St Cyprian's Church, over the river and on the far side of Battersea Park. She and Felix met him in the course of their first case together,[2] and in the intervening year and a half his life has changed considerably and – if the air of happy contentment that the vicar wears nowadays is anything to go by – very much for the better. He was married in May, and there is a rumour that his delightful young wife is looking particularly rosy at the moment.

But if his life is so blessed, Lily asks herself, then what is he doing here?

[2] See *The Woman Who Spoke to Spirits.*

She is rising to her feet to go and find out when Felix ushers James Jellicote into her office.

Are you busy? he mouths.

She shakes her head, saying as she does so, 'Mr Jellicote! How nice to see you. Can we offer you some tea?'

The vicar strides across the office to shake her proffered hand. 'Good to see you too, Miss Raynor. No tea, thank you, for this has been a visiting afternoon and I am already awash.'

Felix has drawn up two chairs, and Lily resumes her seat while both men make themselves comfortable. Felix has brought his slim black notebook and his little silver propelling pencil, and as he turns to a clean page, he says, 'Lily, Mr Jellicote thinks he has something for us.'

She knows that these words usually herald human misery of some sort or another. She knows she should be feeling regret and pity, wishing that whatever has brought a client to her Bureau had never happened and that they could go on peacefully living their normal uneventful life. But she can't help it: every time a new case turns up, she senses that thrill of excitement. And, briefly meeting Felix's clear hazel eyes, she suspects he feels exactly the same.

'Then please, Mr Jellicote,' she says calmly, turning to the vicar, 'tell us how we may help.'

He pauses for a moment, perhaps gathering his thoughts and deciding where to start. Then he says, 'You may recall, perhaps, my church's association with Lady Venetia Theobald's Mission to Limehouse?'

'Indeed.' The aim of the Mission, Lily remembers, is somewhat grandiosely and sensationally expressed in the litera-ture as *A Fight Against the Scourges of Lustful Practices, Illegitimate Births and Disease.* Laudable, of course, but Lily can never see the words without feeling someone is shouting at her and expecting her to wipe these evils out all by herself.

'I feel I should point out here that the Mission is not exclusively concerned with, er, with *prostitution.*' James Jellicote discreetly lowers his voice to a whisper for the final disreputable word. 'And, in fact, the distressing matter I am about to lay before you is nothing whatsoever to do with the evils of the flesh.'

Lily is about to protest that she is a professional and as prepared to confront the evils of the flesh, if not a great deal more so, as the next woman, but Felix catches her eye and minutely shakes his head. So instead she says mildly, 'Please, go on.'

James Jellicote pauses, frowning into the middle distance, and it is only after several moments that he resumes.

'I feel I should provide a little background,' he says apologetically, 'in order that you should fully understand. Is that acceptable?'

'Yes,' Lily and Felix say at the same time. Lily hears quite clearly the subtext, *Oh, do get on with it!*

'Oh. Ah, yes.' The vicar, who has clearly heard it too, recovers himself. Then, barely pausing for breath, he begins.

'You have heard, no doubt, of the dreadful happenings in Russia? The assassination of Tsar Alexander II, and the rumours that it was the work of foreign influences?'

Lily, who has been fully occupied with the affairs of the World's End Bureau and found little spare time for the study of international affairs, has only a vague notion of unspecified horror and brutality in that distant land. Felix, however, is much better informed: for one thing, he is well travelled and consequently of a more cosmopolitan nature than his employer, and for another, his landlord is a journalist called Marmaduke Smithers, and Marm always keeps his eyes and ears wide open.

'Yes,' Felix says, his face grave. 'A spark has been lit, and far too many have already died.'

'Indeed, and thousands more are on the move,' James Jellicote agrees. 'But when your house has been burned down, your synagogue attacked by armed militia and you fear for your life if you stay, what choice is there? And it is all *so wrong*,' he goes on passionately, 'for there is no evidence whatsoever that the Jews were responsible for the Tsar's death, and more than a little to suggest that this was a falsehood put about by the Russian press and based on the slimmest evidence, and—'

'Wasn't one conspirator of Jewish origins?' Felix interrupts.

James Jellicote brushes that aside. 'Oh, who can say the truth of it?' he demands. 'But it is always the way to blame the outsider, the foreigner,' he goes on, 'and on this wretchedly, shamefully flimsy evidence, pogrom after pogrom is now being launched, and thousands are reduced to abject poverty as they try to escape to safety. And where can safety be found? Answer me that if you will!'

His voice has risen steadily, and now, as he stops speaking, the echoes of his words take a moment or two to die away. 'I am sorry,' he mutters, clearly embarrassed. 'I did not come here to harangue you.'

'Why did you come, Mr Jellicote?' Lily asks gently. 'Please, tell us what we can do.'

He shoots her a grateful look, then says, 'The Mission runs a charitable ward for the destitute sick, and presently it has been expanded, and indeed a second ward opened, to care for immigrants arriving off the ships who have no knowledge of life here, little money and nowhere to go. In addition, many, of course, are also ill.' He pauses. 'It is tempting to observe the masses of those who need our help, and to baulk at the task and turn away. I feel that instead we must seek out how and where we are able to assist, and perhaps, by using our minds and our might to help the individual, so add a counterbalance to the vast evil over which we are powerless.'

'You have an individual in mind?' Lily smiles at him, and instantly he smiles back.

'Of course I do, Miss Raynor,' he says softly. 'A Russian woman of the Jewish faith, not long off the boat. I do not have the details – some terrible account of fleeing halfway across Russia to escape the violence of the pogroms, and I understand that members of her family died, or were killed, along the way.' He pauses, then goes on, 'She arrived in London with her young grandson, desperately sick. She collapsed on the quayside, and they bundled her up and took her off to the London Hospital in Whitechapel. When after a couple of days or so she came round and understood where she was, the first question she asked was, "Where is Yakov?", Yakov being her grandson. She went on asking, with increasing desperation, until finally and through roundabout means, the matter was referred to me and I made a few tentative enquiries. But I am not skilled in asking the right questions in the right places,' he said earnestly, leaning forward in his eagerness, 'whereas I know that you two are.' He looks from one to the other, his face eloquent with silent pleading.

'We—' Felix begins.

Taking this as encouragement, the vicar says, 'The boy – he's about eleven or twelve – was last seen on the quayside. Someone said he'd been approached by a man who was trying to help him, probably from either Barnardo's or the Poor Jews' Temporary Shelter, although there are other charitable organizations, and I'll give you the details. But the lad had no idea what was happening, he was scared and he'd lost sight of his grandmother, and he took fright, kicked his would-be helper in the shins and fled.'

'And you have no idea where he fled to?' Lily asks. Leaving us the entire East End, if not the whole country, in which to search for him, she adds silently.

As if he reads her mind, James Jellicote turns to her with a disarming grin. 'No, no idea at all,' he says. 'But I can provide a fair description.'

For the next few minutes Felix writes to James Jellicote's dictation. Observing, Lily reflects that the rigorous clerical training has produced a man who is able to amass his thoughts swiftly and express them efficiently and succinctly. Or, she adds with a private smile, perhaps these abilities were Mr Jellicote's forte to begin with.

Presently Felix leans back in his chair, flexes his fingers and flips back through the pages he has just covered in his neat, even hand. 'Yelisaveta, probably in her sixties, and grandson Yakov, about eleven, family name not known for certain but sounds like Hadzi-something, maybe Hadzibazy. Boy is thin, wiry, dressed in ragged clothes and broken shoes. Dark hair, drastically cut as if by someone shearing off filthy tangles. Intensely dark eyes. Sharp teeth.' He meets Lily's eyes, and there is a spark of humour in his. 'It would seem, would it not, that it wasn't only his feet that he lashed out with?'

'I believe I too would have defended myself with every

weapon at my disposal,' Lily says. Her heart has gone out to this poor unknown boy, for she can imagine only too clearly how frightened he must have been.

James Jellicote is watching her closely. 'You will try to find him, Miss Raynor?' he asks softly.

She nods firmly. 'Of course we will.'

He is standing up, clutching his hat. 'Now you are sure you have the details?' he says, turning to Felix. 'She is in the London Hospital in—'

'Whitechapel,' Felix interrupts. 'Yes, and I know where that is, thank you.'

The vicar looks faintly surprised at this unexpected knowledge of the East End. Lily smiles to herself, reflecting that, unlike her, he doesn't know about Felix's scrap-metal dealer grandfather in Limehouse.

'Ask at the front desk,' James Jellicote adds. 'I told them I'd approach you, and they'll be expecting you. Not assuming you'd agree, of course,' he goes on, his handsome face flushing slightly, 'but—'

'We quite understand, Mr Jellicote,' Lily says smoothly. 'We will do our best to reunite grandmother and grandson.' She walks round her desk as she speaks, gently but firmly ushering the vicar towards the door.

As he steps out into the street, she thinks that, with business concluded for the present, it would be correct to enquire about his wife. 'How is Mrs Jellicote?' she asks.

He turns back to her, his face illuminated by such joy that she is quite sure the rumours of a baby on the way are most likely true. 'She is blooming, thank you, Miss Raynor,' he breathes. Then, touchingly, he leans closer and whispers, 'Truly, I had no idea that life could be so magical.'

Then with a tip of his hat he springs down the steps and hurries away.

Felix must have overheard; the vicar's first remark, anyway. He has come through into the front office and now says with a grin, 'Albertina's expecting, then. The old biddies have it right.'

Lily sends him a repressive frown, of which he takes absolutely no notice.

*   *   *

The church clock strikes the quarter as Lily tidies away the last of her papers in preparation for closing up for the day. She is just about to suggest to Felix a plan for tomorrow – definitely to include one or other or both of them visiting the Russian woman in the hospital – when the knocker on the street door sounds loudly in two sharp raps.

'A last-minuter,' Felix says with a sigh. 'And Marm and I were planning on a pie and a pint in the Cow Jumped Over the Moon this evening. Ah, well.' He goes to open the door, and Lily sits down at her desk again.

This, she thinks, is likely to take some time: *last-minuter* is the name she and Felix have coined for the more nervous sort of client who has had to nerve him or herself to come to the Bureau; who quakes in horror and embarrassment at the very idea of spilling shameful secrets; and who, having been driven to this dramatic measure only by sheer desperation, turns up right at the end of the working day.

She hears a man's voice asking if this is the investigation bureau. Patiently Felix refrains from saying, *Yes of course it is, it says so on the brass plaque.* Apart from anything else, some of their clients aren't very good at reading. Instead he just says, 'It is. Please come in.'

Lily looks up as a young man in his twenties precedes Felix into the office. He is quite tall, powerfully built and strong-looking, of regular features and nondescript colouring. He is dressed in workman's clothes: canvas trousers, a navy blue pea coat, heavy boots, collarless shirt and a checked necker-chief at his throat. He turns his battered felt hat in his hands, which have clearly been washed but on which black dirt lingers under the fingernails.

'Sorry to come so late,' the young man says. 'Even as it is, I've had to bunk off work.' He adds in a rush, 'It's a relief to find you still here.'

He is sweating. Beads of moisture are popping out on his handsome face, and he mops at them with a large handkerchief. Since it is without doubt cooler inside the house than outside, Lily surmises that the perspiration is because he is very nervous.

'What work do you do, Mr . . . ?' she asks mildly. Felix has pulled the visitor's chair forward again, and invites him to sit down.

He does so, clutching the felt hat on his lap as if it were a lifeline.

'Docks,' he says succinctly. 'And it's Spokewright, Jared Spokewright.'

Felix, who has clearly also spotted the nerves, says in a friendly manner, 'Still very hot, isn't it? May I fetch you a cold glass of beer?'

Jared Spokewright looks up at him, an expression on his face suggesting whatever he had expected from a private enquiry agency, this wasn't it.

'Yes please,' he whispers. Felix nips out to the scullery, Lily hears a brief exchange with Mrs Clapper, and in no time he is back with a tray bearing three glasses of golden brown beer so cold that already condensation is forming on the outside of the glass; yet again Lily is grateful for an old house with a deep cellar that always feels chilly.

Lily takes a polite sip; Felix and their visitor a rather larger one. Then, hoping these pleasantries have allowed Mr Spokewright sufficient time to collect himself, she says, 'Now, how may the Bureau be of assistance?'

Very carefully he puts his glass down on her desk. It is almost empty. Then he takes a deep breath, squares his shoulders, looks her straight in the eye and announces, 'There's been a miscarriage of justice. Someone told me to come to you because you take on cases other folks don't care about. I've got money – I've been putting some by for the best part of a year – and I want you to sort it.'

She wonders who this someone could have been. She also wonders where he has heard the phrase *miscarriage of justice*. The way he spoke the words made them sound alien on his tongue. Then, cross with herself for her hasty judgement, she says courteously, 'Would you care to explain?'

Strong emotion seems to be searing through young Mr Spokewright. His face is working, he emits a gulp that might have been a suppressed sob, he fumbles once more for the handkerchief and presses it to his mouth. For the second time in half an hour, Lily is filled with pity. Whatever has happened, whatever this man has done, he is in deep distress.

He manages to control himself. Felix, who Lily judges is as affected as she is, asks quietly if he would like more beer but the young man shakes his head and mutters, 'Better not.'

Then, in a rush as if this is the only way he can get the words out, he says in an over-loud voice, 'They hanged my brother, they didn't ought to have done because he never did what they said, someone has to be brought to account because if he didn't someone else did and I've come to ask if you'll do it.'

As she absorbs this burst of words, part of Lily is thinking that, not long ago, she was wishing she and Felix could have a case that didn't involve the sordid extra-marital goings-on of spoilt rich people with an over-inflated sense of entitlement. You should have been more careful what you wished for, she tells herself, for now you seem to have two.

TWO

Having broken through the dam of shame and reticence, now young Jared Spokewright can't seem to stop talking.

'It was last September,' he begins, 'and we'd gone hop-picking down in Kent, just like we do every year, us and Ma and her sister and some of our other kin that's not so close and most of our neighbours and all. Always the same place, a little village called Crooked Green, and the same farm, Nightingale Farm, which is Mr Chauncey's place. The work's all right and the pickers' huts aren't bad, but what we go for is being out in the fresh air and a chance for the little 'uns to dash about a bit and feel the grass under their toes and get some pink in their cheeks.' He pauses, and the faint smile of reminiscence reveals, Lily notices, that, when his face isn't screwed up in anxiety, he is actually a very nice-looking man.

'Go on,' she prompts. She notices out of the corner of her eye that Felix once again has his notebook out; that he has already written something and is frowning down at the words.

'Like I say,' Jared Spokewright continues, 'we go every year and have done since time out of mind. Year before last, my brother – my brother Abel, that is, two years younger than me, he was – my brother falls for this local girl, Effie Quittenden, and last year they pick straight up where they left off. Well, her name's Euphemia really, but everyone called her Effie. She was a real sweetheart – kind, ready smile and two little dimples in her cheeks, pleasant word for anybody, and everyone liked her. She worked as a dairymaid at this other farm, not Ted Chauncey's hop farm but a dairy farm run by a man called Marchant and his old mother, along with his nephew and a cowman. Effie wanted to save money, though, and she also worked in the village pub of an evening whenever they were busy. That's the Leopard's Head' – he has noticed that Felix is taking notes – 'and the landlord's Ezra Sleech and his wife's name's Peg, and she's sister to the cowman at Newhouse Farm. That's where Effie worked.'

There will be a time for the accurate recording of this minutiae, Lily reflects, but it isn't now. Careful not to sound disapproving, for if Jared Spokewright thinks he's doing it wrong he'll undoubtedly be overcome with embarrassment, it will all take much longer and it'll be hours before Felix gets his pie and pint and she can slope off upstairs to her own quarters and take her corset off, she says, 'What happened, Mr Spokewright?'

He nods rapidly several times. 'Yes, yes, you don't need all this, course you don't.'

'We do,' Felix says kindly, 'but let's save it till later.'

Spokewright flashes him a grateful smile. Then his face falls into dismay and he says quietly, 'Effie was killed. Murdered. Some bastard – sorry, miss – someone wound a length of hop twine round her lovely neck and choked the life out of her. They said it was Abel, and for all we kept telling them it wasn't, that he loved her, he was saving up to marry her, putting aside a bit every single bloody week just like she was, that he'd never have hurt a single hair on her head, course he wouldn't, we couldn't make them see the truth.' Abruptly he stops, and the echoes of his words, of his profound and lasting pain, slowly die away. Two tears form in his dark blue eyes, and quite unselfconsciously he takes out his handkerchief and wipes them away.

'They took him off in handcuffs,' he says in a voice that aches with shame. 'Then he was put in prison – Lewes, that was – and tried for murder. Found guilty and hanged.'

Neither Lily nor Felix breaks the silence.

Presently Jared Spokewright sits up straight again.

'It'll soon be a twelvemonth since he was arrested,' he says. 'Brings it all back, though in truth it's never far from our minds. It's my old Ma I'm really concerned about.' He leans forward, fixing first Lily's gaze and then turning to Felix. 'She's grieving, has been all year, and it's not getting any better. She barely eats, for all my Auntie Bea and me do our best.' He pauses, clearly searching for the words. 'See, if he'd died in a *normal* sort of a way, sickness, say, or an accident

– he was on the docks along of me and there's accidents aplenty, I can tell you – I reckon Ma would have borne up better.' Again he pauses. Then he whispers, 'But what's normal about being *hanged*?'

Even saying the word has made him look pale and sick.

Lily and Felix wait.

'Trouble is, he's buried somewhere inside the prison walls, along of all the villains and the thieves and the cutthroats, and they don't let you in. Maybe they don't even mark where each executed man lies, I don't know.' He gives a weary sigh. 'He didn't do it – *couldn't* have done it – but when we went to the authorities and told them, would they listen? Would they hell!' For a moment his face is dark with fury. 'They just say he's had a fair trial and the jury found him guilty, and that's an end to it.' He shakes his head. 'We don't know where else to turn, and that's a fact. Now I know nothing'll bring him back,' he goes on, 'but it'd ease Ma's soul, give her a bit of solace, if she could kneel at his graveside, lay a posy and say a prayer over him, only that's not allowed.' He pauses, and his expression suggests he's working hard to suppress emotion. 'Wherever he lies, it's not consecrated ground, and that hurts Ma worse than anything. It's the shame, see, miss, mister, the *shame*' – suddenly he is almost wailing – 'and the kids down our street don't help, the little sods, making faces outside the window with their hands up round their bleeding scrawny little necks and their tongues poking out, and poor old Ma just can't get any *peace*!' The last word is a desperate shout. There is a pause, then he adds softly, 'Poor old gal, what with the shame, and the grief, and not eating and barely sleeping, she's being ground away before our very eyes and it looks like we're going to lose her and all.'

Lily tries to speak but her throat is too dry.

Felix says, with what she thinks is admirable calm considering what they have just heard, 'You wish the World's End Bureau to look into the matter?'

Jared spins round to look at him, his face alight with hope. 'Is it what you do?' he demands. 'Investigate miscarriages of justice?'

Felix glances at Lily and she nods.

'This is an investigation bureau,' he says. 'We have no power over the police or the law courts. We can't make the police re-open the case, or force a re-trial. What we can do, and will do if you engage us, is to examine the events of a year ago all over again, starting at the beginning, speaking to those who were involved, listening to the views of anyone and everyone prepared to speak to us. Should we find out mistakes were made, should we dig out evidence that points the finger of blame at someone else, then we will put what we have discovered before the appropriate authorities.' Lily is about to add a proviso, but Felix hasn't finished. 'However, I must tell you, Mr Spokewright,' he says firmly, 'that the chances of uncovering anything that has the power to persuade the police and the courts to act are very slim. They don't—' He stops, and Lily is all but sure he nearly said, *They don't like admitting to mistakes, especially when someone had been hanged.* Instead he concludes, 'You may very well be wasting your money if you ask the Bureau to act for you.'

Jared Spokewright doesn't say anything for a few moments. Then, with a wry grin, he says, 'Reckon I've more faith in you because you told me you probably won't succeed than if you'd said course you could do it, it'd be a piece of cake. Mind you' – he shoots a glance at Felix – 'that might just be you being clever.'

'I don't—' Felix begins.

Jared waves a hand. 'Pulling your leg,' he says. 'Can't put my finger on why, but I trust you. Tell me where I sign, and what I need to pay up front. and I'll do it.'

Felix stands on the step, watching Jared Spokewright stride away down Hob's Court and turn left up World's End Passage. He moves gracefully for a big man. Felix wonders if his dead brother was of similar build, and despite himself he can't prevent an image briefly invading his mind of a big man overpowering a slight, slender, girl. Very firmly he dismisses it.

As he returns to his desk in the front office, Lily comes to join him. She is looking at him through narrowed eyes.

'What did you write down just as Mr Spokewright embarked on his tale?' she asks.

He is not in the least surprised that she noticed.

'It was the name of the village,' he replies.

'Crooked Green.'

'Yes. I thought it was familiar.' He doesn't go on.

Her face is alive with curiosity. 'He said it's only small, and it sounds as if it's in the depths of farming country; he mentioned the hop farm and a dairy farm.' Now she looks mystified. 'Why on earth should a widely travelled urban sophisticate such as you know of a quiet rural backwater like that?'

He suppressed a smile at her description of him, but, watching as she does the same, realizes she is gently poking fun at him.

'I have an idea of where I've heard it,' he says. 'I'll check, soon as I'm back at the lodgings.'

She shoots a rather pointed glance at his desk drawers, where he is in the process of building up a comprehensive reference system, as if to say, *Why can't you check here?* But then, with a faint shrug, she returns to the Inner Sanctum.

'Two new cases,' she says over her shoulder. 'Tomorrow we will discuss both of them, and decide on our initial steps and how best to allocate the tasks between us. Perhaps we should—'

But just then there is an eruption of sound from the rear quarters of the house, a tattoo of quick, brisk footsteps along the passage, and with a loud, 'I'm off, then, Miss Lily, I'll be back day after tomorrow to attack the back court and the necessary. G'd evening, miss, evening, Mr Felix.'

It has taken the length of time that Felix has worked for Lily for the volatile, fiercely loyal and very easily offended Mrs Clapper to unbend to the use of his Christian name, and, as it is a relatively new departure, he is very keen to encourage this tentative indication of approval. 'Good evening, Mrs Clapper!' he calls back with ludicrous enthusiasm, adding a pointless little chuckle that sounds imbecilic even in his own ears. Mrs Clapper clearly thinks so too, if the way she bangs the street door is any indication.

Lily rolls her eyes.

*   *   *

Felix is hot and sweaty by the time he arrives back at the apartment he shares with Marm. It is usually a pleasant walk home to Kinver Street – down to the river, east along the Embankment, up into the maze of streets between Royal Hospital Road and the King's Road – but the August evening is still too full of the heat of the day, and far too many tired and irritable people are pushing and shoving alongside him, all eager to get home and take their jackets off.

Marm is in his usual place to one side of the fireplace, and as Felix shuts the door he calls out, 'Cold beer waiting for you. Come and put your feet up, dear one, and tell me all about your day.'

It is one of Marm's more irritating habits, to greet Felix as if he was a weary husband returning home to his cosy little wife at the end of the working day. Felix has resolved always to rise above it, for in most other respects Marm is the ideal landlord, and has become a good friend as well.

'I'm going to have a wash,' he calls back. 'Hot as Hades out there. I'll join you presently.'

Shortly afterwards, much refreshed by dunking his head and upper body into a large basin of cold water, wet hair still dripping onto a fresh shirt, he emerges to take his place on the other side of the hearth. He takes a long draught of beer, nods in appreciation, then opens the thick notebook he has brought from his room. At least half of its pages are covered in writing, and cuttings from newspapers and magazines have been pasted in.

'What's that you've got there?' Marm asks.

Felix is riffling through the pages, muttering. Without looking up he says, 'It's my Personal Records book.'

'Personal Records,' Marm repeats. 'As opposed to the copious files you are busy amassing at work for your elegant employer?'

'Yes,' Felix says absently.

'Splendid,' Marm remarks. 'Good to see you are learning from the master.'

Marm has shelves and drawers full of notebooks, files, press cuttings, built up over the quarter of a century of his career as a journalist. One of his most faithfully kept records – and one for which Felix, on behalf of the World's End Bureau, has been grateful more than once – is the Lost Women file, which includes the details of women and girls whose disappearance, in Marm's view, has not been sufficiently well investigated by the relevant authorities. And that, as Marm once said with a mixture of grief and fury in a moment of despair, was, in the case of the sort of women who usually go missing, 'bloody near all of them'.

It is a sad comment on the state of the world that this file is added to with monotonous regularity.

Now Marm edges forward in his armchair, trying to crane his neck so that he can see the page that Felix is staring at. 'That looks like a list of addresses?' he says, a hint of an enquiry in the remark.

Felix looks up. 'It is.' Obligingly he turns the big book round so that Marm can see. He sweeps a hand across the page. 'The names and addresses on this and the next couple of pages all belong to members of my family.'

Marm affects amazement. 'I thought you had no time for your family? That your father booted you out of the ancestral home when you were expelled from Marlborough College and refused to be suitably penitent? And,' he adds with a sly smile, 'I'm quite sure you told me that before you turned your back on them all for the last time you called him an arsehole.'

Felix chuckles. 'It was the head groom who called him that, but I wholeheartedly agreed with him.'

'So?' Marm prompts. 'Why have you compiled a list of all their names and addresses if they're arseholes?'

'They're not all,' Felix protests. 'The East End branch are quite different. They work hard, and if originally their money came via means that don't entirely stand up to thorough investigation, go back far enough and the same can undoubtedly be said for practically every other wealthy family in the land, including the ones with titles and a bit of blue blood.'

'Especially those,' Marm mutters.

Felix turns a page, reads a few entries and exclaims, '*A-ha!*'

'Found it?' Marm sounds excited, entirely caught up in the chase.

'Yes.' Felix stares down at the five lines of writing; his own

writing. Then – for he is afraid Marm will burst with
impatience – he explains. 'This afternoon a young man came
to the Bureau. His younger brother was charged last year with
the murder of a girl, down in the hop country, tried, found
guilty and hanged. The young man – he's called Jared
Spokewright and his brother's name was Abel – swears he
didn't do it. When he told us the place where the murder
happened, I was all but sure I recognized it.' He taps the page.
'Now I'm certain.'

Marm reads over his shoulder, 'Noah Smith, 2, Spinfish
Cottages, Ford Lane, Crooked Green, Kent.' He looks at Felix.
'This man – a relative of yours, you seem to be telling me
– lives in the village where your client's brother killed, or
didn't kill, the girl?'

Felix nods. 'He does.'

Marm frowns. 'And you know this relative? You've been to
this outlandish-sounding village to visit him?'

'No, we've never met. He's my great-uncle, on the
disreputable side. My grandfather's younger brother.'

'He must be knocking on somewhat.'

'It was a large family,' Felix says. 'The Smiths always liked
plenty of children and it may be that my grandfather came
much earlier in the birth order.'

'Why do you say disreputable?' Marm demands.

'Because my mother's ancestors were impoverished
aristocrats, desperately in need of a large injection of cash and
none too fussy where it came from, so my grandmother was
married off to Derek Smith, who was a scrap-metal dealer
whose family were tinkers from Essex and who moved to the
East End because that was where the money was.'

'Tinkers?' Marm sounds incredulous.

'Grandad Derek had improved his lot from trailing round
the country lanes with a handcart by then,' Felix says with a
smile. 'He and his kin worked all the hours there were, and he
was living in considerable comfort by the time he married
Althea Courtney. Then soon after the wedding she decided they
needed to move to somewhere a little more socially acceptable.'
His expression softens, for he has very fond memories of his
Grandad Derek. 'I'm not sure my grandfather ever entirely

forgave her, and I know for a fact that he maintained most of the friends and associates of his youth because he used to head back to the East End whenever he got the chance and quite often he'd sneak me away with him.'

Marm nods slowly, absorbing the information. Then he says, 'The lovely Miss Raynor will have cause to be grateful for your family background and your comprehensive record-keeping, young Felix.'

Felix grins. He takes Marm's reference to Lily being lovely entirely in the spirit it is meant, knowing full well that Marm has a lot of time for her and, Felix suspects, has something of a crush on her. 'She will indeed,' he replies.

He can't wait to tell her.

Some time later, when he and Marm have returned from their visit to the Cow Jumped Over the Moon, enjoyed their pie and several more than one pint apiece and he is listening to the rhythmic sound of Marm's snoring coming through the wall, a thought occurs to Felix.

He had been wondering how a London docker with limited knowledge of the world and not much spare time for reading the newspapers – if indeed Jared Spokewright can read – could have come across the details of the World's End Bureau as the answer to his desperate hopes of clearing his brother's name.

Now he believes he may know. If Jared Spokewright has returned to the place where the crime happened, then might he not have slipped into the local – the Leopard's Head, Felix recalls – for a quiet pint before going back to London? And might he not have said to the old man beside him at the bar that he had made up his mind to clear his brother's name, if only the police would give him the time of day instead of dismissing him out of hand? And might that old man – Noah Smith, of course – have leaned across and muttered, 'I have a young great-nephew who works for a private enquiry bureau.' He would know this because other members of the family still living in London would have read about Lily and Felix's most notorious cases and perhaps even cut out the relevant sections from the newspapers, and passed the information to their country relative. 'Why not go and talk to him?' Noah would have continued. 'Here, I'll jot down the address.'

   With that nagging little loose end tied off to his satisfaction, Felix falls asleep.

THREE

'So if you agree,' Felix says to Lily early the next day, 'I thought I'd go down to Crooked Green, have a nose around, then look up my great-uncle and have a few quiet words with him about the murder of Effie Quittenden. I have my portmanteau in case I decide to stay.' He points to the battered old leather bag – small but surprisingly capacious – beside the door.

He is in Lily's office, standing in front of her desk, and she is eyeing him thoughtfully, a slight frown drawing her brows together. It is uncomfortably reminiscent of being summoned to the headmaster's office at school, and to break the illusion he draws up the spare chair and sits down. You never, ever, he recalls, sat down in the headmaster's office, or at least Felix didn't, but then since he was invariably there for a thunderous ticking-off and probably a beating, this was not surprising.

'I've decided on my cover story,' he informs Lily. 'I'm going to present myself as a London journalist writing a piece for a magazine about the effects of the annual inundation of East End hop-pickers on the Kent countryside and its inhabitants.' The idea, in fact, was Marm's, and over supper in the Cow last night he provided Felix with pages of useful information to help him pad out his character.

When Lily still does not reply he says, 'I've been doing some research. The hop-picking season starts in about a week, and I feel strongly that I ought to begin my investigations – both the real one and the fictitious one – before the population increases about fiftyfold and everyone's too busy to stop and talk to me.'

She nods slowly. 'Yes.' He waits, managing to suppress his impatience. Just. Then she says, 'We're assuming it is to be you who goes down to Crooked Green rather than I?'

'Well, I'm the one with the relative there. And I'd have

thought it would raise less interest for a male journalist to
visit on his own than a female one.'

For a moment Felix thinks he's made a mistake. Lily has
been known to take grave offence at any suggestion that her
sex means she carries an automatic handicap when compared
to a man. 'I mean—' he begins hurriedly.

She smiles. 'I know what you mean, Felix.' Thankfully she
doesn't sound cross. 'You are quite right, and I admit I would
be hard put to think of a reason for my being in the village,
other than the true one.' She frowns thoughtfully. 'I am sure
there *are* women journalists, but I suspect the presence of one
in a small village in the countryside would raise eyebrows.
And, as you say, you do have a contact there.' She pauses,
clearly thinking. 'Just one thing, which I dare say you've
already considered. If we are to accept that Jared is right and
Abel did not kill Effie, then someone else did. Whilst I have
no wish to slander your great-uncle, neither you nor I know
him, we have no idea what sort of a man he is, and therefore
we cannot swear that it is not him who killed the girl.'

It is Felix's turn to sit in silence. Lily is right to point this
out, but wrong to suggest he has already thought of it. He
hasn't, and now, as he reflects on it, he realizes that the reason
he hasn't is because his East End Smiths have always had a
romance and a glamour to them; an aura which makes it hard
for him to believe one of them could be guilty of murder.

This is not, he tells himself firmly, the attitude of a
professional private investigator, who should always embark
on a case with his mind wide open and a good, healthy dose
of cynicism concerning the human condition.

'I haven't considered it and I ought to have done,' he says
now. Then, meeting her cool green eyes, 'I was very close to
my grandfather. I wasn't happy at home – my parents and my
two elder brothers were so bound by convention that they
utterly refused to consider there was any other way of life
than the traditional one of the narrow and tightly bound wealthy
gentry. Of course, shutting themselves in so rigidly meant that
they closed themselves off to all other ways of life and everyone
in them.' He stops, because this is not relevant and in any case
it's far too self-revelatory. 'Grandad Derek picked up that I

was the odd one out, and once I was sent off to Marlborough and life got even worse, sometimes he seemed like my only friend.' *Enough*, he commands himself. 'But just because I loved and admired my grandfather, it's no reason to assume his little brother isn't capable of murder.' Firmly he shuts his mouth before he can say anything else.

After a short silence Lily simply says, 'Thank you.'

He has no idea if she's thanking him for so readily accepting the possibility that Noah Smith is a murderer or for his disarming and, he now thinks, entirely unintentional burst of breast-baring. Either way, it is high time to move on.

'You'll head off for Whitechapel and go to speak to this Russian woman in the London Hospital?' he demands; rather too briskly, if her raised eyebrows are a guide.

'Yes,' she says. Then she adds worriedly, 'Her little grandson is eleven years old and adrift in a very unsafe part of London, undoubtedly without much more than a word or two of English and probably not a penny in his pocket. There's not a moment to lose.'

Even as she speaks she stands up, and Felix observes that she is dressed for a day pounding the streets, with a sensible-looking heavy linen skirt and her stout boots (the pair with a long, thin blade concealed down the inside of the left one). She reaches behind her for her jacket, putting it on and buttoning it up, then shoves a small and unfussy straw hat on her fair hair and picks up her leather bag. 'Shall we walk up to the King's Road together?'

Felix has already checked the details of how to get to Crooked Green. Marm has a fine collection of railway timetables covering most of the country, and he makes sure it is kept up to date. Felix will travel into Kent from Charing Cross, taking the line that goes through Tonbridge and Ashford and on to the south coast, changing onto another line for Paddock Wood and then a small rural branch line that will deliver him to Binhurst, the nearest settlement to Crooked Green which has a railway station. He reckons he'll have to walk the last mile or so, just as all the hop-pickers do.

He bags a window seat facing forwards, his favourite place,

and settles down to enjoy the journey. The train rocks and
trundles its way across Hungerford Bridge, and he gazes out
at the sparkling Thames down below. It is a dull khaki colour,
and he suspects that, close to, the pleasure of watching the
light leaping and bouncing off the rivulets and ripples would
be heavily outweighed by the stench, not to mention the sight
of unidentifiable but highly suspicious objects floating past.

The suburbs pass by, houses, apartments and tenements
folded in on each other as people try to find a space to live.
He ticks the successive stations off his mental list, and soon
they are out in the green fields and the wooded slopes of the
countryside. Tunnels delve deep beneath the North Downs –
he remembers at the last moment to put the window up – and
presently it is time to change trains. Then another change,
and now they are deep in the sleepy rural landscape.

Emerging at Binhurst, he is half-entranced by the heavy air,
the warmth, the deep buzz of bees and sundry summer insects
and the rich smell of roses and pinks from the tubs that the
station master has planted up along the platform. Giving
himself a mental shake – *I'm here to work!* – he surrenders
his ticket and strides out into the main street of the village.

It has grown up at the place where a bridge crosses the River
Beuse (Marm's reference library again). It appears to be a very
old bridge. The road rises steeply on either side, and on the
north side there is an inn called the New Cock. From some
long-ago lesson, Felix recalls that the reason so many old inns
are called the Cock, the New Cock, the Old Cock or any other
sort of Cock is because, back in the old coaching days, a fresh
horse was added to the team at the foot of a hill and this animal
was known as the cock horse.

Whatever the history of the name, the inn looks a welcoming
sort of establishment, an impression that proves to be accurate
when he goes into the oak-beamed reception area and asks if
there is a room available. There is, he is told by the friendly
young man in attendance, who furthermore says it is quite
acceptable for Felix to leave his portmanteau behind the desk.

Then, free of his encumbrance, he goes out into the sunshine.
He strides over to a crossroads, studies the four finger boards
for a few moments and spots the name Crooked Green. If the

sign is to be believed, the village is a mile and a quarter away. He starts walking.

The countryside is a delight. On either side of the narrow lane hedges are alive with birds, and his path is crossed by both a grey squirrel and a pair of coneys. Fields golden with ripe corn stretch away up gentle slopes, bordered by the rich greens of trees, in every shade from emerald to the deep near-black of fir plantations. There is water all around: the main river, the Beuse, runs somewhere down at the foot of the valley to his left, he crosses at least three little tributaries, and he can hear the constant quiet bubbling of water in the ditches beside the road.

It is a beautiful morning for a walk, and he doesn't hurry.

Signs of habitation start to appear: a farm track heavily rutted from the passage of carts; a pair of tiny dark cottages with minuscule windows huddled beside the lane, the thatch half-rotten and hanging down raggedly like old men's eyebrows. Then he rounds a gentle bend and suddenly he is walking between hop fields, stretching away on either side as far as the eye can see.

A hand-painted sign beside a track on his left reads Nightingale Farm. 'Mr Chauncey's place,' Felix says aloud, echoing Jared Spokewright's words, and the place to which Jared and his family have always gone for the hop-picking. Felix pauses, staring down the track towards the farm. There is a cluster of buildings, and, dominating the rest, a red-brick structure with a round tower at one end, its steeply sloping roof clad in tile and in the shape of a cone. Its top is a rotating structure made of white-painted wood, and one side is open in an air vent and has a long wind vane projecting from it. Felix watches, observing that this cowl is turning slowly in the light breeze. There is something captivating about it, and it takes an effort to tear his gaze away.

The land beyond the oast – he has recalled the name of this unlikely building from his reading – slopes away to the left, which, from the position of the sun, must be the south. At some distance from the oast and the main farm buildings there is a row of small wooden huts, conjoined, each with its own door and single window. At the end of the row is a pump. The huts, he presumes, constitute the hop-pickers' accommodation: adequate, and far enough away from where the farmer lives, eats and sleeps for whatever noise the Londoners and their children make not to be a nuisance.

As he stands watching, a tall, strongly built young woman emerges from one of the farm buildings carrying a bucket. She empties it into a ditch, then pauses, a hand to the small of her back, staring out over the countryside. She has her thick hair tied up in a brightly coloured scarf, although quite a few strands of it have escaped and her handsome face is framed in bouncing auburn curls. Her body is enveloped in a capacious apron, although it isn't capacious enough to hide the fact that the woman is very shapely. Observing as she strides back across the farmyard that the curls aren't the only things that are bouncing, Felix muses that the woman has the sort of figure that is just perfect for a tight-laced corset and black stockings. Briefly he is back in a Paris music hall and a line of women in basques and wide frilly skirts dance across his memory, turning periodically to raise their petticoats and stick their calico-clad bottoms out at the audience. For a moment he can almost hear the thump of the band's percussion section, beating out the rhythm . . . Returning to the present, he sees that the auburn-haired goddess now has a broom in her hands, which she is banging vigorously against the wall of the building she emerged from, releasing clouds of dust from its bristles. The sound echoes in the still air. She is fully engaged in her cleaning task and hasn't noticed Felix.

Ah, memories, he thinks.

He is smiling as he walks on. The lane climbs steadily, and presently comes to a T-junction. The wider road onto which he emerges has a sign: Upper Road. 'You can't accuse these country folk of having overactive imaginations,' Felix mutters.

A row of cottages line the road to his right, and beyond them is a wide field with a border of deciduous trees. There is a pub a little further along, and even before he is close enough to read the sign, Felix knows it's the Leopard's Head. Just before the pub a lane branches off to the left: Church Road, and sure enough it leads to an ancient church – Saxon origins? – whose board proclaims it as All Saints' Church, and informs him that the vicar is the Reverend Mr Peter Tewks.

Walking slowly down Church Road, Felix looks over at the village green, enclosed by the road he is on, Upper Road and a third; the green is shaped like a right-angle triangle with the long side turned from a straight line to an inward-facing curve, and this curved, crooked shape is no doubt what gives the village its name.

Past the church, and he takes the fork up to the left, the intriguingly named Earlyleas Lane. Then Felix comes to a sign that reads Beuse Lane leading to Ford Lane.

And, remembering that Ford Lane is where 2, Spinfish Cottages is to be found and within his great-uncle Noah Smith, Felix stops and stares down the sloping track.

It is tempting to seek out his great-uncle straight away. Felix is full of curiosity about him; will he look like Grandad Derek? Will he have the same independence of spirit, the same insouciance, the same sense of humour that always appealed so much? Will he, in short, be a replacement grandfather for the man who still misses the original one?

Felix turns away from Beuse Lane, heading back for the green. It's not the moment to meet Noah Smith, and if he were to be discovered nosing around Spinfish Cottages in his guise of London journalist, what possible excuse could he give for being there? Someone intent on researching a magazine article on the invasion of the hop-pickers would in all likelihood head straight for that source of all village information and gossip, the pub.

As Felix emerges onto Upper Road after crossing the green, he hears bolts being shot back, and the ancient wooden door of the Leopard's Head creaks open.

It is a long, low building, beamed, whitewashed, with a tiled roof. There are outbuildings to the left, stretching out behind the main building and with it forming three sides of a square and enclosing a yard. Beyond is a field, with a thicket of trees along the right side. The heavy oak door is set in a frame so low that Felix has to bend so as not to bump his head. He reads the hand-painted sign above it: *The Leopard's Head by*

Ezra Sleech, licensed to sell ale and distilled spirits and for the provision of vittles.

Another name that is familiar from Jonah Spokewright's account, Felix thinks. And the landlord's wife, if memory serves, goes by the unromantic name of Peg.

I'm a journalist, he tells himself, I'm here to ask the publican, his wife and his customers for information, for their opinion on the impact of the hop-pickers' presence in the village. Since I want to hear about the place where they live and an aspect of their lives here, I shall in effect be asking them to talk about themselves. Normally, he reflects, the problem is to persuade people to *stop* talking about themselves.

Smiling to himself, his confidence growing, he walks into the public bar.

He is the only customer.

A thick-set man with broad shoulders and a bit of a beer belly straining against a clean white apron is standing behind the bar, frowning at a beer pump. The frown serves to increase the man's piratical good looks: he is dark-haired, dark-eyed, the brows heavy and well shaped. The pump's handle is made of porcelain, decorated with a lively scene of a hunt chasing after a pack of hounds. The man in the apron bends down below the counter, and there is the sound of something heavy being hammered against something made of metal. There is also a stream of muttered curses. There is a sudden violent spluttering from the beer pump, a froth of amber liquid bursts out of it and the man in the apron mutters, 'So you've decided to play nicely, have you, you bastard?' Then he shoves a jug beneath the pump and draws the beer through until it is running smoothly.

He glances up and meets Felix's interested gaze.

'Temperamental bugger, that pump,' he says cheerfully. 'Be with you in a moment. What'll it be?'

The aroma of the beer pouring into the jug is wonderful. 'Pint of that, please, when you're ready,' he replies.

He wonders whether to add that entrée into a publican's favour, the quietly murmured *and whatever you're having yourself*. But this man may not be the landlord . . .

A door behind the bar opens just far enough to reveal a
woman's head and shoulders. She has fine, light brown hair
drawn severely away from her thin face and wound into a
small, tight bun. Her eyes are a nondescript light colour, and
frown lines crisscross her forehead. She has a long, thin neck
that somehow puts Felix in mind of a snake, and wears a
paisley patterned blouse with a small round collar, the carefully fastened row of tiny pearl buttons giving an impression
of primness. She too wears a white apron. She glances at Felix,
faint surprise registering on the lean face.

'Ezra, I've asked you three times now to see about the
potatoes,' she hisses. So he *is* the landlord. 'I can't manage
the sack by myself, it's too heavy!'

'Be there soon as I've seen to the gentleman, Peg,' the man
in the apron replies.

The door closes again – rather firmly – and Ezra Sleech
grins at Felix. 'The wife,' he says. 'Has a bit of back trouble.'

'Oh dear,' Felix says. Then, as Ezra puts the brimming pint
jug before him, 'One for yourself, landlord?'

Ezra Sleech's grin widens, revealing a fine set of even white
teeth. 'Now I call that very kind. Don't mind if I do.'

When they have raised their glasses to each other and drunk,
Ezra puts his glass down and disappears into the kitchen. Felix
heard the mumble of voices: Peg Sleech's plaintive, her
husband's conciliatory.

When the landlord returns, Felix takes advantage of the fact
that he and Ezra are alone to introduce himself and present
his cover story.

And Ezra, as if the chance to talk about the hop-pickers
and the villagers' response to them is the very thing he's been
yearning for, begins to talk. And talk. And go on talking,
pausing at one point to explain – as lengthily as he explains
everything else – that the Leopard doesn't usually open at
midday but that he's more than happy to draw a pint or two
if someone comes asking. Glancing out of the window, Felix
observes a quartet of men, who by their appearance must be
farm labourers, pass by. Their ages range from about fifteen
to perhaps seventy, eighty or even older, three tend towards
the upper age limit and only one is younger. He suspects

they've all had a hard-working morning, probably out in the fields or elsewhere on one of the surrounding farms. They all carry napkin-wrapped bundles, and he suspects that while he sits in the cool of the pub over his beer, these hard-working men will sit under a hedge with a hunk of bread, a piece of cheese, an onion and a flask of cold tea.

They must have settled somewhere close by, because presently he hears a quiet, continuous murmur of sound from the old men, floating in through the open window: soft country voices, chewing over the day's events, reflecting on the village's recent small happenings. 'Stood out there, she was, *yelling* at him!' one old boy exclaims loudly. '*Yelling* at him!' echoes another, and, 'Would you credit it?' the third joins in.

The ale, the walk in the unaccustomed fresh air, the monotonous, gentle mutterings, combine to form a powerful soporific . . .

Felix jerks awake, and a glance at Ezra Sleech tells him the momentary lapse has not been noticed.

He resumes his pretence of note-taking. He is just wondering how to stop the flow of words when, with a look to either side to see if anyone is listening – although nobody else has come in – Ezra leans on the bar and says very quietly, 'Then of course there was that business last year.' He stares at Felix, one eyelid dropping like a shutter in a rapid wink.

'What business was that?' Felix asks innocently.

'A young woman was strangled,' Ezra whispers, mouthing the last word, near-black eyes rounding in horror. He nods as if to verify the truth of what he's just said. 'One of our own and all, pretty young lass as used to help out right here in this very pub, when we were busy, and a good little worker she was too! Slain in her prime, she was, out there on the far edge of that field!' He pauses, astonishment written all over his expressive face as if he's amazed all over again at such a thing happening so uncomfortably close to home. Then, leaning right up to Felix again, he murmurs, 'One of them very East End hoppers you've just been asking about got himself hanged for it, but none of us reckons it was him at all.' He nods several times. 'Now, Mr Wilbraham, what d'you think of *that*?'

*   *   *

Sounds from the room behind the public bar break the sudden silence. Peg Sleech must be busy cooking up something with her sack of potatoes, Felix thinks absently. Is she making dishes to serve when the pub opens this evening? Do country pubs like this one in fact serve food, like their London counterparts, or are the sounds of conscientious culinary industry all in aid of keeping a steady flow of substantial meals on her husband's table? Ezra does look like a man who can do justice to a good square meal . . .

There is a steady hum of conversation from outside. Then two of the men stand up, and one peers in through the window at Felix. He says something to the others, and to a man they turn to stare. One smiles – the young man – two remain expressionless, the last sends him a suspicious frown.

Felix is quite sure that as soon as he leaves, Ezra Sleech will nip outside and tell the four of them who he is and what he's doing there. This can only be to Felix's advantage – or so he hopes – because anyone with anything to tell him will come and find him. He moves away from the bar to finish his beer, and almost straight away one of the older men beckons to Ezra through the window, exchanging a few muttered words with him. Both cast a quick look at Felix: it is plain he is the topic of conversation.

Good, he thinks.

He drains the last drops of his second pint of beer. It tastes even better than it smelled. Then he returns to the bar, slaps down his empty glass and says, 'Thank you, landlord, that was a tasty drop. I'm going to have a look round the village and enjoy the sunshine.'

'You do that!' Ezra replies cheerfully. Once again he drops the eyelid, as if saying, *You and I know full well what you'll really be doing!*

Outside, Felix turns to look at the four labourers, all packing away the now-empty napkins. 'Good day to you,' he says. There are a few grunts in reply, and one deep bass voice rumbles, 'Good day.'

Even as he walks off down the path from the door to the road, he can hear the talking begin.

*   *   *

He crosses the green and heads for the church. He walks in beneath the lychgate and stands looking up at the tower. It is squat and square, and the black-faced clock on its front face reads ten minutes to two. The tower is flanked on either side by matching aisles under steep-sided gables. There are clues to the antiquity of the church's origins in the surrounding churchyard, where two huge yew trees soar up protectively. Both have the multiple trunks and hollow centres that reveal great age, and one has several thick, heavy branches that sweep down to the ground and are supported by stout timber props. There are more mature trees all around the church – oak, chestnut – and, other than those areas closest to its ancient walls, the grass has been allowed to grow long and is dotted with wild flowers. A patch of concentrated colour over on the far side of the churchyard catches Felix's eye: tiny dots of pink and orange, an impression of green foliage. He walks closer. On a grave over by the high boundary hedge, marked only by a small, unmarked, weatherbeaten cross, someone has left a posy. Some carnation-like flowers which exude a scent of cloves, a couple of marigolds. The long fronds of foliage have a smell that takes him straight back to a particularly sumptuous meal of lamb and spring vegetables in a dilapidated château on the Loire in the height of his thrilling days with his eccentric, captivating French countess, but he can't place it . . .

He wanders on.

He pauses by a large headstone in the long grass which is so densely covered by twining ivy that he can only make out half the inscription at most: . . . *London 1770, . . . ked Green 1870*. Whoever lies beneath it, Felix reflects, lived to a very good age. Then three women's names, somebody *Hill, . . . ssie Crump, . . . arjorie Burgess*, and finally, *All the wives of . . .*, the identity of this much-married Methuselah hidden by more ivy. Since it would be decidedly awkward to be caught pulling greenery off someone else's gravestone, Felix turns away and strolls across the short grass to inspect the biggest of the mausoleums.

It is constructed out of pale stone which he thinks might be marble, and in the form of a classical temple. It is roughly rectangular, perhaps three paces by two, with a pitched roof and pillars at each corner. Steps lead up to it, and the surrounding grass has been clipped neatly. At the front there is a stout wooden door, set plumb in the middle, and directly above it on the pediment is etched the name LEVERELL.

Clearly this is the name of the most prominent local family. Or at least it was once . . . Felix is going through his memories of all that Jared Spokewright said to see if there was a mention of any Leverells and concluding that there wasn't when a quiet voice with a hint of amusement says, 'You can't really miss it, can you?'

Felix spins round and discovers that a man in a dog collar under a cream linen jacket is standing behind him. He touches the brim of the old straw hat and says with a friendly smile, 'Peter Tewks. I'm the vicar of All Saints.'

I know, Felix thinks, I read it on the board by the lychgate an hour ago.

'Felix Wilbraham,' he responds, shaking the proffered hand; Peter Tewks has a very strong grip, which is quite a surprise as he has white hair – thick and abundant, it is revealed, as courteously he raises the battered straw hat – and his bright blue eyes are set in a face full of character lines, most of which seem to go upwards. Felix has an impression of a man who smiles easily; whose long life has produced more to be cheerful about than sorrowful.

The Reverend Mr Tewks is smiling now, but with a definite look of enquiry; he is evidently waiting for Felix to explain himself.

He embarks once again on his cover story.

'And I've just had a couple of pints in the Leopard's Head,' he concludes, 'on the grounds that if I'm to write a piece about the hop-pickers then I need to be able to describe the end product from personal experience.'

Peter Tewks smiles again. 'As good an excuse as I've ever heard,' he remarks. 'Ezra keeps a fine pint, does he not?'

Felix agrees that he does.

'And he provides an equally fine line in local information, not to say gossip.' The vicar is looking at him expectantly.

He knows Ezra will have told me about the murder, Felix thinks.

'Indeed he does,' he says. Then, softly: 'It was dreadful, what happened to poor Effie Quittenden.'

The vicar nods. He is looking fixedly at Felix, and he's not smiling now.

'Is that why you chose Crooked Green among all the other places where Londoners come down into the country to pick hops, Mr Wilbraham?' he asks.

Felix is thinking, hard and rapidly. He has warmed to this elderly man, and he is tempted to come clean and reveal that he is here in his professional capacity as a private enquiry agent. But he thinks he can almost hear Lily's voice in his head, see her intent expression as she hisses, *Do no such thing! You have only just met him, and you have no idea where his loyalties lie, who he may want to protect or who he bears a grudge against and would like to see accused! Why, for all you know he might have killed Effie himself!*

Not the moment for a full confession, then.

But he doesn't think he can stand there and claim not to have known about the murder; perhaps Lily would have commanded it, but then Lily isn't standing here under the intent scrutiny of those wise blue eyes that look as if they don't miss a thing.

He knows what to do.

'I did know about the murder, before Ezra told me about it just now,' he says quietly. 'I—'

But before he can complete the sentence, the Reverent Tewks interrupts. Eagerly, the words spilling out, his face alight, he says, 'And you don't think young Abel Spokewright did it either, do you?' He has grasped Felix's arm, the fingers digging into the muscle. 'Oh, I've been waiting, *hoping*, for someone like you to turn up!'

FOUR

Lily, on her way across London to the Limehouse Hospital, is full of apprehension concerning how she is to help an elderly woman newly arrived after an unimaginably frightful journey when they do not have a common language and the old woman is half out of her mind with grief and anxiety.

She sits on the top deck of the tram, trying to relax, telling herself to enjoy the feel of the breeze on her face while she can. Today is even hotter than yesterday, and she is not looking forward to the sort of smells there will undoubtedly be in a place that offers free medical care to the poorest and the most desperate. Then she berates herself for the uncharitable thought. I should be rolling up my sleeves and offering to help, she thinks, not acting like a sheltered, easily shocked girl at the thought of what I'm going to encounter. I used to be a nurse, for heaven's sake!

By the time she is walking up to the imposing entrance of the hospital, fighting her way through a throng of people and driven to retaliate after one too many elbows in the ribs, she is restored. The hospital smell – carbolic, sweat, disinfectant and, here in the busy foyer, the overriding, miserable odour of poverty – adds another level to her confidence: this used to be her world, and she is at home here. She will do her best for this poor woman and her best will have to suffice.

'I am here to see a Russian woman newly arrived,' she shouts across the desk to the large, stern-faced young nurse sitting behind the wide reception desk. She is bent over an enormous, thick ledger filled with pages covered in dense writing.

'Name?'

'Yelisaveta. The family name is Hadzibazy, or at least, I'm informed, that's what it sounds like.'

'Jewish, fleeing from the pogroms, with the boy that ran

away?' The woman has raised her head and is looking at Lily with interest.

'Yes. I've been asked to try to find the boy, and—'

'Pity you didn't come three days ago', the nurse says lugubriously. 'Lad's not likely to turn up now.'

Lily raises her chin. 'That is defeatist talk,' she says firmly. When she was nursing she would, she reckons, have been senior to this woman, and she's not going to let that dismissive, uncharitable remark pass without comment.

The nurse shrugs. 'Suit yourself. All the foreign immigrants we've got here are down there' – she points to the left – 'through the big double doors and then follow the sounds of Babel.'

Babel . . .

Of course. As Lily pushes the doors open and strides off along the corridor, she is met with a cacophony of raised voices talking, shouting, yelling and sobbing, and very few of them are uttering in English.

She tries two wards before she finds the woman she is looking for. An older nurse in the uniform of a sister nods when Lily explains her mission, leading her into a small side ward with two beds in it. On one a skinny young woman barely out of her teens sits feeding a tiny baby. In the other is a woman dressed in black, a close-fitting black veil drawn low over her forehead and covering her hair, extending down to conceal her neck. She looks up as the sister shows Lily into the ward. Her face is deathly pale, her dark eyes look like holes in a mask, her mouth turns down in a permanent grimace of pain.

She looks, Lily thinks in that first instant, like someone who has lost everything that matters to her and really cannot see much point in going on living.

The sister is saying something, but Lily doesn't hear. She crosses the floor – very clean, she notes absently – and crouches down beside the woman's bed, staring into her eyes.

'You are Yelisaveta Hadzibazy?'

Even in her grief, a brief spark of humour lights the woman's black eyes, and Lily guesses she has mispronounced one or both of the names. She wishes she'd taken the time to ask someone how she ought to say them: this woman has surely suffered enough, without some admittedly well-intentioned stranger saying her name wrongly.

Then, her face falling again, the woman nods. 'I am.'

'The Reverend James Jellicote came to see me,' Lily continues. 'He says you need my help. I run an enquiry agency, and—'

She has been wondering if the woman understands. She seemed to recognize James Jellicote's name, but that doesn't mean she is picking up anything else. But as Lily says *enquiry agency*, a thin, long-fingered hand in a darned black lace mitten flies out and grabs her sleeve.

'You look for Yakov? You find my grandson?' The words shoot out like darts.

'I am going to try,' Lily replies.

Briefly the woman closes her eyes, and her mouth moves rapidly. Lily guesses she is praying. She opens her bag, takes out a pencil and a notebook. She is looking round for a chair when the sister, who has been observing from the doorway, reaches behind her into the corridor and carries a three-legged stool across to Lily.

'I hope you can help her,' she says softly. Then she is gone.

Yelisaveta has opened her eyes again and is staring at Lily as if she has just thrown her a lifeline.

'May I sit down?' Lily asks politely, and she nods. 'Now, I would like you to tell me everything you can about Yakov, and where you think he might have fled to—'

But Yelisaveta, it seems, has only heard *tell me everything you can*. Even as Lily turns to a clean page and writes the date and the place, she is already launching into an account of all that has happened to her in the last few months.

Lily tries a couple of times to stop her, to divert her onto something more pertinent – such as a full description of the missing child and where he was last seen – but the old woman goes right on talking. And presently it dawns on Lily that Yelisaveta needs to pour out the terrible details of her dreadful account, almost as if she were ejecting some foul poison from her body, and that it doesn't much matter who to. Lily closes her notebook, puts down her pencil and simply listens.

Yelisaveta Hadzibazy, she learns, lived in Odessa, in the

south-west of Imperial Russia, and the pogroms against her people really got into their stride earlier this year, sparked off – as James Jellicote said – by the assassination of the Tsar. Jewish homes were attacked, burned, looted, and many men, women and children were injured.

'Then it is April,' Yelisaveta goes on, 'and in city of Kiev is big disturbance, and violence, and suffering, and now our people defend themselves and their property, and fighting is bad, more bad, much more bad than before, and men die, and my husband, my son, they say it will get much, so much worse, and we must leave, save our lives even if we not save our homes and everything we have is taken from us.' She pauses, eyes wide with remembered horror. 'Then we are on the road, my husband, my son, his wife, my grandson, and I try to care for Rachel – she is wife of Yefrem, and he is my son – and she is big with baby, her belly swollen, and travel is bad for her.' She stops again. 'Then there is more fighting, worse than all other.' Now she is whispering, and Lily can only just hear her. 'Men who fight to defend us make attackers even more savage. My husband Abram, my Yefrem, they are not fighters, not soldiers with guns, but they try, they try, try so hard, but both are wounded, both fall, and my son, my boy, he try to protect his old father but attackers are brutal and have no mercy and they club them to death even as they lie at their feet.' Two fat tears roll down the sunken cheeks.

Lily's hand creeps out to still Yelisaveta's, frantically pleating and re-pleating the fabric of her skirt. Mistaking the gesture, Yelisaveta grabs hold of it, cradling it in both of hers, thin fingers caressing the back of it.

'Rachel and Yakov and I, we hide, we do as my husband tell us before he is taken from us, and when all is quiet we run away. We reach station, we board train, but is crowded, so, so crowded, and people are not kind, they show no charity even for a woman great with child who is sick, and even when she begins to labour, nobody will make room on seat and she must lie on floor, and floor is *filthy*, with mud, dirt, blood, urine, faeces, and labour, it begins too soon, baby not ready, and when it comes out there is no life, no breath, little body all blue and even though I try, I go on trying, baby is dead.'

Lily, horrified, pictures the scene: a railway carriage packed with people, every one of them terrified and concerned only to save themselves, the floor heavily soiled and no place for a woman to give birth to a premature baby.

'Rachel she die too,' Yelisaveta whispers. 'My son her husband dead, baby dead, she so afraid, so hurt, body torn and nobody to help but me, and I, I have *nothing* to comfort her!' Briefly she takes one hand away from Lily's and violently punches the thin mattress, overcome with fury at the memory of her impotence. 'And then after my dear daughter-in-law die, is just Yakov and me.'

Lily does not speak. Yelisaveta, she thinks, is deep in the memory of this ghastly time, and probably wouldn't hear anyway.

'Journey go on,' Yelisaveta says, 'and train goes north, always north, and other people die, and then they tell us we go no further and we are all thrown off, and we take boat from . . . Netherlands?' She says the syllables tentatively, as if unsure. Lily nods. 'From Rotterdam. Sea is so very rough, everyone sick, I am very, very sick, and have fever, and forget who I am, what is happening, and then I fall into sleep like death and know nothing until I am here.' She stares blankly around her. Then she whispers, 'And Yakov is not.'

And she begins to weep.

Lily gives her a few moments. She can see that the poor woman is still not well – some sickness she contracted aboard the train, perhaps, or even on the ship, for both would have been very dirty and overcrowded and contagious diseases would have spread unchecked – and that the weakness has undermined her. But already Lily has sensed a core of steel beneath the desperation and the grief: Yelisaveta is someone to be reckoned with.

Presently the woman straightens up and dries her eyes. She turns to Lily with raised eyebrows as if to say, *What are you going to do?*

Lily meets the stare. Something occurs to her: 'You speak very good English,' she says.

Yelisaveta nods graciously. 'Now will be of use, I think.' Then, gazing round at the green-painted walls of the small ward, she adds, 'My husband was teacher of languages. French,

English. He try to teach Yakov, but always Yakov he want to be outside, will not study, will not listen . . .' But the mention of her grandson's name has brought his current peril right back to the forefront of her mind. Her eyes returning to Lily's and staring fixedly, she says plaintively, 'Yakov.'

Lily has opened her notebook and says briskly, 'Yes. Now, I need a description of him. I have been told he is eleven or twelve years old, and—'

'Twelve,' Yelisaveta interrupts, 'but small.'

'Thank you.' Lily makes a note. 'He is . . .' James Jellicote had said the boy was thin, wiry, dressed in rags and broken shoes, his dark hair filthy and roughly sheared. It was possibly not a tactful description for a doting grandmother to hear, so she says instead, 'Why not describe him to me?'

Yelisaveta needs no further urging. 'He is dark, his hair, his eyes, dark like my son and my husband. Hair is not washed, and I try to cut it but scissors were stolen and I use knife, and not good.' Her lip trembles briefly. 'Teeth are white, even, very fine, sharp, with . . . hole *here*.' She indicates her two top incisors, and Lily decides that she isn't saying one of them is broken or decayed but that he has a gap between them. 'He is *quick* boy, always darting, running, busy with next thought, next thing to do. He likes sea, ports, canals and rivers, boats, and always that is where Rachel look for him when he did not come home for meal. He wears good clothes when we flee our home, but journey is long, with many troubles, and trousers, jacket, become very dirty and torn.' Her face works. 'Now my Yakov looks like beggar child, and good leather boots broken, one heel flaps loose.'

For a proud grandmother, Lily realizes, how that must hurt.

After a moment she says, 'You did not see what happened on the quayside?'

'No. *No!*' She repeats the denial in a suppressed scream. 'I am not awake, I am sick, fever . . .' She snaps her fingers, staring at Lily as she searches for the word.

'You were unconscious,' Lily says. 'I imagine you became increasingly unwell as the ship crossed from Rotterdam, fell into a coma and had to be taken by stretcher down the gangplank.'

Yelisaveta nods. 'Yes, is right. They tell me—' She swallows, tries again. 'They tell me Yakov stay right beside me, will not leave me even when they try to tell him I must go to hospital, where I will be cared for, but he will go straight to place that is special for immigrants.' Her lip curls at this description. 'Yakov, he sees man come towards him, try to take hold, and he takes fright, kicks, bites, runs away.' Briefly she shuts her eyes. 'He is afraid,' she says. 'All this time since we are driven from our home we have been running from those who would harm us, kill us. Of course Yakov is afraid.'

'Yes, I would have been too,' Lily agrees. 'Really, I do believe the people from the Mission, or wherever they came from, only wanted to help him. He would not have been allowed to come here to the hospital with you, but I'm sure they would have looked after him until you were better and the two of you could be together again.'

But Yelisaveta is looking at her doubtfully. 'Many bad people in big port city,' she says darkly. 'Many bad *men*.'

I know, Lily thinks.

She says brightly, 'Then the sooner I start looking for Yakov, the better.'

Yelisaveta raises a sceptical eyebrow. 'It is kind that you try, but . . .' She leaves the sentence unfinished.

But how am I going to set about my seemingly impossible task? Lily thinks. Good question.

She puts her notebook and pencil away, thinking quickly. Then, raising her eyes to meet Yelisaveta's, she says, 'Other people who travelled here with you are being cared for at the Mission, which is not far from here. I shall go to talk to them, and to the people who run the place, and pick up anything and everything that any of them can tell me about what happened on the quayside, when Yakov ran away.'

Yelisaveta doesn't look very pleased to hear this plan of action; in fact, Lily thinks, she looks decidedly dismayed, although this might well be because it really isn't much of a plan.

'Were there friends who undertook the journey with you?' Lily asks, determined to persist despite the lack of enthusiasm. 'Perhaps people you knew back in Odessa, or to whom you grew close as the long weeks passed and you all endured the same hardships?' She is envisaging the sharing of various horrors – hunger, fear, grief as the weaker of the company succumbed, fell sick, died – and the way human beings have of drawing together for comfort. 'Perhaps you—'

But Yelisaveta is violently shaking her head in denial. 'No! No friend, no one *close*!'

Her face has flushed with some strong emotion, and she has put up both mittened hands, palms outwards, in a warding-off gesture. Lily has no idea what she has said to provoke such a reaction, and after a moment Yelisaveta subsides again and mutters something that could have been an apology.

Reflecting charitably that the poor woman is still weak from her illness as well as beside herself with worry, Lily puts it to the back of her mind.

She stands, looking down at Yelisaveta.

'I will come back as soon as I have news,' she says.

If Yelisaveta is grateful, she doesn't show it. She simply gives a curt nod, wraps her shawl more tightly around her, lies down on her bed and turns away.

The sister who showed Lily in is at her post at the end of the corridor. Looking up at Lily, she asks, 'How did you get on?'

Lily makes a face. 'Not very well, I'm afraid.' She pauses. 'What do you call Russian women?' she asks, for it seems disrespectful to go on referring to a much older woman who she has only just met by her given name, especially when every other dignity has already been so violently ripped from her. The sister looks perplexed. 'What is their title?' Lily goes on. 'We would say Mrs Hadzibazy, but what do they say?'

But the sister merely shrugs.

So Lily is forced to say, 'I'm afraid Mrs Hadzibazy doesn't have much confidence in my ability to find her grandson.' *And neither do I*, she might have added.

The sister nods. 'It's a dirty, dangerous world out there What do you plan to do?'

'I'm going to the Mission – Lady Theobald's Mission?'

'Yes, I knew where you meant.' The sister smiles faintly. 'Good idea. They took many of the passengers off Yelisaveta's

– er, off Mrs Hadzibazy's boat, and I believe a few of the men were scooped up by the Poor Jews' Temporary Shelter, in Church Lane. So many have nowhere to go, although not a few have family here already, so presumably *they'll* be all right.' She shakes her head, sighing. 'God alone knows what'll happen to the rest of them.'

'I told her I'll be back,' Lily says.

'She won't be here much longer,' the sister warns. 'We've done what we can for her, and she's getting better. We need the bed,' she adds.

'The perpetual cry of the nurse,' Lily remarks. She and the sister share an understanding grin. 'Where will she go next? To the Mission?'

'Yes, I expect so,' the sister says. But Lily senses her attention has moved on; gone back to more pressing concerns. With a quick 'Good day,' to which the sister grunts a reply, she leaves.

Lily goes next to Lady Venetia Theobald's Mission to Limehouse.

It is a tall and forbidding red-brick building on a corner where a narrow street called Lord Sidney's Passage branches off at an acute angle from the Commercial Road East. The right angle of the corner has been cut across to form a wide pillared entrance with steps leading up to it, above which a large sign advertises the name of the mission with the words FOOD AND SHELTER underneath.

Lily strides up the steps and goes in. The foyer is lined with narrow wooden benches, about half of which are occupied, mainly by women, some of whom cradle babies. An awful lot of small children seem to be tearing around, and there is a smell of unwashed skin and clothes and a reek of soiled napkins. She takes her place in the short queue of people lining up to speak to a severely dressed woman with a patrician face sitting behind a big oak table.

When her turn comes, she leans over the table and says quietly, 'Lily Raynor, private enquiry agent. The Reverend James Jellicote has told me about a boy who has gone missing, and—'

'Ah, yes, he said he would ask you to help.' The stern expression softens into a smile of welcome. 'I'm very glad to see you.'

'It's an almost impossible task,' Lily says warningly.

'Of course it is,' the woman replies. 'But at least you are prepared to try.'

'I would like to speak to others who arrived with the boy and his grandmother,' Lily begins, 'and—'

'I hope they will be able to help,' the woman interrupts.

She rings a small brass bell, holding its delicate porcelain handle between forefinger and thumb with the other fingers gracefully extended in the manner of the lady of the house summoning the maid to bring tea. In moments a young red-headed lad in a worn and ill-fitting suit appears from a door behind her. It's hard to guess his age: he is quite short, slightly built and wiry, but in all likelihood this is due to a poor diet, and the faint suggestion of facial hair suggests he's older than he looks. Fifteen, sixteen, perhaps?

'This is Alexei,' the woman behind the table is saying. 'He's been here some time, he knows more than the rest of us put together' – she flashes the young man a smile – 'and he helps the new arrivals find their feet. He will show you where to go.' She beckons to the youth and he leans down to hear what she is saying. He looks up at Lily and says, 'This way, Miss Lady,' and she follows him off along a wide passage to the left.

'The fresh lot off *Oude Maas* boat are down 'ere,' Alexei says over his shoulder. English is clearly not his mother tongue – Lily thinks he is almost certainly Russian – and the overlay of idiom and the Cockney accent on top of the Russian one makes for an interesting result. 'Reverend Jellicote, he send you? Good bloke, is he.'

'He did,' she affirms. 'He has strong contacts with the Mission, I understand.'

'For sure,' Alexei agrees. He is opening a door. 'This is Russian Jews' day room,' he says, 'and 'ere all people, allowed to mix in daylight hours.'

Lily concludes from this that the sexes are segregated for sleeping.

Alexei is scanning the vast room, which is crammed with

trestle tables, benches, and, all along the far wall, a long refectory table. There seem at first glance to be more than a hundred people here. Many look up as Alexei pauses, Lily beside him. Several nod or mutter a greeting. Lily feels that strange sensation that comes when someone is staring with more than casual curiosity, and, slowly turning her head, she looks round, trying to see where the intense scrutiny is coming from.

A group of men of various ages sit at a table beside the door. They are playing cards, one of them expertly shuffling the dirty, greasy pack. One is heavily built, dark and bearded, and, unusually in that group of ragged people, the hair and the beard are close-trimmed. Something about him catches her attention. He is better dressed than most of the others, although his well-cut, good-quality garments show signs of hard wear and a long journey in the one outfit. But almost immediately she notices that he has a facial defect: one of his conker-coloured eyes is wide open and looking straight at her, the other is half-closed, the upper lid bisected by a scar. Feeling embarrassed, as if she's been caught gawping at this minor disability, hastily she averts her gaze to the slighter, younger man next to him – the one shuffling the pack – who gives her a cheerful grin, flicking back the long fair hair that flops over his forehead.

'*Ya!* Over there,' Alexei exclaims, nudging her to catch her attention. He points to a group of some twenty men and women sitting around a pair of tables pushed together. 'They all are *Oude Maas* arrivals.' He hesitates, and she thinks he is about to leave. Then, leaning close and speaking softly, although in truth the level of noise in the room is so high that nobody is likely to overhear, he murmurs, 'The tall man with long grey beard, 'e speaks for them. Is called Semyon. The woman sitting opposite, with small child beside 'er, is Serafima.' He touches a finger to the side of his nose. 'She 'as eyes always open, sees everything.' Then he turns away, about to leave.

But Lily, who has just thought of something, grabs his sleeve. 'Which quay was it?' she asks. 'Where did the *Oude Maas* tie up?'

He was already nodding his understanding, even before she added the extra words.

'Saint Katharine Dock,' he says, enunciating carefully. His evident pride at being able to answer the question makes her glad she asked. With a nod, he slips out through the door.

Lily weaves her way between the long tables, very aware just how many pairs of eyes are now watching her. Some look interested, some are wary, some are hostile. She tries to keep a calm, pleasant expression on her face, but it is wearing thin by the time she reaches Yelisaveta's fellow passengers.

She stops beside the man with the long beard. 'Good morning,' she says. 'I am told your name is Semyon, and that you and your companions arrived on the *Oude Maas* from Rotterdam, and a lady called Yelisaveta Hadzibazy and her grandson Yakov were with you.' Again there are smiles, and even a snigger or two, at her pronunciation, and she hopes the amusement may serve to ameliorate the somewhat chilly reception. 'As you probably know, Yakov is missing. I have told Mrs Hadzibazy' – more chuckles – 'that I will try to find him, and I have come to ask if any of you have any information that might help.'

She has spoken very slowly and clearly, and therefore is not a little embarrassed when the man with the grey beard replies in more than adequate English, 'Yes, we were on that boat, and some of us travelled very much further with Yelisaveta and her grandson.' He glances at the woman with the little girl – she is young, very dark, and the heavy hair is knotted in a bun so solid that it seems to draw her head backwards – and she gives an almost imperceptible nod. Then, with a shrug, he says, 'What can I tell you? We were all crowded onto the quay, and there were many sick like Yelisaveta who could not walk and were on stretchers. Many were there who tried to help us, and behind the barrier were the people trying to pick out their family who had just arrived. Also, many charitable men and women offering support.' He shrugged again, smiling faintly. 'Chaos.'

Lily expected this response but nevertheless is keenly disappointed. 'Did anyone see him running away?'

There is a brief silence, then a dark-haired man says something in Russian. Semyon listens, then turns to Lily. 'He saw a man approach the boy and bend down to talk to him. He believes the man was trying to help, because other men in the same clothing were collecting children who seemed to be alone and already a group of boys had been gathered.' Another man speaks up, again Semyon listens, nods and says, 'Men were from Salvation Army.' He enunciates carefully. He indicates the man who has just spoken. 'He hear one say that some of the children will be taken to Barnardo's?' He turns the sentence into a question.

'Yes, the home for boys,' Lily replies. 'They will be looked after there,' she feels compelled to say.

Semyon gives another shrug.

The dark man is speaking again. Nodding, Semyon translates. 'He say Yakov was frightened because he did not understand. Also, very anxious because grandmother so sick. He kick, he bite, man cries out and hand bleeds, lets go of boy and boy runs away.' He listens, nods again and concludes, 'Crowd was very thick, and boy soon is lost.'

Lily waits, but nobody volunteers any more. She has learned almost nothing she didn't already know. She wants to ask about Yelisaveta: What was she like? Were any of the group particularly friendly with her? Does anyone know her from home? But the eyes intent on her are disconcerting, and in any case she feels strongly that even if anybody is prepared to speak to her, it isn't likely to be in front of all these people.

She notices that the woman called Serafima is watching her closely. Meeting her eyes, she thinks Serafima inclines her head slightly towards the door.

Lily makes up her mind.

'This is my card.' She takes it out of her bag and lays it on the table. 'If anybody remembers anything that could help me find Yakov, I would be grateful to be informed.' She glances round the nearest people – she is sure they have more to say, and suspects they are aware she knows this – wishes them a courteous 'Good day' and turns away.

She is halfway down the corridor when she hears hurrying footsteps behind her. Expecting Serafima, she turns to see it is Alexei.

'Come with me,' he whispers. He leads the way down a side passage, turns to the right and the left, and presently opens a low door on to a dark, enclosed yard that smells of drains. Standing in the one thin shaft of sunlight is Serafima.

'Does not speak English. I tell you words,' Alexei says.

Serafima begins to speak, very rapidly. At regular intervals Alexei holds up his hand to stop her and translates.

'She know Yelisaveta, know Hadzibazy family. They live close but not friends.' He frowns. 'She say house is big and fine, but tight-shut, closed-in, like something must be kept hidden. Always Yelisaveta keep apart, and on train when Serafima try to be kind she pretend not know her.' Serafima is speaking more urgently now, and Alexei frowns as he tried to keep up. 'She say Yelisaveta scared to be friend, want to keep private, 'ide 'erself behind blanket, take no aid from other women even when wife of son lose baby and die, and Serafima, she not understand this.' Serafima adds a few curt words, and now she sounds angry. Alexei frowns again, then, his face clearing, says, 'Women very sorry for loss of wife of son and baby, but they do not like Yelisaveta because she 'ave food, she *buy* food when train stops, but will not share, say always is just for Yakov, all for Yakov, 'e must grow big and strong because 'e is all she 'ave now.' Serafima speaks again, and there are tears in her large brown eyes. 'Other children so 'ungry, bellies ache, starving, see food, smell food, they cry, they sob, but Yelisaveta hides away behind her blanket and stony 'eart does not soften.'

Serafima falls silent. Now she is looking straight at Lily, eyebrows raised in enquiry.

'Please tell her I understand,' Lily says to Alexei. She hesitates, then adds, 'Has she a child? Is it—' She doesn't know how to ask.

But Serafima is already speaking, smiling now, nodding and reaching out to touch Lily's arm.

'Yes,' Alexei says with a grin. 'Little girl who sit with 'er is daughter. And she say she needs to go back to daughter now.'

Lily takes Serafima's hand. 'Thank you,' she says.

And softly Serafima repeats, 'Thank you.'

FIVE

'You don't believe Abel Spokewright murdered Effie Quittenden, then?'

Felix and the Reverend Peter Tewks have gone inside the church, and the vicar has led the way into the vestry and firmly closed the door; Felix has the strong impression that Mr Tewks doesn't want this conversation to be overheard.

'I most certainly do not,' the vicar says vehemently. 'Effie was a member of my flock, of course, and a most lovely girl, with a warm and affectionate nature. She loved her young Londoner from the East End, he returned her love in full, and they had already been to see me to say that they had made up their minds to be married as soon as they could. And then she was killed.' He stops, his face displaying his sorrow. 'Abel was not capable of harming her, never mind killing her, for, you see, she brought out all the qualities of *tenderness* in him.'

There is a silence. Felix observes the vicar quietly wipe his eyes.

Then he says briskly, 'But in truth I was not well acquainted with Abel Spokewright, for he was only ever here in the village for the annual hop-picking. However, if you are sincere in your quest, there is someone to whom you should speak.' He looks enquiringly at Felix.

'I most certainly am totally sincere,' he replies.

Peter Tewks nods, smiling in grim satisfaction. 'The person I shall send you to is the clergyman who officiated at poor Abel's execution. He spent much time with the poor boy in the final days. His name is Tristram Cox, he's vicar of St Matthew's on the Downs, and I know him quite well.' He pauses, frowning slightly. 'How to describe Tristram? He is a young man, idealistic, a little naive, perhaps, and he feels strongly that capital punishment is barbaric.' He leans closer to Felix. 'It was appalling that the forces of circumstance

arranged it so that a man such as Tristram should have to
minister at a hanging such as Abel Spokewright's. In addition,
the poor fellow feels dreadful because he mistimed his final
prayers, and the executioner had to wait, with Abel standing
trembling on the trapdoor, for him to finish before pulling the
lever.'

Felix feels a deep shudder of revulsion go right through
him.

'The burden of guilt that Tristram struggles with is almost
unbearably heavy,' Peter Tewks says. 'I have tried to tell him
that the grave weight of capital punishment is not his to
carry; that he was there in an official capacity, employed by
Her Majesty's Government, and only summoned because the
chaplain of Lewes Gaol had broken his leg and was quite
incapable of mounting the scaffold steps.' He pauses. Then
he says, 'Tristram's parish is in a small village on the South
Downs, as I say, and really no distance at all. You could be
there and back by this evening.'

Felix takes the train down to the village where the church of
St Matthew's is to be found.

The village is tiny: two rows of houses either side of a lane
that runs along at the foot of the South Downs, a pub, a village
shop with a butcher on one side and a baker on the other.

And a church.

This one is no historically interesting and beautiful old
building such as All Saints', Crooked Green, but an unimagina-
tive Victorian rectangle with a pitched tile roof and a
steeple that looks very much like an afterthought. The path
leading up to the partly open door is also of brick, and as
Felix walks up it he hears organ music coming out of the
church.

He slips silently inside and finds a seat in a pew towards
the back. Whoever is sitting at the organ is practising hymns:
Felix recognizes a very tender version of 'Love Divine all
Loves Excelling' and then, carried away, apparently, by the
stirring melody – which he plays superbly – the organist begins
to sing, quietly at first, and then in a full-throated tenor which
sends echoes up into the soaring roof. And Felix, who hasn't

sung a hymn since he was ejected from school, finds himself standing up and hears his own baritone joining in.

The organist must surely have heard – Felix has quite a loud voice – but it doesn't deter him, and he plays right through to the end of the second verse. Then there is the sound of feet on wooden steps, and a young man of about twenty-eight or thirty appears from behind a curtain beside the door.

He strides towards Felix, his hand out, and with a grin says, 'I don't suppose you've come to join the choir, have you? We're rather light on baritones.'

'I'm afraid not.' For a moment Felix wishes his visit had such a simple and pleasant purpose, for already he is warming to the young vicar of St Matthew's – if indeed this is he – and he enjoyed the singing enormously.

The vicar (he is certainly a vicar, for he wears a dog collar) seems to have detected that Felix's business is grave, for his smile has gone. He indicates to Felix to sit down again, and settles beside him. 'What can I do for you?' he asks.

'My name is Felix Wilbraham, and I am with a private enquiry agency in London.' He has a card ready, and hands it over. 'You are the Reverend Mr Tristram Cox?' The vicar nods. Now he looks decidedly apprehensive, so Felix plunges straight in. 'I have just come from Mr Tewks, in Crooked Green, and he said you were the man to speak to concerning—'

Tristram Cox is already nodding. 'Abel Spokewright,' he says. 'You are going to prove he wasn't responsible for the death of that poor girl, and perhaps even acquire a posthumous pardon for him.'

'I am going to try,' Felix says. 'Unfortunately there is no guarantee that I shall succeed.'

'He did not kill Effie,' Tristram Cox says very firmly. 'His love for her was deep and true, Mr—' he glances at the card – 'Mr Wilbraham. He was saving his money and taking on extra work in order to buy her a ring and provide for her as his wife, and his heartfelt wish was to spend the rest of his life with her. He could not have killed her. He loved her strongly and profoundly, so much so that in truth he saw little point in living after she was dead.' He pauses. 'It was my duty to take the place of the prison chaplain, who broke his leg a week or so before the execution, and I spent as much time as I could with Abel in those last days.' He shakes his head, his expression a mixture of shame and grief. 'I believe I may have offered a modicum of comfort during those sessions, but to my shame I undid all the good I might have done at the hanging itself, when I—'

But there is no need for him to go through the pain of confessing all over again: 'I know,' Felix interrupts gently. 'Mr Tewks told me.'

Tristram hangs his head.

Into the painful silence Felix says, 'Will you tell me what happened the day Effie died? If you can, that is, and if you are willing?'

'Yes, Mr Wilbraham, I will. I probably know as much as anybody, for I was there for every single moment of the trial, and in addition poor Abel could not stop talking about it, before they – before the end. He kept going over and over all the details that came out during the trial, searching, always searching, for some overlooked little fact that would prove he didn't kill her.'

He stops speaking, gazing down the aisle at the altar. Then he continues.

'It happened last September, on the final day before the hop-pickers went home. It was the day of the annual cricket match. It's a tradition, apparently, that the villagers challenge the East End hop-pickers on their last day, and the match is held on the field behind the pub, which I believe is called the Leopard's Head.'

'It is,' Felix confirms. 'I had a couple of pints there only this lunchtime.'

Tristram nods absently.

'The match was played in very good spirits, helped along by a barrel of beer and some good solid food from Peg – Peg Sleech, the landlord's wife, that is – in the pub kitchen, where Effie Quittenden was helping her. The East Enders won, apparently.'

'It was a perfect late September day,' he goes on after a pause. 'A true Indian summer day, sunshine all afternoon and a long, long twilight that seemed to go on for hours. You can picture it, can't you? The cricketers sweaty and hot, the sound of the ball on the bat, cries of triumph and howls of dismay, applause, people sitting on the grass, and barefooted, sun-brown hop-pickers' children, wild with the last day of freedom and fresh countryside to play in.' He paints a good picture, Felix thinks.

'Effie crept outside to watch when she could, and made sure she was there for Abel's time at the wicket. He did very well, apparently – took a tricky catch, and later, when his side were batting, got his eye in and hit a couple of boundaries and a six. He was a tall, powerfully built young fellow.' Briefly he closes his eyes, as if picturing the dead man.

'Then finally Effie's work was done and at last she could slip away, amid much ribald teasing from the locals, all of whom knew about her and Abel.' He stops, frowning, and mutters, 'I did wonder, Mr Wilbraham, if there might not be resentment among some of the local young men.'

'Because they looked on Effie as one of theirs and didn't like an outsider winning her hand?'

'Precisely so,' Tristram agrees. 'She was very pretty, by all accounts, and I am quite sure many of the village men would have liked her as their wife.'

The thought had already occurred to Felix – naturally it had – but he takes his notebook out of his pocket and writes down a few words. The vicar nods in satisfaction.

'She went to meet Abel?' he prompts.

'She did.' Tristram sighs. 'Apparently Ezra Sleech – he's the landlord – put out his hand and pretended to detain her, then, according to one of the witnesses, demanded "Just one little kiss from my pretty, pretty barmaid before she slips away to her sweetheart!" but Effie just laughed. It was all very good-natured and friendly, they said – Ezra and Effie got on well together, and I don't imagine Ezra would have spoiled his relationship with a hard-working, useful barmaid by compromising her.'

He stops for several moments and Felix, appreciating that this is difficult, waits in silence.

'And then there they are, those two young lovers, out in the soft, kindly darkness,' Tristram says quietly. 'They used to meet under the concealing branches of the chestnut trees on

Badgers' Bank, which was close to the village yet secluded
and private. Abel told me they kissed, and he held her tightly
in his arms, and once he ventured to slip his hand inside her
bodice.' He glances quickly then looks away. 'I am sorry to
be so crude, Mr Wilbraham,' he mutters, 'but I feel you should
hear the story just as Abel told it to me. They whispered their
words of love, they renewed their promises to be married as
soon as they had enough money.'

Again he stops.

'Then what happened?' Felix prompts.

Tristram jerks out of his sad reverie. 'Abel saw her back to
the house she shared with her elderly grandfather, in Newhouse
Lane. Then, dancing on air, he went back to the hop-pickers'
sheds at Nightingale Farm, and let himself into the one he
shared with his mother, his aunt and his brother.' Now he turns
to Felix and, with a puzzled frown says, 'But then for some
reason it appears that Effie went back to Badgers' Bank. Abel
had no explanation – was it for one more kiss, one more
exchange of promises? One last reassurance that their plans
would work out? Simply to live again those precious moments
with the man she loved? But Abel had gone – happiness lent
him speed, and he sprinted off across the cricket field and
down the lane to Nightingale Farm as if he were flying. We
can but imagine Effie standing forlorn under the bank.' He
stops, swallows a couple of times. 'And there was her killer,
stepping calmly out from the shadows to dispatch her with a
length of hop twine.'

There is a silence which, it seems to Felix, both of them
are reluctant to break.

Then after a while Tristram sighs heavily and says, 'Nobody
missed her till early the next morning, when she should have
been in the dairy at Newhouse Farm for the morning milking.'

'Did her grandfather not wonder where she was?' Felix
asks.

'He did not,' Tristram says disapprovingly. 'He is a selfish
old man who sat back in his chair complaining that he didn't
understand anything any more and expected Effie to look after
his every need, despite the fact that she worked long hours at
the farm and helped out in the pub whenever she was asked.

As long as she kept the house clean and there was food in the larder, he largely ignored her. It seems he was not in the habit of lying awake listening out for her until she came home. He certainly didn't that night.'

He stops to draw breath. Then: 'It was George the cowman who raised the alarm. To begin with he was simply cross that Effie wasn't there and he had to do twice as much work. The Marchants were angry too. By that I mean Harold Marchant, who is the farmer, his mother Beryl – Harold is not married – and his nephew Mick, his late brother's son, who works there. They were all accusing Effie in her absence of drinking too much after the cricket match – she didn't, she was working in the pub till the moment she left – and then getting carried away with her young man, and, as a consequence of all that, sleeping so soundly that she overlaid – that's what they call oversleeping down in this part of the country – and in short not having a jot of consideration for others who had to do her work for her. Old Mrs Marchant, so they say, was particularly vindictive, which was probably something to do with the fact that she had to be summoned out of the house to do Effie's share of the milking.'

'But then someone found her,' Felix says.

'Yes,' Tristram breathes softly. 'A lad on his bicycle, heading up Badgers' Bank towards Hopgarden Lane. He'd stopped to check on a particular badger's sett he'd been keeping an eye on, and Effie's body was lying in the deep shade beneath the trees.' He swallows, making a gulping sound. 'The twine was still tight around her neck and her face was—' But it seems he can't go on, and he drops his head into his hands.

But then suddenly he leans forward, eyes fixed on Felix, who can sense the tension in him. 'In those first shocked minutes and hours, people started to say that they knew who had killed her,' he cries, his voice loud in his distress, 'that it was obvious, that it could be nobody but Abel Spokewright, because he was full of beer and cocky with his success in the cricket match, and, wild with lust, he tried to make Effie go all the way, she wouldn't, he forced her and, when she tried to scream, he strangled her.'

Just as the last words of the hymn had done not long ago,

the echoes of his loud, angry voice repeat a few times before fading away.

'They were wrong,' he says presently, his voice soft and sad. 'Abel didn't kill her, and in fairness I believe that is now the general opinion. That first violent reaction was born of panic, I imagine, and once the villagers had had time to reflect, doubtless most of them realized they were wrong. And Abel didn't try to force her against her will, either,' he goes on firmly. 'For one thing, he told me he hadn't, and I believed him. For another' – he shoots a quick glance at Felix – 'the police medical officer's report on the body was read out at the trial. Effie's underclothes had not been disturbed, and she was still a virgin.'

It is late evening now, and Felix is back in Crooked Green.

He did not linger in St Matthew's Church once its passionate young vicar had told him all he could. Felix thanked him for being so frank and informative, promised several times that he would do his utmost to help Jared Spokewright clear his brother's name, and that he would keep Tristram informed of the progress he made. 'If I manage to make any,' he muttered under his breath as finally he made his escape and headed off for the station.

He stops off in Binhurst in order to confirm that he will be staying for the night, and possibly the next one too, at the New Cock. He is shown to a modest but adequate single room – the friendly young man he met earlier carries the portmanteau for him – where he unpacks his few personal possessions and has a wash. It is after seven o'clock by now, and he goes down to the bar to eat a meal of sausages and mashed potato. He has another pint of the local ale, discovering with pleasure that the tapster here keeps his ale as well as Ezra Sleech does.

He lingers over a second pint, but even so it is still too early when he has finished it to think of going to bed. So he emerges into the soft twilight and walks back up the lane to Crooked Green.

He wants to look round the village on his own, and hopefully with nobody watching. As he passes Nightingale Farm and comes to Upper Road and the first of the houses, it seems he is to get his wish. There are lights in many of the windows, and here and there he hears voices talking quietly in the small gardens set behind the houses. There are signs of life emanating from the Leopard's Head, but he is not tempted to call in. Pausing beside the hedge, he looks over into a well-tended vegetable garden with neat rows of flowers growing at one end.

It is very quiet, very peaceful . . .

He stops in the middle of the green, staring first at the church and then over to his right, towards the lane that leads down to the cottage where his great-uncle lives. Tomorrow, he tells himself.

Finally he returns along Upper Road, this time turning up to the left, along the side of the field behind the pub. The lane is narrow, with a belt of trees concealing the field. To the right a bank rises steeply, more trees and some shrubs on its slope and a stand of chestnuts mixed with oak and hazel along the top.

This is Badgers' Bank.

This is where Effie Quittenden's dead body was found.

This is the place where she was strangled by an unknown assailant with a length of hop twine. Whoever he was, he definitely was *not* Abel Spokewright: after everything Felix has learned today, he is as sure of this as they are.

He stands perfectly still for some time.

He is thinking about a lovely, warm-hearted girl on the brink of womanhood. About the strong young man who loved her, who was powerful enough to drive a cricket ball right over the boundary and who worked almost every day of his life in that toughest of environments, the London docks. Whose ability to care and to commit were aroused by her. Whose qualities of tenderness – that is the word of today that keeps coming back to him – were drawn out of him by her love.

There is a movement, over there in the profound shadow at the foot of the bank. Very slowly Felix turns his head to look, barely breathing, freezing to stillness. If it is a badger, he would like to see it, and he has heard that they are very shy.

It isn't a badger. In the split-second Felix can see it, he

thinks it must surely be a man. A big man, a tall man, bending over as if in the deepest, most agonizing grief.

But even as his eyes focus on him, he is gone.

Not there.

Felix stands breathless, waiting for his racing heartbeat to slow down.

Of course it wasn't a man, he tells himself. Nobody could have disappeared so fast, and besides there was no noise.

It wasn't a badger either. It wasn't anything; just the shadows.

He doesn't want to admit to himself that he is spooked, but nevertheless he is. He rapidly comes to the decision that he's had enough of Crooked Green for one day and hurries back down Badgers' Bank. Soon he is striding out for Binhurst, the New Cock, a rather badly needed nightcap and bed.

SIX

Felix wakes in his room in the New Cock. It displays hints of past opulence: the walls are panelled in wood below the dado rail, and the wallpaper above this is thick and was obviously of good quality (Felix knows this because it is peeling away on the damp patch behind the door and he has inspected it). The floorboards are oak, warped now and heavily stained in places, and they creak as loudly as gunshots when he walks across the room. The bed is wide, high and with elaborate head and foot boards, and unfortunately for Felix, the gap between them is just too short for a man of his height. Nevertheless the mattress is fairly new, the bedclothes adequate, and he has slept surprisingly well. 'Must be all that country air,' he says to as much of his reflection as he can see in the tiny mirror, crouching before the wash stand to shave. Someone had left a jug of very hot water outside his door – in fact their loud banging on the door and shout of 'Take it while it's 'ot!' were the noises that woke him – and now, washed, shaved, he is ready for the day. He eats a surprisingly good breakfast and pays a last visit to the lavatory in the yard – not so good. Then, recalling that he undertook to notify Lily of his address as soon as he had one, he writes a swift note to that effect and calls in on his way out at the post office. Then he sets off for Crooked Green.

He very much wants to seek out his great-uncle and justifies this by telling himself he needs to know a lot more about the village and its inhabitants, because if Abel didn't kill Effie, then someone else did. He needs to find out about the likely contenders, and he can scarcely do this in the Leopard's Head.

He walks swiftly and heads off down Beuse Lane. He passes a very narrow track on the right, little more than a path. He continues down the lane. Presently it narrows until it is a cart track, descending gently into a valley. He spots a footpath that leads off to the right, climbing back to the higher ground. It has a belt of trees on one side, and it looks shady and very appealing: Felix is already overheating in the sunshine. The sound of water from the ditches either side of the road, hurrying on to join some larger water course, draws him on. Presently another, wider track leads away to his right.

After perhaps a quarter of a mile the track takes a last downward plunge, and there running along the bottom of the little valley is a wide stream, or perhaps it qualifies as a small river. The water is shallow just here, and there is a stretch of rocky ground clearly visible on the stream bed into which two deep grooves have been worn over the centuries by the passage of cart wheels. To either side of the ford the banks rise again, and willow, alder, oak and ash grow in profusion, casting their deep shade over the dark greenish-brown water. A few paces down to the right, the river takes a leisurely curve, and the effect of the current over the years has undercut the bank and carved out a deep pool. Felix spots movement as a trout rises smoothly up to the surface, snatches a fly and descends again.

It is an idyllic spot.

With an unmistakable twinge of guilt, for he is working and what he is about to do most definitely is not work, Felix unlaces his boots, removes them and his hose and, balancing carefully, walks out into the water.

It is so good that he hears himself groan with pleasure.

After a few moments of this bliss, an image of Lily's face floats into his head. She wears her disapproving frown. He steps carefully back to the bank – the rocks are slippery – and dries his feet as best he can with his handkerchief. Replacing his socks and boots, he turns and walks back the way he has come, to the point where he spotted the only track of any size leading off Beuse Lane, for surely this has to be Ford Lane and his goal.

To begin with he thinks he must be mistaken. There is no sign to indicate that this is indeed Ford Lane, and he can see no dwellings. But then, emerging from a thickly wooded stretch, he sees signs of human habitation: a barn, standing by itself in a paddock whose fences are in good repair and which contains two skewbald horses, a fat-bellied chestnut, a couple of bays and a very pretty grey mare with a foal keeping very close beside her.

Felix walks on, his pace increasing, for he has spotted a pair of handsome cottages standing in their own gardens, the latter vibrant with the flowers of late summer and, as if to demonstrate that whoever tends them has an eye for dutiful practicality as well as the joy of delphiniums, pansies, stocks, roses and many other plants that Felix can't name, there are also runner beans, peas, a bed of potatoes and rows of soft fruits. At the rear is a small orchard of apple trees, whose shade augments that of the oaks that grow on the sloping ground behind the cottages.

They have thatched roofs and are white-painted, their walls criss-crossed with beams. Small windows poke out of the thatch, marginally larger windows are set into the ground floor, and each cottage has a rose-covered porch that half-conceals its ancient wooden door.

A painted sign hangs at the place where the two cottages adjoin. It reads *Spinfish Cottages*, and the date *1785*. Number 2 is the further cottage.

Slowly, treating lightly – there is a slight squelching sound from his inadequately dried right foot – Felix approaches the white-painted gate opening onto the path to its door. The door is ajar: he creeps into the porch and peers through the gap.

He is looking at what appears to be the main living area. There is a range set into the right-hand wall, and next to it a stone sink with a pump beside it, its spout debouching into the sink. Shelves on the wall hold cups, plates, pans and a couple of glasses, neatly arranged. The floor is stone-flagged, and there is a colourful rag rug in front of the hearth on the rear wall. On the left of the fireplace there is a fine oak settle, the wood dark and glossy with age, on the seat of which someone with an eye for comfort has placed a series of cushions. The cushion covers have been enlivened with skilful cross-stitch designs of pansies in purples and yellows that are practically identical to their real-life counterparts outside.

There are two people over on the far side of the room.

A man in perhaps his mid-thirties sits on the settle. He is

re-stitching a stirrup leather. He has dark blond hair and light-coloured eyes, he is powerfully built and, as far as it is possible to tell with someone sitting down, looks to be tall. He reminds Felix of someone.

He is laughing up at the woman who has just risen from the settle. She is putting on a sturdy shoe, and as she straightens the tongue to get her foot inside, she rests a hand on the man's shoulder for balance in a gesture that manages to suggest profound affinity and regular habit. She is square-shouldered, quite tall, blue-eyed, blond-haired and pale-skinned, and she is absolutely beautiful. She is dressed in a white – no, cream – blouse of some thickish cotton fabric and a skirt in coarse beige linen, and she is as graceful as a dancer, long-necked like a ballerina.

Her shoe back on her foot to her satisfaction, she leans across the man at the table to pick up a wicker basket lined with red and white checked gingham. He puts down the stirrup leather and darts out his arm, encircling the woman's waist, pulling her towards him. She bends down and kisses him on the mouth, mumbling something, but with her lips to his the words are indistinct. He understands them, whatever they are, and as he releases her, both of them are laughing.

Without even pausing to consider it, Felix knows these two are lovers and have been for some time. This is not the fizzing thrill of a new passion, for the mood between them speaks of deep love and long familiarization. Instinctively, and even more quietly than he approached, he tiptoes away from the door and hurries back up the track, slipping into the shelter of the trees and hiding behind a sturdy oak.

Presently the beautiful woman emerges from number 2, Spinfish Cottages, shaking her head and leaning back inside the cottage for some final remark. There is the faint rumble of a male voice as the man replies. Whatever the remark was, it was funny, and briefly the beautiful woman laughs aloud: a surprisingly earthy guffaw, Felix thinks.

There is clearly more to her than meets the eye.

He moves further behind his tree as she passes. He is so efficiently concealed that he only catches a glimpse of her. She is walking fast, striding out in those sturdy shoes, and the basket is over her arm. She is humming to herself. Once she has gone past, he ventures out to the edge of the trees, looking up the lane after her. She comes to the place where the footpath branches off to the left, and, hitching up her skirt, climbs up the bank and sets off along it. The path crosses a field, following a line of trees that soar above a hedgerow of blackberry and blackthorn. That, he thinks, explains the basket: she's out gathering the wild fruits of the late summer. It's too early for the sloes, so it'll be blackberries.

When she is out of sight, he goes back down the track, up the path and raps smartly on the door of number 2, Spinfish Cottages.

It has been closed, but now it is flung open and Felix is face to face with the man who had been sitting on the settle. The two of them are much the same height and build, and once again Felix has that strange sense of recognition. But there is no time to reflect on this, because the man is scowling and his large right hand is bunched into a fist.

'What the hell do you want?' he demands.

Felix, who, if he had prepared his opening words has now forgotten them, says questioningly, 'I thought Noah Smith lived here?'

The man's frown intensifies and he says suspiciously, 'Who wants to know?'

It is surely not the moment to produce a World's End Bureau card, and instead Felix says, 'My name is Felix Wilbraham. Noah Smith is my great-uncle, or so I believe.'

The frown is still there, but Felix thinks – hopes – that the man's light golden-brown eyes crinkle slightly with amusement. After what seems like a very long moment, he says, 'Your name is not unknown to me,' and, standing back, he opens the door widely and jerks his head in a gesture that seems to invite Felix to enter.

He doesn't hesitate but steps down into the room.

The first thing he notices is an oil painting, on a part of the room's walls that wasn't visible when he was peering through the crack. The painting is a portrait of a grey-haired man in what appears to be his vigorous middle years, perhaps edging towards old age. He is balding, although the greying hair on his temples is still thick, and he has a moustache and beard. He is dressed in some sort of a robe, dark and with a heavy collar, and he wears leather gauntlets on the hands that rest on the table in front of him, one of them holding a rather beautiful pewter goblet. He stares out of the painting with an expression that seems to issue a challenge; the brows are drawn together, and the light eyes are narrowed in an assessing glare.

He reminds Felix powerfully of his grandfather Derek Smith, and simultaneously, just as this realization dawns, Felix also knows that the person who the man before him reminds him of is himself.

The man draws a chair from beneath the table in front of the sink, perches on it and, indicating the settle, says, 'Sit.' Felix obeys. There is a silence, during which he endures the intent scrutiny of the man, who presently says softly, 'So you're looking for Noah Smith.' He pauses, then adds, 'You're Frances Smith's son.'

It isn't a question, but Felix feels he should answer it anyway.

'Yes, although by the time of her marriage to my father, plain old Frances Smith had been elevated to Frances Althea Courtney-Smythe.' Struck by a sudden urge to defend the woman who bore him – admittedly something that doesn't happen very often – he adds, 'Not entirely her fault. Grandad Derek's wife had been trying to make him more socially acceptable for years, they say, and my mother probably picked it up from her.' The man watches him, his face impassive. 'My parents included Derek as one of my Christian names,' Felix blurts out, 'purely because he was the wealthiest out of all their relations.'

There is an all but imperceptible nod.

After a brief and increasingly uncomfortable silence, the man speaks at last. He says, 'I do not doubt that you are who you say you are.' He pauses, then says softly, 'Since you've come all this way from London to seek out Noah Smith, I suppose you want me to tell you about him.'

And Felix, intrigued, thinks it best to answer simply, 'Yes, please.'

The man closes his eyes briefly, then starts to speak.

'I don't believe they make men in his mould any more,' he

begins. 'He lived to nearly a hundred, and it was only about a decade ago – 1870, to be precise – that he died.' He gives Felix a sardonic grin. 'You've not missed him by much,' he observes.

'Why did he—' Felix begins, but if the man hears he takes no notice.

'He was a strong, virile, charismatic man,' he states. 'Married for the first time when he was sixteen years old, his bride a year younger, and their daughter was born the next year. Ena – that was the first wife's name – died of cholera in the 1810 outbreak, and five years later Noah married Flossie Crump.' He glances at Felix. 'He wasn't going to risk the health of a second wife and her children amid the deadly diseases of the East End's poverty-ridden streets, so he brought his pregnant young bride down here. Flossie was only seventeen, and the countryside was a frightening mystery to her, but despite the twenty-eight-year age gap she was deeply in love' – he glances up at the oil painting – 'and would have followed her new husband anywhere.'

The man stops, regarding Felix closely. Felix feels a brief urge to say, *Don't worry, I'm paying close attention*, but he decides it's not necessary; besides, any interruption might give this strangely compliant man a chance to think again about confiding his family history to a stranger, even if he is a relative.

But of course – the thought hits Felix like a gentle punch – *it's my family history too.*

'Noah and Flossie settled in a tied cottage deep in the countryside,' the man is saying. 'Noah had inherited his forefathers' talent for spotting an opportunity, and soon he was salting away money, prepared to take on anything promising a profit. The years passed, one of the daughters married a local man and another moved back to London.' He stops, once again looking up at the portrait. 'Then in 1841 Flossie died, worn down with the grief of losing three of her five children.' The light eyes turn to Felix and the man says softly, 'Children and wives die in the country too, and it wasn't the idyll Noah believed it to be. There he was, a widower again with his two surviving daughters, and more of those he loved in the ground than living upon it.' Before Felix can comment on this somewhat startling way of putting it, the man says, 'You'd think he'd have had enough, not risked his heart again, wouldn't you?'

'Er – yes,' Felix says.

The man smiles. 'Not Noah Smith. You see, both Ena and Flossie bore boys but none survived, and, fond though he was of his girls, what Noah wanted was a son. So in 1846, at the age of seventy-six but looking a decade or two younger' – yet another twitch of the eyes towards the portrait – 'Noah took his third and final wife.'

'Seventy-six!' Felix says softly. He hadn't meant to say the words aloud, but the man gives no sign that he has heard.

'Her name was Marjory Burgess, and she was always known as Jory,' he is saying. 'She was clever, capable and, at thirty, considerably older than either of her predecessors. She was a widow whose husband had died young, too soon for her to have had children by him.'

He wanted a son, Felix thinks but doesn't say. *Surely it would have made better sense to wed a woman who had proved she could give him one?*

The light eyes are staring at him again, narrowing intently, and Felix has the disconcerting impression that his companion has read his thoughts. By now he is pretty sure of the man's identity, and it's really not the time to offend him by suggesting Noah Smith's third wife was an unwise choice . . .

'Was she a local woman, this Jory Burgess?' he asks, hoping to divert the man.

There is what seems to Felix like a very long pause. Then the man says neutrally, 'Local enough. Horsmonden way. Her father bred horses.'

And the man smiles faintly as he replies, as if to say, *Just you be careful and guard what you're thinking, Felix Wilbraham, because I take offence very easily.*

But surely that is nonsense. People can't read one another's minds, and all those stage performers who claim they can are actors who fool their admirers with the clever use of well-placed stooges in the audience. Felix gives himself a silent reprimand for allowing his imagination to run away with him.

Rather more forcefully than he intended, he says, 'Go on.'

It sounds like a command. For a moment, his eyes meet the man's and he can almost imagine the clashing of invisible antlers . . .

After a brief and somewhat tense moment, the man continues.

'By now Noah Smith was a rich man,' he says, 'although he never advertised the fact. It was never clear how he'd succeeded in amassing so much wealth. He lived frugally, and Jory was a better manager of the household than either of his former wives, and there was money in abundance. He had long since moved his family out of the tied cottage and now lived in his own house, although this was something else he kept to himself. He had a reputation as a breeder of fine horses, and regularly attended the local horse fair on the second Saturday of every September.'

Any minute now, Felix thinks, *he's going to tell me* . . .

And, sure enough: 'In 1847,' the man says portentously, 'Jory gave birth to the longed-for son. He was to be her only child, Noah's sole son to survive infancy, and they named him after his father, adding a "the second" after his name for the sake of clarity. He was big, healthy, and he inherited his father's strong constitution, his mother's insight and intelligence, and the good looks of both of them' – his handsome face twists into a smile that is heavy with self-mockery – 'for Jory had been a true beauty when young and she was still a looker when she died twelve years ago.'

'Twelve years,' Felix says gently. He is certain, now, and sends the man a compassionate smile which he can see goes completely unnoticed.

'She was the love of his life,' he says quietly. 'Only a few weeks after she died, he followed her.' He clears his throat. 'Noah Smith II was twenty-two, and, his father's sole heir, he settled down to life without them. He grieved them deeply, although nobody ever realized.'

Silence has fallen. Felix has the strange sense that the man's last words are still floating on the warm, still air. He sits motionless, occasionally looking up at his father's portrait, and after some time says with a smile, 'He's buried in the churchyard, you know. Ena, Flossie and Jory are all with him

– he had Ena's body brought down from Limehouse. You can
go and read the headstone for yourself, but I'll tell you what
you'll find.'

I already know, Felix thinks. *I know the words not concealed
by ivy, anyway, and now I can fill in the rest.*

'Noah Smith, born Limehouse in London 1770, died
Crooked Green 1870,' the man recites, his eyes closed. 'Also
Ena Hill, Flossie Crump and Marjory Burgess, all the wives
of Noah Smith.'

He opens his eyes again and, staring straight at Felix, says,
'I am Noah Smith II, that is my father' – he points at the
portrait – 'Jory was my mother, and you are my second cousin.
Now I think you'd better tell me what you want,' he goes on,
a note of warning in his voice, 'because, gratified as I am by
your interest in my branch of the family, I don't believe finding
out about us is why you're here.' He pauses, then, his eyes
narrowing, adds softly, 'Could it, I wonder, have anything to
do with the fact that there was a murder in this village a year
ago, for which the wrong man was convicted and hanged?
And,' he goes on remorselessly, not allowing Felix to comment,
'because you work for a private investigation bureau?'

'How did you know?' Felix demands.

'Your successes are reported in the London press. I know
quite a lot about you and your cool-headed lady employer.
My London kin keep me informed.'

Just as the full picture is finally coming together in Felix's
mind, Noah says, 'Who do you think sent Jared Spokewright
to the World's End Bureau?' Now at last he smiles. 'I've been
expecting you, Felix Wilbraham.'

SEVEN

L ily wishes very much that she felt more at home in the East End, but it is as if she has strayed into a mystifying foreign country, which in a way she has. People talk, laugh raucously and shout out to each other all around her, and among the languages they use, English only features occasionally. Very few of these people look anything like her. It is both intensely interesting and more than a little alarming.

She has now visited all of the charitable institutions whose details were provided by James Jellicote and which might be caring for Yakov: William Booth's Salvation Army hostel; the Poor Jews' Temporary Shelter; Dr Barnardo's boys' home in Stepney Causeway. There are boys of twelve aplenty in each, and a large number of them have recently arrived from Russia; almost all are dressed in dirty, worn clothes and broken boots, and many have dark hair and dark eyes. But the only child who is totally alone is not a boy but a fourteen-year-old girl, brown-haired and blue eyed, who shoots Lily one shifty look before melting away. 'Says she's called Victoria,' the man checking his lists tells Lily, adding in a low voice, 'What I reckon is that she's run away and the last thing she wants is to be reunited with her parents.'

It occurs to Lily that if Yakov is as bright as his grandmother claims and if his fear has made him determined to hide, he might well have bribed some other lad to say they are brothers, or to have come up with a story persuasive enough to make a family temporarily take him under their wing. She tries not to think about that, because if it has indeed happened, her chances of finding him have just dropped from very slim to non-existent.

The big, harassed-looking but kindly man at Barnardo's is the most sympathetic of the people she speaks to, listening to her in silence and asking several questions, which prompts her to recall Yelisaveta's mention of the gap between the boy's front teeth. But the man shakes his head. 'I'm sorry, miss, but there's just such a *flow* of them coming out of Russia, and I can't say I've had a moment to notice anyone's teeth.'

'No, of course not, it was foolish to ask.'

'Not at all,' he says gently. 'You're trying to help, and that's good. But, like I said, there's so many arriving now, and they need all the help they can get. The East End's fast becoming an enclave, that's what's happening.' He seems pleased with the word *enclave*, repeating it under his breath a couple of times. 'Mind you, they don't let the grass grow under their feet, oh, no, they find work like tailoring and carpentry, and there's new synagogues springing up, and they have their own theatres, schools and what have you. They look after their own,' he says, leaning towards her for emphasis, 'and that's admirable, that's what I say. If one of them come across this little lad you're looking for, hungry, dirty, alone and afraid, he'd not have turned him away, mark my words.'

Now it is late in the day, and Lily has no idea what to do next in her mission to find a small Russian boy of twelve years old adrift and alone in an alien land. She would very much like to return to Hob's Court – and a world she understands – but this would be self-indulgent and defeatist, she tells herself firmly, since in the absence of Felix, she would only be able to think about the problem by herself, which she can do equally well here.

'What do I know?' she says very softly. 'What have I discovered today?' There are people all around her, and she is being swept along in roughly a southerly direction on an incredibly crowded pavement, but the noise level is such that nobody would have heard her quiet words. Yelisaveta was unfriendly towards her fellow travellers, she muses, some of whom she knew from home. The others didn't like her. Why was she determined to keep herself apart? Did she feel herself superior to them? Possibly she was, but surely any such niceties of social status would dissolve in the face of the harsh conditions and the extreme suffering all were forced to endure. Serafima said Yelisaveta hid behind a blanket, presumably so that the others couldn't see her feeding the food she had acquired to her grandson, and implied this might have been the reason for her unpopularity.

But Lily can't help wondering if every other mother or grandmother on the train might not have done the same.

And, rather more worryingly, she is also wondering uneasily if there is some deeper reason for Yelisaveta's insistence on privacy and Yakov's flight . . .

She can smell the river.

Moments later, still surrounded by hurrying people, she erupts with them out of the end of a dark, smelly and very narrow little passage onto a quay. There is a line of ships tied up, many of which are disgorging passengers. She is about to find someone to ask where she is, which quay she has found herself on, when she catches sight of a large sign saying *St Katharine Dock*.

And now she thinks she can work out her location. Immediately to her right – upriver – is the Tower, and to her left there is the southerly bend at whose apex is Wapping. Then the river turns north again, there's the Thames Tunnel, the Shadwell Basin and the Limehouse Basin. But she pulls her mind back to Wapping.

On a previous case, she visited the cramped little office of the river police situated there, and met a man called Alf Wilson who provided rather too much information on what happens to people who fall into the Thames, how their bodies often have to be pulled out in bits, and how he and the other men on his regular shift call themselves the Disciples. He seemed to develop a fondness for her, Lily recalls, even though she did ruin his little joke by spotting that they were called the Disciples because they were fishers of men before he could tell her.

She is tired, her feet hurt, she feels adrift in this world that she doesn't understand, and the thought of Alf Wilson in his little eyrie over the restless water is all at once more than she can resist.

'Now I'm not going to tell you I spotted this *Oude Maas* vessel docking,' he says some time later, 'because I didn't.'

She is sitting on a stool in his office, and the huge relief of

no longer standing on her sore feet is immense. Alf has made
her one of his alarmingly strong cups of tea and proffered an
open tin with currant buns in it. She has drunk half the tea
already and consumed most of the bun and is feeling almost
totally restored.

'But you do remember it being by the quay?'

'Alongside, we call it, miss, and ships are *her*, not it.'

'Sorry,' Lily murmurs.

'Not to worry,' Alf says magnanimously, 'you're not a
woman of the water.'

She refrains from telling him she lives very close to the
river and is on rather intimate terms with a boatman. Chewing
and swallowing, she says, 'I'm looking for a boy who fled the
quay soon after arrival. He's—'

But Alf wags a reproving finger at her. 'Now then, miss,
you and I need to have a little chat, I'm thinking.' He gives
her a roguish grin.

'Do we?' She is dismayed.

'I do not think,' Alf goes on, 'that you were entirely honest
with me, last time we met.'

'I didn't—'

'You asked me about bodies in the river, and what happened
to them.' Now he looks almost accusatory.

'Yes, and that's exactly—'

'What you did *not* tell me,' Alf goes on relentlessly, 'is that
you were seeking this information on a professional basis.'
There is a smile playing round the corners of his mouth. 'That
you are, in short, the proprietor of a private investigation
bureau, and that you were pursuing enquiries into a very nasty
case indeed!'

'Yes, Mr Wilson, I was, and I'm very sorry I didn't say so,
but—'

He waves a hand. 'Don't you distress yourself!' he cries cheerfully. 'No doubt you had your reasons, but when I read about it
in the newspapers, what you'd done and all, and told my missus
and the kids that I'd had a hand in it, they said it was cause for
celebration and we had a fine old night down at the Queen's
Arms! And' – he leans closer – 'there's no call for any of this
Mr Wilson, when I distinctly recall telling you me name's Alf!'

Lily, picking up that he clearly enjoyed his night of celebrity, not to mention the more than a few pints of ale he was probably treated to, decides to capitalize on the moment.

'Well, then, Alf, I'll freely admit it, and that I've come to you now to ask for your help again.'

He visibly preens. 'Anything I can do, miss, you only have to ask.'

Plunging straight in – Alf is on duty after all, and could any moment be called away – she says, 'The boy who's missing is called Yakov,' and succinctly tells him the tale.

Even before she's done, Alf is shaking his head. 'Oh, miss, I wish I could help but I can't,' he says mournfully. 'We'd have entered the *Oude Maas*'s arrival in the log, same as every vessel, but like I said, I didn't witness it for myself, and—' Abruptly he stops. Then he says musingly, 'But Henry saw something.'

'Henry?'

'One of the Disciples. He's not here now, gone out in the boat with the lad' – he doesn't explain and Lily doesn't ask – 'but I do recall him saying something about an old girl on a stretcher screaming like seven devils about something, trying to get up and grabbing at someone, and a lad wriggling away and straight into two men from the Salvation Army and evading them and all.' He frowns thoughtfully.

'Were they in uniform?' Lily asks.

Alf flashes her an understanding look. 'They were. Reckon that was what scared the lad off, from Henry's account. Poor little tacker'd have bad memories of men in uniform, after having been what he's been through. Soldiers, and that,' he adds.

'He would,' Lily agrees.

Alf sighs gustily. 'Shame, really, when all they'd have had in mind was giving the poor little sod something to eat and a bed for the night.'

The maze of dark and narrow little streets around the docks seems even more forbidding to Lily after the friendly welcome she received in Alf's office. She heads away from the river, thinking to make her way up to Fenchurch Street and a tram going west. But the alleyways are bordered by high walls and quite soon she realizes she's going in the wrong direction.

As if being lost in a strange and increasingly alien part of London wasn't bad enough, someone is following her.

She's tried telling herself it's her imagination but it isn't. There are soft footfalls echoing hers, almost but not quite synchronized. When she stops, they stop. When she spins round, as fast as she can, there's nobody there.

She hurries on. Don't run, she tell herself, don't show that you're afraid. She thinks of the knife concealed in her left boot, and it helps, a little.

She bursts out of a particularly dank and forbidding alley. She's on the riverside again, the water behind her, and the Thames Tunnel is to her immediate left; she can hear a train emerging. She knows which direction she should take – left, going west – but facing her is the same complicated network of dark, twisting alleys and passages, not to mention a very high wall unbroken by any doorway or alley, and her courage fails. She hears the footsteps again, and in her mind they sound heavy and threatening. She hurries on.

Past Shadwell Basin, and all at once she's on a bigger road, and there are trams, hackney carriages, people. *He won't attack me now*, she thinks desperately, *too many witnesses*. She can't seem to slow her pace, even though her stays are cutting into her flesh and she can't expand her lungs to take a proper breath. Even though she's still going in the wrong direction . . .

And then, almost as if something or someone has been guiding her, she finds herself by a canal basin. She has to step hurriedly out of the way for a horse, pulling a boat the last few yards to its mooring for the night.

Boats. Horses. A big old black-and-white horse.

She looks at the line of horses. Then at the boats, but the one that has become so familiar to her is not there.

She says softly, 'I may be lost in this vibrant, crowded and suddenly frightening world, but I know someone who isn't.'

A man and a boy are coming along the towpath. The man is carrying a newspaper-wrapped parcel that smells delicious and makes Lily's mouth water. It is some time since Alf's currant bun. He gives her a not unfriendly nod as he passes, and, encouraged, Lily says, 'I wonder, can you help me?'

The man gives the parcel to the boy, mutters, 'Take this to your Ma, I'll be along in a minute,' and turns to Lily. He looks at her in silence for a moment, his face impassive, then says, 'What do you want?'

'I'm looking for *The Dawning of the Day*,' she replies. She is about to mention the name of the boat's master, but the man is nodding, for he already knows.

Since Lily met him two years ago – under circumstances that somehow projected them straight into the sort of deep and trusting friendship that usually takes far longer to develop – she has come to realize that quite a lot of people in his watery world know the name of Tamáz Edey.

'Gone up to Birmingham,' he tells her.

Lily's spirits sink.

But now the man is leaning closer, studying her face. 'I know you,' he says softly.

She looks at him properly, and realizes she knows him too. Not well – she has no idea what his name is, and she didn't know he had a son – but she's recognized him; he's passed on a message to Tamáz for her before. Not that the information is any use now. 'Gone to Birmingham,' she repeats dully.

Picking up her disappointment, the man says, 'Mind, that was a week, ten days ago, if not more. Reckon he'll be well on the way back by now.' He studies her, smiling faintly. 'Want me to send him round to the basin at Chelsea when he turns up?'

She is embarrassed that he clearly knows of her friendship with Tamáz, although this emotion is outweighed by relief at what he's just told her, what he's offered to do. She says simply, 'Yes, please.'

The journey home to number 3, Hob's Court seems interminable. Evening is fast drawing on, and the trams are full of people going home after a long day. Everyone is tired, and, as Lily ruefully accepts when someone treads hard on her sore foot, it's not a time to expect good manners and self-effacing

politeness. And, indeed, the force with which she jabs an elbow
into the ribs of a large, sweaty man who has just pushed her
hard as he heads for the steps suggests she is somewhat short
of these characteristics herself.

As she turns down World's End Passage, her low mood
descends even further as she realizes she's going to have to
start the search for Yakov all over again in the morning.

And she just can't shake off the frightening memory of
those stealthy, echoing footsteps.

The next day is as bad as she feared. It helps that already she
is more at home in the East End: not much, but whenever
she comes to a street whose name she knows, or, pausing on
a corner, thinks, *I know where I am, I was here yesterday*, she
feels a minor triumph. There are many landmarks she already
greets like old friends, including a vast scrap-metal yard she's
walked past more than once that has a sign reading *Smith and
Sons, Fine Quality Scrap Metal Every Need Served*. She
wonders if this is Felix's family of Smiths, but it is after all
a very common surname so perhaps it isn't.

A full day's hunting, however, brings virtually nothing in
the way of helpful information, the one exception being an
elderly man in Salvation Army uniform who says he thought
he saw a lad who answered Yakov's description trying to steal
a bun off a market stall in a court behind the Whitechapel
Road. 'The stall-holder spotted him – well, anyone would
have, you'd have had to be blind not to spot him, he was that
clumsy about it,' he adds, 'and the boy took to his heels.'

'Where did he go?' Lily demands.

But the man can only say vaguely, 'North, I reckon.' Then
he adds kindly, 'Go and talk to the stall-holder, miss,' and
gives her directions.

The stall-holder is still peeved, it seems, because although
he did indeed spot the boy, it was too late to prevent the theft.
'And it weren't no bun,' he goes on aggressively, 'it were a
bleeding *pie*, good firm pastry and crammed with steak and
kidney, bursting with gravy an' all!'

Lily very nearly says she has no doubt the boy was very
hungry, but manages to hold back what would undoubtedly

be taken as an inflammatory remark: she does, after all, want this angry man's help. 'That must have been very galling, when you'd taken such trouble to make it so tasty,' she says sympathetically.

'Well, it's the wife what makes 'em,' he admits. Then, with the suggestion of a grin, 'Didn't tell her one got nicked, did I?'

'Very wise,' Lily whispers. Then, while he is still grinning, 'Did you get a good look at him?'

'I most certainly did,' the man says, puffing out his chest, 'and I stored it all in here, didn't I?' He taps his head. 'Need to be sure to recognize the little bugger if he comes back, don't I?'

'I'm looking for a boy of about twelve,' Lily tells him, and she repeats yet again the description of Yakov. Long before she's got as far as the flapping boot sole and the gap between the front teeth, the man is nodding. 'Can't swear to it, but it sounds like him,' he confirms when she's finished. He is absently rubbing his left foot up and down his right shin, which Lily thinks probably implies that Yakov – if it was Yakov – kicked him as hard as he did the Salvation Army man on the quayside.

'I don't suppose you saw which way he went?' Lily asks. She is so thoroughly prepared for a negative answer that it is a total and very welcome surprise when the man says, 'I did, as a matter of fact. Now me,' he confides, 'I'd have headed out onto the Whitechapel Road and on up Mile End Road and lost myself among the crowds, but he ran off down there' – he waves a hand in the opposite direction, into what looks like a dark warren of high-walled little alleys and passages.

'Where would that lead him to?'

The man rubs a hand against his bristly chin. 'Now you're asking,' he remarks. He frowns thoughtfully. 'The East End Cemetery and the gas works, and assuming he went on in the same direction – and there's no saying he did, mind – he'd end up on the towpath.'

She pounces. 'The towpath?'

He looks at her, grinning. 'Regent's Canal.'

She thanks him swiftly, impatient to get away, but he takes

hold of her sleeve. 'Sorry, miss, but two things I must tell you.'

'Yes?' She knows she sounds peremptory but she can't help it.

He is shaking his head. 'First off, if you're reckoning on following the lad down in there, don't. It's dangerous, see, and the boy'll be long gone by now. Two—' He pauses.

'*What?*' she almost cries.

Now he looks shamefaced. 'You're not the only one after him, miss. I should have followed him. To get my pie back, for one thing, but more because someone else did.'

'Did what?'

'Follow him! I just said, didn't I? Big, hefty feller, dark clothes, black hat, and he had a thick, full beard and that was dark and all.' He leans closer. 'And whatever he wanted with that lad, it were a deal more sinister than a matter of a stolen pie.'

'Why do you say that?' She hardly dares ask.

But the answer, when after a few moments' thought it comes, isn't what she is expecting. 'Because he were evil, miss,' he says quietly. 'It weren't just physical violence I reckoned threatened the lad, it were . . .' But it seems he can't find the word. Shaking his head, already turning away, he says over his shoulder, 'If you've got your own grievance to settle with the boy, you'd better find him sharpish.'

There is no need for him to elucidate, because Lily understands only too well.

And as she wonders wildly if this big, heavy, sinister man somehow contrives to walk with a soft and stealthy tread, the full force of yesterday's terrified certainty that someone was following her comes crashing back.

She makes her way to Regent's Canal and spends a frustrating and ultimately pointless few hours seeking news of the boy who stole the pie. Who may or may not be Yakov, she thinks more than once, further depressing herself with the possibility that she is following a totally false trail and Yakov is miles away by now.

Eventually she gives up.

*   *   *

It's late when at last she opens the front door, and she's hot and tired. Among the post waiting on the mat is an envelope addressed to her in Felix's hand. Even as she swoops down to pick it up she knows it is not the full and expansive missive she has subconsciously been waiting for; it's far too thin. Tearing it open, she reads:

Putting up at the New Cock Inn, Binhurst. Contact made with my relative. Writing. Felix.

The letter, she observes bitterly, is no more expansive than a telegraph. Hoping he means that he'll be writing more fully sooner rather than later, she bends down and removes her boots.

Mrs Clapper, she notes, has gone home. Wandering through to the back of the house, Lily sees with gratitude that one of Mrs Clapper's cold suppers has been left ready for her on the coolest shelf in the larder. The Little Ballerina, she detects, has recently left for her evening's performance; currently she is in a production of *Coppélia* in a small theatre in the less fashionable part of the West End. Lily knows her tenant has just been in the hall because she always leaves behind a sort of miasma made up of chalk dust, pomade fumes and body odour. The Little Ballerina looks beautiful and ethereal on stage; out of sheer curiosity, Lily and Felix went to see her at Christmas in a performance of *Sylvia*, and she danced the role of a nymph who was turned into a bear with competence if not a great deal of conviction, although as Felix remarked, it was a tricky transformation to carry off with any degree of credibility (the bear was considerably larger than the nymph, and Lily told him it wasn't really the Little Ballerina under the mask and all the fur). Her fragile looks, however, bely her reality, and in her personal habits she isn't ethereal but all too corporeal, and she is indolent, careless and downright smelly.

Lily relishes having the house to herself. She stands in a large bowl in the cool scullery, washing herself all over and rinsing with jug after jug of cold water, then pats herself dry and goes up to the top floor and her own rooms to dress in a loose-fitting old gown and a minimum of undergarments. Back in the scullery, she washes out her sweaty, dusty, city-dirty clothes – Mrs Clapper has enough to do – and pegs them on the line in the back yard.

She is not expecting visitors. She would not have dressed in so very informal a manner if she had been. She has eaten the supper, and is thinking of retiring to bed – it is now almost eleven o'clock, and cool at last – when there is a soft tap on the street door.

She knows who is there.

Dancing, for she delights in him for himself as well as greatly valuing the help he so freely offers her, she goes to open the door. And, sure enough, Tamáz Edey stands on the step.

He is dressed in a white shirt, his habitual waistcoat and tall hat, and he carries an earthenware flagon. Holding it up, he says, 'It's cider and it's cool. May I come in?'

But she is already standing back to let him pass.

Some time later, he says, 'Why were you looking for me?'

Because I thought someone was following me and I was very afraid, she wants to say. But that is not the only reason, and certainly not the most important one.

She orders herself firmly to stop being so feeble.

Quickly she tells him about Yakov and Yelisaveta, what happened on the quay, how Yakov fled twice, once from the quay and once from the pie-seller's stall – assuming that *was* Yakov and not some other lad – and the abysmal failure of her attempts to find him. Tamáz begins to say something to the effect that she's been looking for a mere day and a half and that isn't very long, but she interrupts.

'The pie-seller said the man who followed him was . . . *sinister*,' she says, trying to find the words to make Tamáz understand the sudden chill of fear she'd felt. 'That the boy would suffer much worse than physical violence if his pursuer caught him.'

'Then we'll hope he hasn't,' Tamáz says calmly. Then – and she is sure he asks in order to distract her from her immediate anxiety – 'Do you know where the old woman and her grandson came from?'

'Odessa.'

He nods. 'A very long journey,' he says softly.

Lily realizes that her knowledge of the geography of Russia is slight; she only knows it's a vast country. 'Is it?'

He turns to her, smiling. 'Have you paper and a pencil?'

'Naturally,' she says. She fetches a notepad and pencil, and he spends some minutes drawing a map. Then he holds it so that she can see. 'Here is the Black Sea, and Odessa is here.' He indicates a dot on the north-west of the sea. 'They would have journeyed north, perhaps to Kiev, and that would be more than five hundred miles. Then possibly on to one of the Baltic ports, searching for a ship, and that is maybe a thousand miles.'

'They crossed from Rotterdam.'

He nods again. 'Then in total a journey of not much under two thousand miles.'

She stares down at the sketch. He seems to have a ready grasp of these vast foreign lands, and even as she watches, he writes in the names of some of the countries. She has never before realized how small Britain is, stuck up here in its far north-west corner.

'How do you know all this?' she asks.

'Men who have survived the same route work on the boats. They talk.'

'Yes. But I really meant how do you know how to draw this map.'

There is a short pause. Then he says, 'I travelled much when I was young.'

She senses that's all the reply she's going to have, and reflects, not for the first time, just how much there is about him she doesn't know.

'And they flee from their homes because they are afraid?' she asks after a minute or so. 'That's what James Jellicote said; he spoke of pogroms against people of their faith, and so much violence.'

'That is the truth of it,' Tamáz says. 'And how great must the fear be, to force people to abandon their comfortable homes, their possessions, everything that makes up their lives, and run?'

Lily shakes her head. 'I can't imagine,' she says. 'I've never experienced anything remotely like it.'

He turns to her. 'And now you are trying to unite one old woman and one young boy.'

'Yes, and I know it's an impossibly tiny gesture, when so many people need help and so many are grieving and deeply shocked by all that has happened to them, but—'

'That you cannot help them all should not be a deterrent.' He puts a big, warm hand over hers. 'You are helping two people,' he says softly. 'If everyone here did the same, think how many that would add up to.'

It's a nice idea, she thinks, but somehow she just can't see it happening.

'I don't know what to do next,' she says. She glances at him, and sees that she has his full attention. 'When you arrived, you asked why I was looking for you. Because of trying to find Yakov, as you'll have guessed, but specifically because I was by the canal this afternoon and I'd been thinking that I wished I knew that world better – the East End, the river, the quays and the boats – and then I thought of you, because you do know it.'

'I do,' he agrees.

'And' – she has been saving this up, deliberately trying not to think about it since it will probably turn out to be as little use in the hunt for Yakov as the dark hair, the flapping heel and the gap between his teeth – 'because, according to his grandmother, Yakov has always been drawn to ships, boats and the water, and it was where his mother always went to look for him when he was late for dinner.'

Tamáz smiles faintly. 'I once knew a boy like that.'

She guesses from his expression that he's thinking about himself.

Then she feels his attention snap back to the present. 'It is true,' he says, 'that men and boys from Russia find work on the boats, as I told you just now. There are great waterways in their country, and it is a world they understand. A man does not need to speak the language of his new country if he already knows how to hitch a horse to a boat, how to negotiate a lock, how to ensure that his cargo is secure and remains undamaged in transit.' The distant look is back, and he murmurs, 'I do not believe, however, that the Grand Union Canal, or even the

Thames, can compete with the Volga, and these men so often look sad.'

'But they are working,' she says, wanting to reassure him as he just reassured her. 'People like you help them, and that has to be enough since nobody can give them what they really want.'

There is silence again as they both think about that.

'Tell me all you can about this Yakov Hadzibazy,' he says. She does, concentrating hard so that she doesn't miss anything out.

'He is young,' Tamáz says when she has finished. 'And alone.' He glances at her again.

'He may be safe!' she protests. 'I've been told how so many of their countrymen already settled here turn out to help them, and there are also the charitable organizations. Perhaps even now he's warm, well-fed and asleep in clean sheets.'

Tamáz is still looking at her. 'Perhaps he isn't,' he says quietly. 'Lily, I do not have to tell you, I think, that open-hearted countrymen and philanthropic Londoners are not the only people on the watch for solitary children.'

She wishes he hadn't said that, because it is something she has been battling to keep at bay ever since James Jellicote told his tale. Now her mind fills with horrible images: opium dens, bands of pickpockets, the unspeakable use of boys and girls for rich men's gratification, and she wants to weep.

He senses this. She feels his arm go round her and he draws her close. 'Do not despair,' he whispers, his lips against her hair. 'I will help you.'

EIGHT

Felix is engaged in a silent and intense argument with himself. On the one hand, his newly discovered second cousin clearly remembers the murder of Effie Quittenden – well of course he does, Felix thinks, he lives right here in the village where it happened – and he has just said that he doesn't think Abel Spokewright was guilty. Felix would very much like to hear what he has to say on the matter; why, for instance, he is so certain of Abel's innocence. After only a brief acquaintance, Felix has the impression of a shrewd and watchful man with considerable intelligence, although he admits that this could partly be because the two of them are related . . .

On the other hand, it's still entirely possible that Noah was involved in Effie's death; the most obvious explanation of his certainty that the wrong man was hanged is because he was the killer.

But every instinct is informing Felix that this isn't the case. He has already gained the impression from speaking to other inhabitants of Crooked Green that Effie was a sweetheart; popular, attractive, kindly, vivacious and loving, and in general something of a pet to all the village men. It's quite possible that someone tried to press himself upon her that night after the cricket match; that some man too full of beer and cheer attempted to replace Abel in her affections and, when she rejected him, strangled her in his frustration and his fury.

That man, however, is highly unlikely to be Noah Smith II.

Because, apart from anything else – and surely, with this reason every other becomes superfluous – Noah clearly has a lover of his own already, and the beautiful and mysterious woman in the cream cotton blouse has apparently been in his life for some time. What could he possibly want with a sweet little dairymaid, no matter how pretty and lovable she was?

Felix discovers that he has been staring at his cousin quite intently, and the faintly sardonic smile on Noah's face suggests he knows exactly what has been going through Felix's mind.

'I've always lived on the edge, like my father before me,' he says softly. 'And those who observe the game from the sidelines see the whole thing. You won't find a better source of information than me.'

Felix grins. 'I've already worked that out.' Then, after a final pause: 'Will you help me, then?'

'I will.' They exchange a glance, aa if to register the arrangement. 'What do you know already, and what do you want from me?'

Felix takes out his notebook and, trying not to let his cousin's fierce stare put him off – he looks very like his father in the portrait on the wall behind him, same light eyes and fiercely challenging expression – briefly sums up what he has learned to date, first from James Jellicote, then from Ezra Sleech and the two clergymen. 'If we are to take it as certain that Abel Spokewright didn't kill her, then—'

'Then we have to decide who did,' Noah finishes. 'It's a question I've been asking myself over and over this past year, and I have reached no conclusion. Probably one of the local men, since quite a few of them made it clear they resented an outsider like Abel Spokewright courting *one of our womenfolk.*' Felix can hear from the way he says the words that he's quoting some such local man. 'Effie was told more than once that Abel would love her and leave her, or, as her own grandfather so crudely put it, "that bloody Londoner will take you and take off", and he was one of many who told her to have no truck with him.' He sighs. 'Who knows, maybe one of them saw that she was serious about Abel – that he was serious about her – and took the view that if they couldn't have her, nobody else was going to either.'

He shakes his head, brows drawn in a deep frown. 'There was such a crowd that night after the cricket, many of them drunk, most of them shedding inhibitions fast as New Year resolutions. If we discount a stray lunatic or, narrowing it down a little, the great gang of Londoners down for the hop-picking – and there's really no reason why we should, except that if it was one of them then he's probably going to get away with it – then I have listed the men who featured most strongly in Effie's life and the total comes to eight.'

'Eight,' Felix repeats faintly. He turns to a fresh page in his notebook.

'First, Effie's kin,' Noah begins. 'Her parents died when she was a girl, there were no brothers or sisters – her mother was not strong – and she went to live with her old grandfather. Don't imagine that this was a kind or charitable gesture on his part because it wasn't. Bert Quittenden is a terrible old man, and he only took Effie in because the vicar insisted it was his Christian duty, everyone in the village backed him up, and, most crucially from Bert's point of view, Ezra Sleech threatened to bar him from the Leopard's Head if he didn't.' A savage grin briefly crosses Noah's face. 'I wouldn't have put it past Bert to have done away with his granddaughter at the beginning – you could hear him moaning about the unfairness of life, morning, noon and night – but as soon as Effie was old enough to be of use, he started to see the advantages of having her around. Pretty soon she was doing everything for him, and bringing in wages from two different jobs into the bargain, and of late he did bugger-all except sit on his chair beside the hearth all day and shuffle down to the Leopard for his evening couple of halves at the end of the day.' He grins again, but this time there is little to distinguish it from a grimace. 'Bloody old hypocrite went into deepest mourning when Effie died. Led the pack of hounds out slavering for Abel's blood, told anyone who'd listen that he always knew the lad was a wrong 'un and that he ought to have locked the lass up soon as Abel came sniffing round and kept her safe.' He pauses, his expression suddenly dark. 'If Bert Quittenden was grieving for anything, it was for the comfortable life that his pretty, cheery, vivacious and loving granddaughter provided for him so uncomplainingly. We can discount him as Effie's killer,' he adds, the anger still vibrant in his voice. 'He's gone down steeply since she died, and he'd no more have murdered his slave than cut off his drinking hand.'

Felix, who has written *Bert Quittenden, grandfather* and then not a word more, so enthralled has he been by Noah's narrative, quietly draws a line through it. 'Next?'

'Next come the men who Effie worked with at Newhouse Farm. It's a dairy farm, and she was the dairy maid. Ah, but you know that already, you just read it out to me from your notes.' Again, Noah looks as if he finds this amusing. 'Harold Marchant is the farmer. He never married. Doesn't like women, and probably took very little notice of Effie, never mind wanting her dead, which apart from any other considerations would rob him of his dairy maid. The household is managed by his mother, Beryl, who is a cruel, sour old bat and probably the reason for her son's lifelong antipathy towards her sex. His nephew Mick lives and works at the farm, and from all accounts he and Effie got on well. I'm guessing they were drawn together, being much of an age and both of them suffering the daily lot of having to put up with Harold and Beryl, and I can think of no reason he'd have wanted to harm the girl. He's courting a lass from over Binhurst way, in any case. We can't entirely rule him out – men perform uncharacteristic acts under a harvest moon with a belly full of beer – but he's never been high on my list.'

He waits for Felix to stop writing, then says, 'Then there's the cowman, George Croucher,' and something in his tone makes Felix look up.

'What about him?'

'He's an odd one,' Noah replies. 'His sister Peg is married to Ezra Sleech, and by all accounts the pair of them had a harsh upbringing. George Croucher has a twisted foot, apparently the aftermath of some act of violence from his father, and walks with a hobbling gait. He used to watch Effie, and then quickly look away when she caught him.'

'And you think that betokens a secret passion that led to assault and murder?'

'I'm keeping an open mind,' Noah replies. 'Then there's Ted Chauncey, hop-farmer at Nightingale Farm, and he's always had an eye for the ladies and isn't beyond peering up a skirt at a well-turned ankle. While I can see him appreciating Effie – she really was a lovely girl – he has his pick of women, what with the farm doing well enough and him being a good-looking fellow, and it's not likely he'd have tried to force Effie when so many others were falling over themselves to catch his eye.'

'We're up to five,' Felix says, wondering if he'll ever be able to make out the scrawl into which his usually neat handwriting has degenerated.

'Six is the aforementioned Ezra Sleech. You've met him, you've talked to him, what do you think?'

Felix puts down his pencil and massages his hand. 'I liked him,' he replies. 'Genial, easy to talk to, and I'd have said he was genuinely fond of Effie and truly sorry at what happened to her.'

'I'd agree,' Noah says. 'Against that we must remind ourselves that Effie regularly worked in the Leopard, that she and Ezra were thrown together, that they were friendly with each other and openly affectionate.'

'Doesn't that make it less likely that Ezra would suddenly have developed a burning passion for her?' Felix demands. 'Aren't we told that propinquity and familiarity are the death knell to fierce attraction? A woman can be full of mystery and allure at arm's length, but human and quite ordinary once you get close.'

Noah laughs. 'You speak from experience.' It isn't remotely a question.

'Er . . .'

'Never mind. You're probably right, and in any case your little Effie wasn't all that gifted with mystery and allure, and most of the men hereabouts had known her since she was a little tacker.' Now he looks sad.

'Including you?' Felix asks quietly.

'Including me,' Noah agrees. Then, vehemently: 'It was appalling, what happened to her. Of all people, Effie Quittenden shouldn't have died like that.' He pauses, then adds, all but inaudibly, 'She had so much love and kindness to give, and now she won't.'

For a few moments they sit in silence, as if paying their tribute to the dead girl.

Then Noah says briskly, 'Just two more, then we're done,' and Felix picks up his pencil. 'Penultimate is a man called Alderidge Cely Leverell. Anyone mentioned him to you?'

'I saw the name Leverell on the mausoleum in the graveyard of All Saints' Church.'

Noah nods. 'Yes, you would have done.' He stops, frowning, staring beyond Felix towards the open door. 'What can I tell you of Alderidge Cely Leverell? He's the landowner around here, and he owns pretty much everything you can see for miles in each direction. All the farms belong to him, including Nightingale Farm and Newhouse Farm, and so does the Leopard's Head. He has never done anything to earn his wealth, and virtually nothing to conserve and increase it. The whole estate is in the hands of a very capable and undoubtedly underpaid manager.'

'Is he on your list?' Felix interrupts.

'The estate manager? No,' Noah says shortly. 'He is not interested in women. Going back to Alderidge, he lives in the big house,' he goes on, 'which is Old Abbey House, built in the early 1700s on the site of Earlyleas Abbey, the ruins of which are in the grounds of the house. The Cely Leverells made their fortune in India – many of them were with the East India Company – and the name derived from the union by marriage of Aurelius Rowley Leverell and Sophia Adelaide Harrington Cely some time in the late eighteenth century. The leopard featured on the Cely coat of arms – from the India connection, no doubt. Over the gigantic fireplace in the Grand Hall of Old Abbey House, if you ever find yourself there, is a very large and crudely executed oil painting of the new crest that came about from the union of the Celys with the Leverells, in which the Cely leopard cavorts unconvincingly with a pallid and feeble-looking unicorn, which for some reason was the device adopted by the Leverells. If Alderidge doesn't invite you to visit,' he adds offhandedly, 'you can also see the coat of arms on the front wall of the Leopard's Head.'

'I'll look out for it,' Felix remarks. 'What sort of a man is this Alderidge?'

Noah doesn't answer for so long that Felix begins to wonder if he's going to. But eventually he says, 'I don't think you'd take to him. He's in his mid-forties, and he's still to grow up. He put off marriage as long as he could, eschewing all respon- sibility and turning a deaf ear to his parents' increasingly desperate entreaties to settle down and start behaving like an adult. They finally managed to bribe him into line by volunteering to move into the Dower House, leaving Old Abbey House for his own use, provided he would take a wife. Old Abbey House was too much of a temptation, and six years ago he married. He was forty, his bride was twenty-three. But if his parents had hoped for the swift arrival of grandchildren,' he goes on, 'in particular a son to follow on after Alderidge, they were to be disappointed. The old father died, sad and embittered, three years ago, furious to the end that he'd given up the luxury of Old Abbey House for the inadequacies of the Dower House, and his sour old wife followed him into that somewhat vulgar family vault a year later.'

'You didn't tell me the name of the young wife,' Felix says, still writing.

'Did I not?' Noah looks at him briefly. Then he goes on, 'Her name was Mariah Valentine. A quiet little thing, of good family but very reserved and, when Alderidge took her to wife, young for her age.' He pauses. 'But Alderidge doesn't respond to naive young women, no matter how nicely raised. He prefers the company of prostitutes, the lower the better, reasoning, no doubt, that if he's paying them he can have what he wants. In short, his desire is for a woman he can be truly filthy with, and—'

Abruptly he stops.

Felix is wondering why – and how, indeed, he comes by his knowledge, although no doubt the villagers love nothing more than spreading gossip about their landlord, the more scurrilous the better – when Noah says sharply, 'What's the count now? Seven?'

Felix runs back through his notes. 'Yes. One to go.'

Noah laughs softly. 'Eighth and last,' he says very quietly, 'is me.'

Felix's head shoots up. 'You,' he echoes neutrally.

'I fit your criteria,' Noah says. 'I knew Effie since she was small, as I just said. I liked her – you couldn't not like her. I felt protective towards her, and it may interest you to know that I took the trouble to look into Abel Spokewright, once it became clear how the land lay.'

'What did you discover?'

'He was sound. Lived with his mother and his brother Jared,

and the three of them cared for the mother's sister, who was not strong. Brothers both worked on the docks, and people spoke well of them. The house was small, especially with the auntie needing a bed in the ground-floor room because of her legs, but tidy and clean. Churchgoers, good reputation.' He stops, perhaps realizing he has given away just how thoroughly he went about checking up on the young man who wanted to marry Effie. 'Anyway, as I was saying, no reason why I shouldn't be on your list of village men who might have killed her.'

Felix is unable to come up with an answer. To say *I just don't think you did it* would be worse than saying nothing, and feeble and unworthy of a private investigator into the bargain

'Fortunately for you,' Noah resumes after a decidedly awkward little silence, 'and for the future harmony of our newly discovered kinship, I could not have killed Effie because I was known to be somewhere else all that night. I was questioned at the time,' he adds, 'as were many of us, but the police seemed to accept that Abel did it and that stopped them looking too hard for any other possible perpetrator. At least, that's what we thought.'

Felix digests that. Then he says, 'Where were you, then?'

'Going to write it down, are you?' Noah's tone is bland, but his eyes are full of mischief. 'I'll speak slowly, then. The cricket match was winding up. The villagers had gone into bat first and we'd set a tidy score of a hundred and thirty-one runs, to which, I might modestly add, I contributed a reasonably decent twenty-seven. We'd got all the hop-pickers out bar the final pair, and I was bowling my fifth over. I was pretty pleased with myself, given I'd just clean bowled a surprisingly handy lad for eleven – he'd already hit two fours, and the rest of the team were hissing at me like a nest of snakes to do something about him, given they were fast catching up with us – and possibly I let my guard slip. Anyway, this lad's replacement hit the ball hard, it flew off the centre of his bat straight down the middle of the wicket, so fast I couldn't get a hand to it, and hit me plumb over the right eye.' He grins. 'Good God, but it hurt. I felt my legs go, and I was only vaguely aware of Ted and his lad helping me off the pitch. We got the bugger out next delivery, and won the match by seven runs.'

'Were you badly injured?' Felix asks.

'I have a thick skull,' Noah replies, 'and I reckon that saved me. Ezra came to help, and Peg ordered him and Ted to carry me through into their parlour and put me on the old sofa. It's battered and worn, but she fetched cushions and a blanket and it was good to be lying down.' He pauses. 'I remember sleeping intermittently, or maybe I was unconscious, but Peg was always there, watching over me, and she kept wringing a cloth out in cold water and replacing it on my forehead.' He smiles. 'You'd not take Peg Sleech for a caring type, but I was glad to have her there that night, I can tell you.'

Felix finishes writing and then says, 'You mentioned Ted's lad?'

'Ted Chauncey, yes. Boy's called Percy, known as Perce. He's not Ted's son – Ted's wife died a while ago and they had no children. Perce is a local boy who lives and works on the farm.'

'What about other boys in the village? Could any of them have killed Effie? Or' – the thought suddenly strikes him – 'what about the girls? Some anguished rival for Abel's affections, perhaps?'

Noah considers this for some moments. 'A girl who'd fallen for Abel,' he murmurs thoughtfully. 'Could have been, I suppose.' But then he shakes his head. 'Can't see it,' he says. 'The local lasses tend to marry lads from the village, lads they've grown up with and set their caps at long ago.' He grins. 'No doubt it sounds limited and dull to you, with your London ways' – the smile deepens – 'but it's the way of it in the country, always has been. As for the lads,' he goes on, 'decent enough, in the main. Most of them work on the land. One's apprenticed to a blacksmith, two are learning to be carpenters with a bloke over the far side of Binhurst, and pretty much every one of them is strong enough. But why should they? What's the motive?'

Felix rubs his eyes and says wearily, 'If we discount Abel strangling her because she wouldn't let him have his way with her, what's the motive for anyone?'

Apparently treating it as a rhetorical question, Noah gets up and crosses the room to where a handsome oak dresser stands against the wall. He takes down two tankards, then collects a jug from the pantry. 'Mug of ale?' he asks, waving the tankards at Felix.

'Yes, please.'

Noah pours out the beer and resumes his seat. They both take a deep draught. 'It's not strong,' Noah says, 'nowhere near as potent as Ezra's, but it's not midday yet and I have work to do.'

So have I, Felix thinks. But he doesn't utter the words; he's quite sure that his cousin is a man of action who isn't likely to accept a job such as being a private investigator as real work.

Noah breaks the short silence. 'The hop-pickers will be here soon,' he says glumly.

'Do you not like having them here?' Felix asks.

Noah shrugs. 'Doesn't bother me one way or the other. They work hard, they enjoy themselves when they're not working, they all seem to love being down here in the fresh air. No reason to resent them.'

'You sounded as if you weren't looking forward to their arrival?'

Noah gives him a long look. 'Well, now, Mister Private Investigator, let's just think why that might be,' he says, raising a scathing eyebrow.

And Felix, secretly angry with himself for his slowness, nods and says, 'We need to have this business sorted before they get here. Obviously,' he adds, as if to imply that of course he's considered this but hadn't thought it worth mentioning.

Noah smiles to himself, goes, 'Hmm,' thoughtfully, and takes another mouthful of beer. Then he says, 'One of the Londoners has arrived already. Been here a week or so.'

'Oh? Why has he come before the others?'

'Not he, she. Name of Dollie Turton. Came last year, but before that she hadn't been hopping for years, not since she was a child, when she used to come with her parents and her brother and sister. She was married young to a bastard of a man who turned out to be a wife-beater, and he didn't like

Dollie jaunting off to the countryside every September, put his foot down and ordered her to stay at home or else who was going to cater to his every need? Likely she'd have been pregnant more often than not, although that doesn't stop other women coming hopping. The poor woman lost more than one infant,' he adds. He pauses, frowning, his expression sorrowful. 'Anyhow,' he resumes, 'Gil – that was the husband – isn't around to control her any more, and these days she can make her own decisions.'

Felix had been about to ask why this Dollie Turton has come down more than a week ahead of the other hop-pickers, but now he holds back the question because he thinks he already knows.

He has just been reflecting that Noah is remarkably well-informed about a woman who only comes to Crooked Green once a year and until very recently hadn't been since childhood. But he thinks he has deduced the explanation for his knowledge: it's more than likely that this Dollie Turton is the blackberry-picking woman with the wicker basket. Felix is a little surprised, since, despite the earthy laugh, the beautiful woman he saw when he peered through the crack in the door looked to be a rather different sort of person, but then he reproves himself for making judgements on the briefest of observations. Women from all levels of society, he reflects, can possess natural elegance and a good bearing.

'Is she—' He stops, not sure how to phrase the question that will tell him what he wants to know. 'You seem to know her well,' he says instead.

Noah shrugs. Then, glancing up and seeing Felix watching him, he adds, 'Not very well. I talked to her, back last September. She had a black eye, and I felt sorry for her.' After a moment, he says softly, 'The other women seemed to be protective of her, and it was clear they were working together to make sure she didn't have to exert herself too much. Word was she'd been given a hell of a beating from which she was only just recovering.'

'And this husband – Gil – allowed her to come down with the other hop-pickers?' It doesn't sound very likely, Felix thinks.

Noah grins sourly. 'Gil was dead.'

'Dead! When you said he wasn't around any more I thought you meant he'd abandoned her.'

'Terminally,' Noah agrees. He shoots an assessing glance at Felix. 'The body was found in Limehouse Reach, wrapped round a pier support. Not much of him left, what with the battering he got from the force of the water ramming him into everything he encountered on his way downriver, and the fishes had enjoyed quite a lot of him. But he used to wear a wide belt with a heavy brass buckle shaped like a fist, and that was intact.'

'He fell in,' Felix says softly.

Noah shrugs. 'Fell or was pushed. There was an injury to the back of his skull, likely caused by the traditional blunt instrument.'

Felix tries to imagine how it would feel. Falling, the fast-flowing brown water rushing up to meet you. Knowing nothing was going to save you, that you'd be hurried and tumbled on your way till you stopped struggling and drowned. Better, surely, to be dead before you fell . . .

. . . and he sees that tall, fair, beautiful woman with a heavy stick in her hands, swinging it like a rounders bat till it hits home against the skull of that brute of a husband, watching his inert body falling into the river.

If he has guessed right – both about the death of this Gil Turton and about Dollie being both the instrument of his death and the beautiful woman he saw with Noah – then on both counts it seems diplomatic not to ask any more questions about her.

NINE

Very early the next morning, Lily is washed, dressed and descending from her rooms on the top floor to the living and working quarters. She was awake soon after dawn; shaken into consciousness by a dream of something darker than violence featuring a thin boy in broken shoes and a gap between his front teeth. As she prepared for the day, she has been telling herself repeatedly that it was only a dream and that dreams are not prophetic.

Giving herself a bracing talking-to has not, however, proved very effective; rather more so were the valuable twenty-five minutes spent starting on a succinct account of the last couple of days to send to Felix down in his village inn.

She passes the Little Ballerina's closed door on the first floor. There is a sort of snuffling sound from within; the Russian woman is a very sound sleeper, and her night hours in the theatre usually mean that she does not emerge until midday or early afternoon.

Lily picks up the smell of tightly closed rooms, untidiness and a general lack of washing. She is all too well aware that the Little Ballerina never opens a window: suspecting this unsavoury habit, she has looked from outside the house, both back and front, and observed gloomily that every one of the generous number of sash windows remains closed, more often than not with the heavy curtains drawn across.

Lily cannot sleep without fresh air; or, she thinks ruefully, what passes for fresh air in Chelsea. Quite a lot of her childhood was spent on the High Peak farm in rural Derbyshire where she was born, and where her grandparents Abraham and Martha Raynor used to take her in the school holidays, leaving her in the care of her other grandmother, Suzannah Owen, and Suzannah's son Thom. The soft air that floated into her bedroom on the farm was a lot sweeter than the miasma-tinged breezes off the river, and Lily firmly believes that her strong constitution has been bestowed upon her at least partly because of these healthy episodes.

Another blessing is her apparent immunity to smallpox. Epidemics of this horrible disease regularly ravage the land; indeed, there is one happening this very year of 1881. A student of the theories and the medical practices of Edward Jenner, Lily wonders if her immunity is thanks to some unknown, unrecorded brush with cowpox during the Derbyshire years. If so, it is yet another thing for which to thank her grandparents and her wider family.

And because of the expenses of running this beautiful, much-loved house that was left to her by those grandparents, Lily thinks, she has to put up with a stinky tenant who has never heard of fresh air.

'Not for one day more than I must,' she mutters through gritted teeth as she stomps on down the last flight of stairs.

She goes through Felix's office and into her own. She wishes he was there; she really misses talking through with him her growing concern for Yakov Hadzibazy. She wonders how soon she will hear from him; how soon he will be back. He'd promised to write to her once he'd had a chance to see how the land lay down in Crooked Green. When he does, she thinks she might suggest going to see him, for if they meet they can discuss both their cases . . .

The street door opens and closes again. Mrs Clapper must have been awake early too, because here she is arriving at 3, Hob's Court and it's only just gone six thirty. 'Going to scrub out the yard and do the mats, Miss Lily, while the sun's out to dry everything,' she declares as she blows down the hall from the door to the kitchen and the scullery. 'I'll give the necessary a good seeing-to and all, while Madam's still sound asleep,' she adds, brows descending in a furiously disapproving scowl. Mrs Clapper loathes the Little Ballerina, partly because she instinctively disapproves of anyone who is still in bed in the middle of the day, partly because the woman is, in Mrs Clapper's oft-repeated words, a dirty slut. While the first reason for hatred is unreasonable – in vain has Lily tried to explain that someone who dances for a living and does not get to bed before the small hours needs to sleep on beyond Mrs Clapper's habitual hour of rising, and, indeed, the only one she considers respectable – the second is not unreasonable at all, and Lily heartily agrees with her.

Lily and Mrs Clapper work away in their separate areas. Mrs Clapper finds a moment to put the kettle on and light the stove, and presently brings Lily a cup of tea and a plate of scrambled eggs on toast, acknowledging Lily's thanks with a nod and a muttered, 'You don't eat enough, Miss Lily, I've always said as such and I always will.'

The tea doesn't threaten Lily's soft palate in the way Alf Wilson's does, and the eggs, seasoned to perfection, are delicious.

She is finishing her tea when there is a tap at the street door. At least she thinks there is, although the sound is soft, as if whoever is out there is pondering the wisdom of calling on the World's End Bureau. Lily waits for a moment, but the sound is not repeated. She stands up, strides through the front office and into the hall, and she flings open the door.

Alexei is standing on the step, his fisted hand up and about to tap again.

'Alexei!' Lily exclaims.

He grins. 'It is I,' he agrees.

'How on earth did you know where to find me?'

The smile widens, lightening his whole face. 'You left card, on table. Serafima pick it up. I look at it over her shoulder, I put address in here.' He points to his head.

'And you managed to find me, all the way over here in Chelsea?'

He shrugs. 'Is not so far.'

It is not so much the distance he has overcome that confounds her, Lily thinks as she ushers him inside, but the complexity of the journey. The crowds of milling people, the trams, the hurrying, impatient traffic, the wide variety of carriages, the heavy drays, the multitude of wagons and carts . . . Still, he's here, and he must have come for a reason.

She is just about to ask what this reason is when Mrs Clapper stomps through from her domain at the back of the house. Lily is on the point of giving an explanation to her cleanliness-obsessed housekeeper – Alexei is none too clean, and she has already noticed Mrs Capper's swift disapproving glance at his dirty boots on the spotless floor – but she has misjudged Mrs Clapper.

'That lad looks hungry to me,' she says, with the authority of the Delphic oracle pronouncing on the future. 'If you take him in your office – the *front* office, mind – I'll see what I can find.'

Front office, indeed, thinks Lily. She might have known Mrs Clapper would not be able to overlook the boots. 'Thank you,' she says. Then, to Alexei, 'In here, please.'

In the brief time it takes Mrs Clapper to rustle up a plate of food – more scrambled eggs, with toast, bacon, a couple of sausages, tomatoes and a thick chunk of black pudding, accompanied by a large mug of tea – Alexei wanders round the front office. He appears to be interested in everything, and spends several moments carefully handling the reference books arranged on the shelves. Lily's current reading matter is stacked to one side of the middle shelf: it consists of medical journals in which she has been avidly studying a series of articles on the discovery of the bacteria responsible for an array of horrible diseases, including amoebic dysentery, gonorrhoea, typhoid, leprosy, malaria, tetanus and pneumonia. Lily has been absorbed in reading how the diseases are spread and how they could be prevented and treated; since she returned from her spell of being assistant matron at a girls' school in the Fens,[3] Lily is finding it harder to suppress her medical past.

But quite obviously Alexei's knowledge of the English language is insufficient for these earnest paragraphs – although he appears fascinated by the illustrations – and soon he moves on, inspecting the drawers of files, Felix's tidy desk, his chair, the pot plants on their corner shelf which, suffering from feast or famine depending on whether or not Felix remembers to water them, still manage to thrive. Lastly, completing his circuit of the room, Alexei picks up the old white pottery leech jar that belonged to Lily's grandfather Abraham Raynor, which

[3] See *The Outcast Girls*.

she keeps in the front office. It is still full of pennies from when there used to be a toll for crossing Battersea Bridge.

Either the lad can read the English word *Leeches* boldly inscribed on the jar in black letters, or he's familiar with similar receptacles and knows their purpose; making a face and backing away, he says, 'Leeches! *Yeuk!*'

He has finished the food. He has clearly enjoyed it, and it's also plain he was indeed hungry, for he tucked it all away too quickly and is now valiantly trying to suppress a burp.

'Now, Alexei,' Lily says, drawing up the visitor's chair and sitting down on the opposite side of Felix's desk, 'why have you sought me out?' He frowns. 'Why have you come to find me?' she substitutes.

He leans forward, lowering his voice to a whisper. 'When you leave day before last day, I watch. I see man with eyes hard on you, and this man I know not to be *good* man. I think, maybe he follow you, maybe he want to know why you come to see us, what you discover, what you will do.' He pauses. He is watching her intently. 'Is right. What I think, is right.'

'What did he look like?' She considers it's a matter for congratulation that her voice sounds brisk and businesslike, when already, before Alexei has answered her question, she is recalling all too vividly the frightening sensation that beset her as she tramped round the unfamiliar streets and alleys of the East End: the absolute certainty that someone was watching her. Someone was following her, his footsteps echoing hers . . .

'Big man, dark garments, dark beard,' Alexei says.

And a scar on his eyelid, she adds silently. *Alexei is right, and so was I: someone was on my trail and in all probability it was that very man.* A frisson of fear goes through her.

Followed instantly by a far greater one as she remembers the pie-stall man saying that the man who followed the lad who might have been Yakov had a dark beard . . .

Keeping her expression neutral, she says, 'You're sure of this?'

Alexei nods. 'Yes, Miss Lady. Not first night, night after you visit, but next night. Last night.' He looks at her shrewdly.

'But I think already you know that someone follow you,' he adds, so quietly that she can only just hear.

Lily does not comment.

'He does not return until very, very late,' the lad continues. 'He come in like this—' he gets up and makes an elaborate mime of tiptoeing, repeatedly glancing over his shoulder – 'and I see him only because I wait for him.'

'Did he see you?' Lily demands sharply. Because if he did, if he knows this bright young man is suspicious and may well take his suspicions straight to her, then Yakov is no longer the only lad in danger.

'No,' Alexei says. 'He pass close by where I sleep, and I make sleep noises. Soft, not-not—'

'Not obvious? Not exaggerated?'

He nods, repeating the new words under his breath. 'I keep watch, and I see him go to his corner and bend over mattress, maybe take out knife but I not see. He go out again, and I follow.'

'Oh, no, Alexei, no, you shouldn't have done that!'

'But you look for boy, for Yakov,' he says reasonably. 'You leave card, you say for us to tell you if there is word of him.'

'Yes, indeed I did, but I didn't want you to put yourself in danger too!'

'I careful,' he says, and the smile is more suited to a mature man than a lad not far out of boyhood.

He's safe, Lily thinks, feeling her heartbeat race in fear for him, *he's here with me in Chelsea and miles from the secret little alleyways where violence lurks. I should at least let him have the satisfaction of telling me what he found out.*

'Where did the man go?' she asks.

Alexei hesitates, and she knows instinctively it's not good. 'He – he go to water. Straight, short water' – he snaps his fingers, trying to recall a word – '*cut*, that goes through from one canal to other.'

And Yakov is drawn to canals . . .

'What did he do?'

'It is what I fear. What *we* fear.' He shoots her a glance, quickly looking away again. 'Because another man steps out from shadows and they go on together. He – *they* – go after little boy,' Alexei whispers. Hanging his head, he mutters, 'I follow as far as tunnel, but then braveness . . .' He looks quizzically at her and she says, 'Bravery.'

He nods. 'Then bravery fails me and I turn and run.' Looking up at her, he cries, 'I am sorry! Yakov is small, smaller than I, and it was for me to save him!'

Lily's mouth is dry. She is imagining going to Yelisaveta. Telling her the worst news, that her beloved grandson – the last member of her family – has perished.

'Is he dead?' she manages to say.

But Alexei just shrugs.

She doesn't even stop to think but leaps up, runs through to the hall, puts on her light jacket, hat and gloves and checks the knife is in her boot. Then she turns to Alexei, watching her with his mouth open, and says, 'Show me.'

By underground and tram, swiftly they make their way back towards the perilous, secret alleyways that Lily has just been thinking about with such dread. Aldgate, Whitechapel High Street, and right down the Commercial Road East. They jump down from the tram, and even as Lily stares around to find her bearings, Alexei has grabbed her sleeve and, at a fast walk that alternates with a jog, is leading the way through a web of increasingly narrow, dank and poverty-ridden lanes and passages until all at once they are out in the open on the eastern side of Limehouse Basin, staring at a stretch of water that leads away to the north-east.

'Limehouse Cut,' Alexei says, pointing. And before she can comment, he hares off again and she follows.

They are on the south side of the Cut. Lily is just reflecting that there is sufficient narrowboat and barge traffic for someone to hear if she should call out, when abruptly Alexei dives off to the right along a waterway that surely can only accommodate the smallest of craft. The path has been eaten into by water and time; she stumbles, and Alexei takes her hand.

It is very dark in this little stretch opening off the Cut. High brick walls oozing water block out the daylight, the stagnant water is black and forbidding. Nothing but a straggle of pale grass grows in this place without sunshine: it is abandoned, forgotten, lost.

They creep along the ruined towpath. It is a long time since any horse plodded down here, and the surface of the path is cracked and rutted.

What was Yakov doing, coming here? Lily wonders. He was drawn to the boats, the horses, the traffic on the waterways, but it looks as if this little cut goes nowhere . . .

As if Alexei has picked up her puzzlement, he leans close and says softly, 'Boy was running away. Heard man coming after him, fled down here to evade.'

She nods her understanding.

The black mouth of a tunnel looms up ahead, and inexorably the high walls on either side reach out towards each other and finally join up. Out of memory she recalls Tamáz explaining how the boats negotiate such places, in the absence of a towpath for the horse: the boatmen lie on their backs on planks extended from the roof of the boat and walk their feet along the curving brick wall, and this process – it is known as legging – is hard work, wearing on the strength.

She wishes Tamáz was here now.

As they approach she sees that there is a path, but it is barely two foot wide, broken in places and far too narrow for a horse.

There is not enough room for her and Alexei to walk abreast. She feels him try to push ahead, but she won't let him. Reaching down to check inside her boot and make sure her knife is there – it always is – she walks on into the darkness.

Her eyes adjust and she makes out the shape of an object lying on the path, draped over the edge with part of it in the water. They go nearer. She sees a bare foot and another that wears a boot with a worn-out sole, a large hole in the leather.

It is the body of a boy, lying with his legs and lower body on the path, his head and shoulders over the edge. His long hair floats on the water, utterly still, for no current flows here to disturb the filthy, matted tangle.

Alexei grabs her arm, and she is not sure if his intention is to stop her going nearer or to give himself courage. She pats his hand and walks on.

The boy is dark, thin, clad in dirty, ragged garments. He is face down, and one pale hand lies behind him by his side, palm up, the fingers gently curling. The ruined jacket has been folded back across his shoulders and the rags of his filthy shirt have been ripped away. His trousers have been unfastened and dragged down so that the waistband lies across his buttocks. The naked flesh is startlingly white; so much so that it appears almost luminous.

There is a pool under his belly, the liquid black in the darkness.

But she knows it is blood: she can smell it.

The boy is dead.

TEN

I t is early morning. In his room at the New Cock with the low sun streaming through the window, Felix, recalling uneasily the hasty note he dispatched to Lily the day before, is finishing off a letter setting out in detail pretty much everything he has seen, heard and concluded (rightly or wrongly) since his arrival.

It is a very long letter.

By noon yesterday Noah Smith had managed to make it very plain that he'd spent quite long enough chatting with his new-found second cousin once removed, and that a hard-working man of the land could not afford any more time away from his multitudinous responsibilities. So Felix had taken his diplomatic leave. He called in at the Leopard's Head for a bite to eat and probably more than a couple of pints of Ezra's ale – already the landlord seems to take it for granted that Felix will drop in at midday and doesn't seem to mind catering for his sole customer – and if he picked up anything in the way of useful information, the extended afternoon sleep that followed the session in the Leopard has erased it from memory.

And accordingly now, as well as writing the pages of neat script, he finds himself suggesting to Lily that, since he would find it very useful to discuss his progress so far with her in person and in the hope that she too has much to tell him, he will travel up to London and meet her at number 3, Hob's Court some time this afternoon, depending upon the train timetable. If she is out, he assures her, he will wait.

Before he can change his mind, he hurries off to catch the first post of the day.

He is back at Hob's Court just before midday.

His letter to his employer lies on the mat, along with several others that have arrived by a recent delivery.

Wherever Lily has gone, she went out before the postman

delivered his letter. Now there is no sign of her. Glancing inside the Inner Sanctum, he observes that her desk is in its habitual state of tidiness, and that the bookshelves are similarly well ordered except for the fact that her stack of medical journals is crooked. Absently he straightens it up. He is wandering back to his own office, reflecting ruefully that he was far too impetuous and acted without sufficient thought, and there is no knowing what time Lily will return, assuming even that she does return today. She can have no idea that he was proposing to come up to Chelsea to discuss their two cases, so it wouldn't be unreasonable in the least if she'd decided to seek out her boatman friend and head off to Derby or Coventry or Bishop's Stortford or anywhere else with him while she sorts out her thoughts on the case amid the peace and tranquillity of England's waterways, no doubt favouring him with a wonderful smile when the boat is tied up for the night and after a brief spell of efficient and highly creative cooking he presents her with an enamel dish full of something totally delicious and they—

Felix shuts off that train of thought as forcefully as a person slamming a door when they've burst out of a room in a temper.

Belatedly realizing that someone is standing in the doorway of the front office, he meets Mrs Clapper's small, bright eyes.

'Lily isn't here,' he says needlessly.

'No, Mr Felix,' she agrees – is it his imagination or is it a soft smile of sympathy she bestows on him – 'she's not.'

'Do you know where she's gone or how long she'll be?'

Mrs Clapper shakes her head. 'Now that I cannot answer,' she tells him, 'although what I *will* tell you is that very early this morning a ragged young fellow hollow-cheeked with hunger came a-calling and she took off with him and in a real tearing hurry and all. Not before I'd fed him a good square meal, mind,' she adds reprovingly, as if he had suggested it, 'and if ever I've seen a lad wolf down food as fast as that, I can't think when, and he—'

'Yakov,' Felix mutters. 'She's found Yakov, and he came here to Hob's Court.'

But Mrs Clapper, reminiscences stopped in mid-flow, shakes her head again. 'Now you're not quite right, Mr Felix, because for all that it *was* one of them foreign names, it wasn't Yakov. Now let me see, what was it?'

Felix waits what seems an aeon while Mrs Clapper thinks.

Then she exclaims, '*Alexei!* That's what it was, Alexei! There, I knew I'd remember!'

And as she disappears back in the direction of the back of the house, Felix sits down at his desk to wait and to wonder who in heaven's sweet name Alexei is and why Lily has rushed off with him.

It is more than an hour later that he hears the street door open.

He leaps up and goes into the hall to meet her.

Her brows are drawn right down and her forehead is creased with worry. She is pale, with a sort of tightness around the lips. Before he can check himself, he exclaims, 'Good God, Lily, you look ghastly! What's happened?' Then, hard on the heels of that: 'Dear Christ, you've been hurt!'

He lunges at her and grabs hold of her arm, but she shakes him off. 'No I *haven't!*' she says sharply. 'Stop crowding me, Felix, I'm all right!'

But she undermines the brave assertion by slumping against him. Only for a heartbeat, but it is more than enough, and he puts his arm round her waist and, half guiding, half supporting, leads her to his chair and sits her down. Immediately she folds her arms on his desk and drops her head onto them. Looking at her worriedly for a moment, Felix turns and runs through to the scullery to ask Mrs Clapper to make her a cup of hot, strong tea.

She is sitting up when he returns.

'I'm perfectly all right,' she repeats sternly. 'It was hot and crowded on the tram, and I walked too fast from the stop to home.' He watches her, but does not speak. 'And I saw something,' she adds after a short pause. 'It—' She shakes her head, apparently incapable of explaining.

Mrs Clapper brings the tea, and wisely Felix waits while Lily drinks it, making a face at its sweetness. Mrs Clapper stands very close on Lily's other side, watching her intently. Felix is about to make a carefully worded suggestion that she should step back a pace, then realizes he's doing exactly the same.

Lily puts the cup down. 'Thank you, Mrs Clapper, I feel better now.' Mrs Clapper doesn't move. 'Mr Felix and I must get on, and I mustn't keep you from your own work any longer,' she adds tactfully.

With many a backward glance, Mrs Clapper returns to her own domain.

'Your colour's better,' Felix observes, regarding Lily through narrowed eyes. 'Do you think – I mean, are you able to . . .' He pauses delicately.

'Oh, good grief, Felix, stop treating me as if I were an easily shockable ingenue of fifteen!' she exclaims. Then, as if it has only just occurred to her: 'What are you doing here, anyway?'

He goes to fetch his letter and hands it to her. 'I sent you the details of the Crooked Green business,' he says, 'and I informed you I'd be here by early this afternoon so that we could talk over our respective cases.'

'That's funny, because I was writing a letter to you too,' she murmurs. 'I missed yours because I went out before the first post.' Then, as if the memory has brought back all the events of this morning, swiftly she goes on, 'What I saw today is the latest occurrence in my search for Yakov, so I propose to relate the whole account in order that you understand the context.'

'Very well.' He draws up a chair and sits down.

From habit he extracts his notebook and silver pencil; this may be her case, but if they are to discuss it together, he'll need to make notes.

She talks for some time. He jots down names of people, names of places, addresses. She mentions Alexei, explaining how she met him, and when she pauses for breath he says, 'He – Alexei – is the young man who came here for you early this morning.'

She meets his eyes. 'Yes. Mrs Clapper told you?'

He nods.

And then she tells him why Alexei needed her in such a hurry.

When at last she falls silent, Felix has a vivid picture in his mind. A dark, abandoned stretch of water, high walls cutting out the light, the black mouth of a tunnel. The body of a boy, hair in the water, upturned hand by his side as if in an appeal for help.

'This Alexei followed him?'

'To be precise, he followed the man he believed was pursuing him.'

'He's a brave young man,' Felix remarks. She nods. 'Where is he now? He didn't come back here with you?'

'No. I *wish* he had,' she says with sudden passion, 'he's in dreadful danger, because if the killer knows who he is and where he's been lodging, and I'm sure he must do, he'll murder him too, purely because he followed him!' She stops, collects herself and says more calmly, 'I don't know where he is. After he led me to the body, I said I must summon a constable immediately. He seemed to accept I had no choice, but he said he wasn't going to be around when I did. We hurried back to Limehouse Basin, I spotted a couple of constables and when I looked round to point them out to Alexei, he'd gone.'

'So you told them about the body by that wretched little cut, and—' But something has occurred to him. 'How on earth did you explain what you were doing in such a place?'

She looks at him scathingly. 'I didn't tell them I'd been in the cut. I said I'd been waiting for a tram up on the Commercial Road and a boy approached me in great distress, telling me he'd spotted a body by the water, and that as soon as he'd told me how to find it he ran off. Which,' she adds, 'is more or less the truth. I knew what would happen if I was to be found beside the body,' she hurries on. 'At the very least they'd have asked me a thousand questions, hardly any of which I'd have been able to answer, and those I could answer I wouldn't have wanted to. At worse they'd have discovered the knife tucked inside my boot, which would have made them suspect all sorts of ridiculous things. Either way, by the time they'd finally decided I was simply a passer-by and innocent of any crime or even the least involvement in a crime, it would be a week next Tuesday and Yakov's trail would be ice-cold.'

'You did right,' he says. 'Besides, I can't think of one single reason why a woman such as you should have been there, short of the true one, and I'm sure you weren't going to reveal that.'

She shakes her head.

Presently he says gently, 'Tell me about – about the body?'

'Oh—' She turns to him, eyes wide. He has the impression she's returning from far away.

'There was sufficient light in the tunnel to see him by?'

She nods again. 'Yes, there was. Thin, dark, with dirty, ragged clothes. And – and the clothes were disturbed, the jacket pulled up, the trousers down.'

An immediate conclusion springs to his mind. 'He had been assaulted?'

She flashes him a swift glance. 'Felix, of *course* he had, his blood was spread around him like a huge black puddle.' Before he can explain, she goes on, 'But I know that's not what you were asking.' She pauses. 'No, I do not believe so. The bits of rag that served as drawers were still in place, and the waistband of the trousers was only just below the top of the intergluteal cleft.'

'The what?'

'The division between the buttocks,' she says shortly. 'I realize it seems unlikely, but it looked to me as if whoever killed him deliberately drew back his garments to bare the flesh for the knife. Like a sacrifice,' she adds in a whisper.

There is a short silence. Then he says, 'He was lying in his own blood?'

She nods. 'He was face down, but Alexei lifted his torso so that we could see.' She stops, swallows. 'One great knife cut, right up from just below the navel to the breastbone.' She stops again, then says very quietly, 'He would have died very quickly.'

Neither of them speak for some time. Then Felix says. 'Have you told his grandmother he's dead?'

She has been staring down at her hands, folded together on his desk, but now her head shoots up. '*No!*' she cries.

'Lily, I appreciate how terrible it is to break bad news and—'

But she clearly hasn't heard. 'It's *not him*!' she shouts. 'It's not Yakov!'

'It must be!' he says stupidly. 'This man who was following you must be connected somehow, and—'

'It isn't him,' she insists. 'Alexei helped me pull the body's head and shoulders up out of the water and I looked inside his mouth. Now his grandmother told me Yakov has well-cared for, sharp and regular teeth with a gap between the front ones, and the dead boy had no such gap. Moreover they were dreadful teeth, many no more than greyish stumps. And anyway he was too old: Yakov is twelve, but although this body was small, thin and undernourished, it was that of a young man. There were patches of stubble.' She points to her chin and her jaw.

Slowly he nods. 'And so Yakov is still missing.'

'Yes.' The word is barely a whisper.

Neither of them speaks for some time. It is, Felix thinks, as if they are silently facing up to the magnitude of the tasks ahead of them. Finally Lily gives a sigh, sits up straight and, fixing Felix with a hard stare, announces, 'It is time to speak of your case. I shall read what you wrote' – she flourishes his letter – 'and then we shall discuss what you should do next.'

But I'm right here in front of you, he wants to cry. *Why can't I tell you instead?*

He watches in suppressed irritation as she reaches for his paper knife, slits open the envelope, extracts the thick pages of his letter and calmly begins to read.

Then he notices that the sheets of paper are shaking minutely.

A rush of emotion floods through him, and he wants to go round the desk and take his stern employer of the rigid self-control into his arms. For the tremble in her hands gives away the fact that she has been far more affected by the finding of the pathetic body in its sordid, dirty place of death than she is letting on; that she needs the few minutes afforded by the reading of his long letter to recover her equanimity.

His irritation has vanished. He sits back in his chair and waits for her to finish.

Eventually she raises her head and looks at him.

'From what you write,' she says – and he notices that the tight note of strain has gone from her voice – 'it appears that, despite your careful cover story, both Ezra Sleech and the Reverend Mr Tewks assumed that the journalist you told them you were was in Crooked Green for no other reason than to ask about Effie Quittenden's murder, it being the anniversary of her death, no doubt with the aim of making a lot of money selling the lurid story to some scurrilous newspaper or magazine.'

'Er—' he begins.

Ignoring the interruption, she goes on, 'It's probably just as well, as it means you can now ask your questions openly.' She looks at him, eyebrows raised enquiringly as if expecting him to lay out his planned schedule for speaking to each of the men on the list of suspects.

Since no such schedule exists, he simply says, 'Naturally!' adding a brief laugh that sounds false even to himself.

She says nothing, but her expression couldn't say more clearly that she too knows full well it doesn't exist.

'I think you'll find they'll talk to you far more readily when you're asking about a murder than about the effect of the hop-pickers' presence in their village,' she goes on. 'That the most salacious, dramatic and violent events are what people prefer to gossip about is a sad fact of human nature, I fear.' She adds quietly, 'I always thought that cover story you came up with was a little flimsy.'

'But if I declare I'm a private investigator hunting for the real killer, there's a strong possibility that any evidence there is to find will be buried so deep I'll never find it!' he protests. 'Anyway,' he adds, 'it wasn't my idea, it was Marm's.'

She just gives him a look.

'What about you?' he counters. 'What is to be your next step?'

She gives a faint shrug, turning his paper knife over from end to end. 'I'm still stunned at finding that poor young man's body,' she admits, and he finds her honesty disarming. 'I will return to the Mission, and try to find Alexei. I am hoping, praying, that he won't have taken it into his head to trail the bearded man – it's far too dangerous, and I can't bear to think of that lovely, bright young man who has come so far and is so determined to make a new life for himself going into such peril.' Before he can protest that he doesn't want her going into peril either, and why don't they return to the Mission together in the morning and he'll go back to Crooked Green afterwards, she looks up at him with a bright smile and says,

'In case you're worried about me, Felix, don't be. There's no need because I know someone who's utterly at home in that part of the East End, the canals and the basins in particular, and he's undertaken to help me.' Her smile widens. 'With Tamáz beside me, I shall be perfectly safe!'

Felix nearly, so very nearly, says, *Good old Tamáz*. He only just manages to bite the words back.

Felix catches an early evening train from Charing Cross.

He is out of sorts, angry with the world, and – although he is trying not to admit it – hurt. He does not want to go straight back to his room in the New Cock; the idea of meekly settling down for the night in a rather basic room in a quiet and law-abiding village where everyone's virtuously abed and asleep well before ten o'clock is quite unbearable at present.

Consulting the timetable when he changes trains at Paddock Wood, he discovers that if he alights at the stop before Binhurst, which is Elm Wood, he can walk along the lanes to Crooked Green and then on to Binhurst. From the map beside the timetable, it appears that Elm Wood is not much further from Crooked Green than Binhurst. It will mean a walk of perhaps five miles in all, but it is a fine night and the country air, at last with a touch of coolness in it, is a delight.

He approaches Crooked Green in the gathering twilight. The clear sky is a smooth sheet of indigo, and the first stars are coming out.

He turns left onto Earlyleas Lane. Recognizing the name, he looks out for Old Abbey House and the ruined abbey, but, not spotting either, he concludes they must be further along the lane, on the far side of the junction. There is a wide pasture to his right, bisected by a long line of trees made vast with the wide spread of their summer foliage. He can just make out the pale thread of a footpath winding along beneath the trees. Stopping to look at the direction it takes, he reckons it is the other end of the one on which he saw the woman in the cream blouse searching for her blackberries.

The lane descends gently and the church looms up in the distance. Beuse Lane turns off on the right, and now he is striding along beneath the thick canopy of the lime trees next to the church. Visualizing the layout of the village, he reckons if he carries on past the church and turns up All Saints' Road, it ought to lead him across the Green to emerge pretty much opposite the Leopard's Head and in nice time for a pint before retiring.

He has been thinking how very peaceful it is, with barely anything to be heard other than the natural sounds of owls and hunting foxes, when suddenly it isn't peaceful at all.

He hears raised voices, somewhere within the shelter of the trees: the lazy, rounded tones of a wealthy man and the loud haranguing of a woman of a different class, the latter well scattered with several expressions the man isn't likely to hear in his own drawing room.

'Come on, admit it, my lovely!' Felix hears those rounded tones declaring once he is close enough to make out the man's words. 'It's what you want, isn't it? I dare say Ted Chauncey's glad of your help, with that dirty, feckless horde of hop-pickers arriving any day now, but you don't fool me for a moment! I've seen you in the Leopard's Head in the evening when you're meant to be working, I've watched you, and what's more I've watched all the local peasants watching you, bulges in their breeches and tongues hanging out, and—'

'You leave me alone! You can keep your filth to yourself!' The woman's voice cuts roughly through the smooth-tongued little speech, which, Felix thinks with amusement, only a bone-headed idiot from the privileged classes could imagine would work as a means to seduction. 'I do an honest day's work for Ted for an honest day's pay, and the same applies when I do a shift for Ezra, and that's an end to it, and anyone who says otherwise is a bloody liar!'

Stealthily Felix steps over the ditch and, under cover of the lime trees, creeps forward. Suddenly the voices are nearer – too near – and hurriedly he leans back behind a thick trunk.

'I shall provide a far more entertaining and diverting episode for you than those clods, my pretty, and that is a promise,' the man is insisting. 'You're a woman of the earth, and I like that – I *really* like a girl who swears and enjoys a mug of ale or two, and knows how to laugh like you do!' There are noises indicative of rapid movement and just as the man is saying in a hoarse whisper that he likes them wild, there is the sound of a fist meeting flesh, a second, muffled, thump and then a loud, startled, agonized cry.

Felix leaps forward. If this aristocratic oaf has launched himself on the woman and hit her, then for sure he's not going to do her any more harm, because Felix will—

He pulls himself to a stop.

In the patch of open ground between the trees, a large man in a beautifully cut pale fawn linen jacket is kneeling on the ground and moaning in pain. He is leaning forward on his elbows, his face buried in the palm of one large hand, and the other hand is clutching at the crotch of his trousers. His backside is in the air. It is, Felix observes, a fat backside.

Beside him, standing over the fallen foe like a boxer in the ring, is a tall, strong, Amazon of a woman. The knuckles of her left hand are to her mouth and she is softly sucking them. Her auburn hair is twisted in a thick bun, escaped tendrils curling round her face. The expression on her lively face as she stares down at the man is that which she might bestow on a cow's spatter on the path.

Felix watches and waits, smiling.

Presently the fat man gets to his feet, staggering a little, ungainly, his expression ugly. The lower part of his face is covered in blood. *She got his nose*, Felix thinks, *or maybe split his lip. Good punch, either way*.

Hobbling, still cradling his testicles and now making a sort of snarling noise, the man makes a feeble lunge towards the woman, but instantly her fist comes up again and he cowers away. His face falling into self-pitying lines, large, wet bottom lip protruding, he says plaintively, 'You *hit* me!'

'I did,' agrees the woman. 'And I also kneed you in the balls. I've told you more than once to keep away from me but you don't take any notice. You follow me into the woods and you tell me you'll give me an *entertaining and diverting episode*' – the mockery of his plummy tones is harsh and very accurate – 'and when I tell you yet again to leave me alone, you try to persuade me with insulting words and your dirty, groping hand up my skirt!'

'But you hurt me, and – oh, dear God, *look* at me!' He has

noticed the blood, still pouring freely from his lip or his nose, perhaps both, and now spreading over the pale yellow silk cravat, the immaculate white shirt and the pale linen jacket like a crimson napkin tucked in a diner's collar. He raises his head, an agonized expression on his face. 'I can't go home like this! Dear Lord above, what will the servant think? What will my *wife* say?'

'Tell them you fell off your horse again,' the woman says unconcernedly, displaying, Felix thinks, a totally appropriate level of heartlessness. 'From what I hear, it's a common enough occurrence.' She leans down to him – he still seems to be having trouble standing upright and has adopted a sort of crouch – and Felix, straining to hear, just makes out the softly spoken words. He almost laughs out loud, for what she has suggested he do to himself is forming a highly comic picture in his head, even if it is anatomically unlikely.

'Keep away from me,' she finishes, 'or you'll face the consequences.'

The man, hanging his head, still complaining, scrubbing at the flood of blood with a soiled handkerchief, stumbles away.

The woman watches him go. Then, still with her back to Felix, says, 'You can come out now. No need to defend my honour, thanks all the same, I've seen him off myself.'

And the woman turns round to face him.

She is even more attractive close up. There is something nagging at him, wanting attention – something he's just over-heard has sparked his interest and he knows he ought to be trying to think what it was and why it's important – but just now he wants nothing more than the sheer pleasure of her captivating smile, her infectious laugh and her vivacious company.

He has not discovered her name but he knows who she is. She works for Ted Chauncey, and he last saw her banging dust from a broom in his farmyard.

'I heard the sound of the punch,' he says, stepping into the clearing. 'I thought *he'd* hit *you*, and I truly was just about to come charging in to protect your honour. But then I realized it was you hitting him. Good punch, by the way.'

She is grinning at him, tucking strands of the wild, curly

hair back into the bun. 'I'll take your word for it,' she says. 'And it was a good one, wasn't it? I've had plenty of practice at swinging a punch,' she adds with a grim smile.

Yes, Felix thinks, the fat man certainly won't be the first to have tried his luck with this woman. 'Who is he?' he asks, nodding towards the narrow path along which the man has disappeared.

She shakes her head reprovingly. 'Your third day here in the village, and you haven't discovered the identity of the lord and master?' she says, the last words heavily ironic. 'Goes by the name of Alderidge Cely Leverell, and he lives in the manor house away over there.' She indicates the direction from which Felix has just come.

'I've been told about him,' Felix says.

She looks enquiringly at him, and when he doesn't elaborate, says, 'Well, no doubt the lads in the Leopard had plenty to say on the subject. Nobody round here likes him, which is putting it mildly as most folk despise him as a lazy bully who has never done a hand's span in his life and is busy running through the fortune he inherited purely for his own self-indulgent gratification. Not that it matters, since old Alderidge is the end of the line, family-wise, unless a miracle happens.' She laughs shortly.

And Felix, recalling both what Noah had to say about the man and the scene he has just witnessed, understands, or thinks he does, just what this miracle would have to involve.

The woman is watching him, hand on hip, sardonic smile on her beautiful, full mouth. 'Going to see me home, then?' she asks.

'With pleasure,' he replies. 'Who knows,' he goes on as he offers his arm, she takes it and they stroll off through the trees and back towards the lane, 'some other amorous local may take it into his head to try his chances, and where would you be without me to fend him off?'

She shoots him a glance, her eyes dancing with laughter. 'Roughly where I was just now when randy old Alderidge jumped on me, and seeing him off by myself.'

She is warm, her flesh is firm and smooth, she carries about her a sweet smell of grass and flowers. Having her so close

– she has somehow moved into his side, moulded herself against him, as they walk along together – feels like a balm. Although he doesn't want to, Felix is recalling this afternoon, and putting his arm round Lily to help her to his chair, and comparing the feel of these two women, Lily and the powerful goddess presently beside him . . . Lily is not a small woman, but her waist felt rigid, and he suspects she is more tightly corseted than this lovely woman. Not that he's likely to find out one single fact about Lily Raynor and her corsets, because she is going to dash off and throw herself under the protection of her bloody, blasted boatman and for all he knows, she may well decide to stay there.

There is a sudden very high-pitched squeal from somewhere close by.

It makes him jump, but the woman says calmly, 'Some little vole or mouse has just become Mr Tod's supper.'

Enthralled by the power of her presence, Felix is slow to understand: 'Mr Tod?'

She chuckles. 'The fox. Just as likely to be a vixen, mind, especially if she has cubs to feed.'

They fall silent. Felix is content not to talk, happy to bask in the moment, in the sweet night, in the company of the woman beside him. London, Chelsea, the World's End Bureau – Lily – seem very far away. And his companion is bewitching him, the incident with that fat rich bastard firmly behind her. *I would have driven him away*, Felix tells himself, *if she hadn't*. He would have loved to have gone to her aid, and punching someone who richly deserved it would have relieved some of the tension inside him . . .

In that moment as they walk under the stars, Felix thinks he would give anything to make sure his companion never had to see any man off by herself again.

ELEVEN

Felix wakes early the next morning from a highly erotic dream strongly featuring the auburn-haired goddess who works for Ted Chauncey; undoubtedly a result of having come to her rescue – not having come to her rescue, he corrects himself – last night. In the dream she is astride a piebald horse and she isn't wearing any clothes, and although the auburn hair has grown even longer and more luxuriant, it still isn't sufficient to cover her wonderful body. Felix lies with his eyes shut for some minutes, a smile on his face, watching the beautiful images slowly fade.

He would have expected that by the time he is striding into Crooked Green an hour or so later, the dream and the sensations engendered by it would be a dim memory. But there seems to be something in the air this morning . . . The ripe wheat glows under the golden sun, the thick foliage of the woodlands is vibrant with life, the hop bines bend under the weight of the crop, and in the pastures, this spring's foals, lambs and calves grow healthy and strong.

He keeps up a good pace and is soon past the green and striding down the sloping lane towards Spinfish Cottages. He is about to go up to the door and give it a thump before going in, but suddenly checks: his mind still full of visions of rich rural fertility, it occurs to him that Noah's woman may well be within, perhaps even now standing before the sink having an all-over wash before setting out to begin her day, soaping that pale skin before donning the cotton blouse, twisting the long fair hair into a knot from which a few stray tendrils remain, damp against her flesh . . .

He pauses by the gate, reprimanding himself for his lustful thoughts. Then he walks up the path and taps on the door, quickly responding to the shout of 'Come in, Felix.'

There is indeed someone washing at the sink but it's Noah.

He is bare to the waist, lathering his firm, muscular torso as he leans over the big china bowl.

'Went out early to the horses,' he says. 'My best mare – the chestnut – is in foal, and I sat with her a while. Needed a wash and a change of shirt when I got back.'

He doesn't explain further. Felix, realizing he hadn't known nor thought to ask how his cousin makes a living – although in hindsight all those horses in the paddock which he spotted on his first visit were a powerful clue – stores the information away.

When they are sitting at the table with a mug of tea before each of them, Felix announces his next step: to speak to the men on the list of suspects.

'Maybe amend that to speak to others *about* the men on the list,' Noah suggests. 'If one of them's the killer, he's hardly likely to throw up his hands and confess just because a London journalist comes sniffing, now is he? No offence meant,' he adds.

'None taken,' Felix responds somewhat stiffly.

They are going through the list when there's the sound of footsteps on the path outside and a thump on the door, which opens to reveal a small man standing on the step.

Noah says neutrally, 'Morning, Bert,' and Felix realizes it must be Bert Quittenden.

He studies Effie's grandfather.

He's not very tall, and what height he once had has been lost in the curve of his back, the hunched shoulders and the hump at the top of the spine. His skin is the brown of a walnut shell and about as wrinkled, and the lips have fallen in around the toothless jaws, the hooky nose protruding to meet the jut of the chin. A few long, stray hairs poke out from beneath the cap, and the cheeks are coated with pale grey stubble. He is clad in corduroy breeches tied at the knees with twine, heavy boots, a thick shirt over a vest, and over the shirt a waistcoat and a shabby shapeless jacket. The garments look well worn and none too clean, and as the old man hovers on the doorstep, Felix can smell him from where he sits.

Noah, he observes, has not asked Bert Quittenden to come in.

'What do you want, Bert?' he now asks.

Bert eyes him cautiously, shoots a look at Felix and then returns his gaze to Noah. 'I'm told there's someone from up Lunnun way asking about my Effie,' he says. 'Journalist fellow, they're saying, here sniffing out the whys and wherefores concerning what happened last year.' He pauses, adopts a woebegone expression, turns down his mouth and adds plaintively, 'When my poor little lass met her untimely end and plunged me into this abyss of grief what I'm still in a twelve-month later.' He sniffs, wiping a cuff across his nose. Not taken in for a moment, Felix's scepticism increases sharply when he observes Bert shoot a glance at Noah, clearly trying to assess the effect of his performance.

Noah stares silently at the old man, who quite soon is forced to lower his eyes.

'I repeat, Bert, what do you want?' Noah says softly.

Bert comes cautiously into the room. His whole demeanour speaks of obsequiousness: Felix is put in mind of one of his father's hounds – a beautiful bitch with a nervous temperament made far worse by being yelled at – who used to approach her master with her belly to the ground and a look that said more plainly than words, *Please be nice to me.*

'Well, see, it's like this.' Bert shoots another look at Felix. 'Likely as not this journalist fellow – that'd be you, sir, would it?' Felix doesn't respond. 'Well, this fellow will have no doubt picked up the fact that most of us in the village – not to say *all* of us, really – don't believe poor Abel Spokewright was guilty and don't reckon he ever oughta have been hung.' He nods decisively, and an expression of sugary sanctimoniousness spreads across his lean face.

'That wasn't what you said at the time,' Noah says tonelessly. 'I clearly recall you yelling and shouting in the Leopard's Head, foaming at the mouth as you cried for vengeance, calling on everyone present to join with you and march to Lewes Gaol to haul Abel out of his cell and lynch him from the nearest tree.'

Bert's eyes move in a succession of swift darts to and fro. He looks, Felix reflects, the essence of shiftiness. 'That was

then,' he says plaintively. Then – and it's abundantly clear this
costs him dear – 'I was wrong, seemingly.'

For the third time, Noah asks, 'What do you want?'

Bert straightens up, whips off his cap, begins to turn it round
in his hands and, now sending one of his quick glances at
Felix, says, 'For all you're not saying, I'm going to assume
you're the journalist, and I'm also going to assume you've
come here after a story, because I know you Lunnun men, and
that's the sort of thing you do.' He nods sagely. 'Now if we're
all agreed Abel is innocent, then it stands to reason someone
else killed my Effie, and I'm guessing there's money for
whoever reveals the truth of the matter, and don't you go trying
to tell me I'm wrong.'

'Wouldn't dream of it,' Felix murmurs. He notices a swift
smile cross Noah's face.

Bert is watching him expectantly. 'Well?'

'Well what?' Felix asks.

He watches the old man struggle with himself. Quite quickly
venality wins out over any notions of decency, and he blurts
out, 'How much are you paying?'

Still staring at him, Felix narrows his eyes as if considering
the matter. After some moments he says, 'You know the truth
of the matter, then?'

'Now I'm not saying that I do, not for sure,' Bert says,
clearly hedging, 'but I have my suspicions, always have had,
and I reckon I could point an interested party in the right
direction.' Eyes fixed on Felix, 'If that's you, sir, then for a
consideration – and I'm by no means a greedy man, but I'm
old and I've lost my granddaughter and helpmeet – then you
shall be made a party to these suspicions.'

Felix maintains his silence and his hard stare. He senses
that Noah is about to speak, and sure enough he does.

'You've always had your suspicions, have you?' he asks
softly.

'That I have!' The old man sticks his chin even further out.

'Strange, then, that you utterly failed to mention them when
you were all for hanging Abel Spokewright with your own
hands,' Noah goes on, his tone reflective.

'Now, I never said that, never said I'd hang the poor lad

myself!' Now Noah's eyes are fixed on him as intently as
Felix's. 'Well, maybe I did, but I was that upset, who can
blame me?'

Neither man answers.

Bert straightens his back, hitches up his breeches and says,
'Going to pay me, then?'

Felix gives the faintest of shrugs.

Taking this as affirmation, Bert leans towards him and says
in a hoarse whisper, 'The man you oughta be suspicious of
is that weird crippled bugger as worked with my Effie.' He
nods sharply a couple of times. 'That cowman with the gammy
leg and the shifty look. That George Croucher!' He nods a
few more times. 'Never had a woman, hasn't George, and
word is he's incapable.' He makes a lewd gesture towards his
crotch. 'Not being able doesn't stop a fellow *wanting* to, I'm
thinking, and there he was, day in, day out, working alongside
a pretty little rosebud just ripe for the picking – my Effie, that
is – and you can't tell *me* that didn't make the frustration
mount up!' He nods again. Then, lowering his voice to a hiss,
'*He's* the man you want,' he concludes, 'you mark my words!'

'We should go together to Newhouse Farm, and I'll introduce
you to the Marchants,' Noah says when Bert has shuffled away.

'Why?'

'Word will have got around, people will be discussing who
you are and why you're here. Some will react like old
Quittenden, and hurry to tell you their version of the tale in
the hope you're going to pay them. Some will take it amiss
that you're here asking your questions, and we'll be charitable
and say it's because what happened here last year is none of
your business and they don't like outsiders anyway.' He pauses.
'And someone will be afraid, because they'll know why you're
really here.' He shoots Felix a look. 'Because, as you and I
have already said, if Abel's innocent, someone else is guilty.
For a whole year they've got away with it, and they're not
going to be best pleased you've come raking it all up again.'

'And why does it improve matters for you to introduce me?'

'Because I live here. They know me.'

Felix doesn't like this assumption that he wouldn't make

any progress without his cousin at his side. But he is realistic enough to accept that Noah is probably right, and reluctantly agrees.

When they arrive at Newhouse Farm it is mid-morning. A chained collie embarks on a fury of barking as they approach, which stops as suddenly as it began when someone within the long cowshed over to the left of the farmyard calls out a few calm words. There are sounds of activity from this shed, where someone is splashing bucket after bucket of water onto the floor, producing a flood of small rivulets that flow out through the wide-open doors to find their way to the big drain in the middle of the yard. Noah trots over to look inside the cowshed, returning to murmur to Felix, 'George Croucher's in there, finishing the mucking out.'

Some ten or twelve paces beyond the cowshed there is a huge pile of straw and manure, gently steaming in the warm sunshine, and a couple of upturned barrows and an assortment of forks and shovels have been abandoned beside it. Turning their backs on it, Noah and Felix go on across the yard and up to the door of the farmhouse. Noah raises the iron knocker and lets it thump against the woodwork, and moments afterwards, he and Felix are inside the big kitchen, sitting across a scarred old pine table from a thin-faced man with a suspicious look and an even thinner-faced older woman with incredibly tightly pursed lips who looks, Felix can't help thinking, as if she has a very aggressive wasp in her mouth.

Before Noah has had time to say more than, 'This is Felix, he's from London and a cousin of mine and he's thinking of writing an article on Effie's murder,' Harold Marchant has interrupted.

'We've heard,' he says shortly. He glances over his shoulder at the third person in the kitchen – a young man in his early twenties with a friendly, open face and bright blue eyes under a thatch of thick fair hair – and adds, 'Mick here was in the Leopard.'

Thinking it's high time he spoke up for himself, Felix says, 'I appreciate it may be a matter you prefer to forget, but if not, I would be interested to hear your views.'

Harold nods. Then, looking over at Noah, says, 'No need for you to stay now you've done what you came for.'

If Noah is offended by this curt dismissal, it doesn't show in his bland expression. With a nod to all those present, he takes his leave.

Harold Marchant is no Bert Quittenden, and some sense of his own dignity prevents him asking if there's money in it for him. His mother, however, has no such qualms.

'Going to pay us for our time?' she snaps out. 'Farmers are busy people, you know. A dairy herd doesn't look after itself while we sit in here drinking tea.'

Felix refrains from pointing out that this is precisely what they were doing when he and Noah arrived; after all, he's here to seek their help. 'I imagine not,' he says with a smile. 'As for payment, any remuneration that might be due to you would have to wait until the piece had been written, published and paid for, naturally.'

He has tried to suggest that such payment is a fairly unlikely possibility; anything else would feel too like misrepresentation. He's already feeling uneasy about sailing under false colours, but he's sure these misgivings will pass.

Mick Marchant steps closer to the table and says, 'Is it right what they're claiming? That you're saying you don't reckon Abel killed her?'

'It's not what I'm saying,' Felix corrects him quickly, 'it's what others are saying to me. But yes, that appears to be the general view.'

Mick shoots a triumphant glance at his uncle and his great-aunt. 'See, I said as much! Didn't I, Uncle? Aunt Beryl, *you* remember, I always said—'

The tight mouth slackens just long enough for the words 'Enough, Mick! Be about your work,' to emerge like shot from a gun before closing again. Beryl Marchant, a faint flush on her sunken cheeks and an angry light in the tiny dark eyes, watches as her great-nephew stomps out of the room.

Into the silence Felix says, 'I understand that Effie worked with a cowman, George Croucher?'

Harold and the old woman exchange a glance. 'She did,' Harold says.

'And just now he's over in the cowshed?'

'He has work to do,' snaps Beryl. 'I won't have you disturbing him.'

'I'm not proposing to *disturb* him,' Felix replies, laying emphasis on the word, 'unless you feel that some mild questions about Effie's nature, what she was like to work with, will have that effect?'

Realizing too late that she has set a trap for herself, Beryl says crossly, 'I didn't mean it like that, and of course a few harmless questions won't do any such thing.'

'What my mother means is that George is a very shy, limited, unworldly man,' Harold supplies, earning a furious look from the old woman, who is clearly livid at anyone having the presumption to explain what she means. 'He's worked here since he was a boy, for my father before me, and while he can deal perfectly well with everyday life when it continues calm and regular, any untoward event throws him.'

'And you can't get an event more untoward than the brutal murder of the dairy maid,' Felix murmurs.

For a moment he thinks he has gone too far. Harold Marchant rises a few inches from his chair, hands forming fists, and it feels as if Beryl's tiny black eyes are shooting out flaming sparks of furious hatred.

Then slowly Harold resumes his seat. Clearing his throat, he says, 'If you're thinking to lay the blame for that terrible act on George Croucher, or anyone else under my roof, you can think again. Now we'll bid you good day. Be on your way,' he adds, in case Felix hasn't understood, 'and don't even think about going into the cowshed as you pass.'

Felix stands up, bows to mother and son, and with as much dignity as he can gather, walks out of the house.

He has almost reached the gate at the end of the track leading back to the lane when he hears footsteps pounding up behind him. Stopping, he turns to see Mick Marchant, scarlet in the face, running towards him.

'Did they throw you out?' he pants.

Felix grins. 'Not quite.'

'Were you asking about George?'

'I said I'd like to talk to him about Effie, but—'

'That'll be what did it,' Mick says, nodding. 'They pay him a bare pittance and he lives in a stall off the cowshed,' he adds, lowering his voice, 'and poor Georgie is too innocent to understand they are cheating him and have been doing so all his life. They don't like anyone from outside talking to him in case they discover the truth and reveal it to him. Poor old Georgie,' he adds, 'he's always worked hard, always given his best, and has bugger-all to show for it.'

'Your uncle said he'd worked for his father before him?'

'That he did. The old bastard – my great-uncle – made out to the Crouchers he was doing them a good turn, taking their idiot boy off their hands,' Mick says angrily. 'That's what everyone says, anyway, though it was all before I was born.'

'Is he an idiot?' Felix asks.

'No, course he's not!' Mick sounds scathing. 'He has the best way with cows as I've ever seen, and that's saying something. With all animals, come to that. He's quiet and patient, specially with heifers carrying their first calf, and my sod of an uncle and his old witch of a mother are lucky to have him.'

'I'm told he's crippled?'

'No!' Again, Mick leaps to vehement defence. 'His father used to take it out on Georgie when the hardships brought about by his own indolence frustrated him beyond bearing. The Crouchers lived out at the bottom of Mill Lane,' he goes on, 'down beyond the mill. Old man Croucher had a streak of cruelty a mile wide, and his wife and children lived in fear of him. He took against poor Georgie pretty much as soon as he was born, or so they say, and the lad couldn't do a thing to please him. There's tales of how old man Croucher'd get drunk in the Leopard, stagger home, find his wife and his children cowering in the corner, fire gone out, no firewood, no food, and he'd give the lad a leathering as if it was all his fault, and the lass and her mother too, though Georgie got it worst. He hurled poor Georgie out through the door one night, and Georgie fell awkwardly and must have broken his ankle, only of course nothing was done about it and the leg ended up deformed.' Mick shakes his head, his cheery face sorrowful.

'You say he's good with his cows?' Felix prompts after a respectful pause.

'Yes, yes, he's gentle, see, talks to them in this special soft voice, calms them.' Felix remembers the wildly barking dog, and the few quiet words from the cowshed that instantly silenced him. 'Seems to understand their moods – and believe me, cows have moods, don't you go thinking they don't.'

'No, of course not,' Felix murmurs absently. Then: 'He's gentle, you said?'

Mick's bright eyes fly to meet his. 'I did,' he says, 'and you've no need to ask your next question, because I know full well what it is and I'll tell you straight, Georgie Croucher would no more have laid a hand on Effie than take a stick to a frightened cow struggling over a first birth!'

He is panting again, but from emotion this time rather than exertion. Such is the quality of honest sincerity shining out of the young man that Felix believes him.

'I am sorry if I have offended you,' he says quietly.

'Not me, but Georgie,' Mick mutters crossly. Then, gazing away into the distance, he says, 'It's what folk do, isn't it? Someone's different, not the same as everyone else, and straight away, soon as there's trouble, sooner or later someone points the finger of blame and says, *It'll be him, he's not like us, he's odd, he must have done it.*'

And sadly Felix has to agree that it's exactly what folk do.

'We loved little Effie, Georgie and me,' Mick says softly after a moment. 'Not like that, I don't mean like that—'

'I know you don't,' Felix murmurs.

'I mean, we were her friends, her *good* friends, and we cared about each other, the three of us, we looked out for each other. She was a joy, with her pretty face, her smile, her kindness and the way she looked after Georgie like she did. She made my life bearable too, and the two of us made a joke of it when the old woman got into one of her moods.' He glances back upon the track towards the farmhouse. 'She'd had it tough, Effie had – not as bad as Georgie, of course, but she lost her parents when she was little and had to go and live with that old bugger Bert Quittenden, him being her only relative, and he treated her no better than his slave. But then she met Abel, and she was so happy, and Abel was a decent man and Georgie and I reckoned Effie'd do all right with him, and we were glad for her, even if it meant she'd probably leave the village and go off to be his wife in London. But then someone killed her,' he concludes with a deep sigh, 'and Georgie and me have mourned her every single day since.' He pauses, then adds very quietly, 'It's not the same here without her.'

Then he gives a curt nod and heads back up the track towards the farm.

TWELVE

Lily has to steel herself virtually every step of the journey back to the East End the next morning. She tries to focus her mind exclusively on finding Alexei, and with his help uncovering who it was who thought he was killing Yakov last night and why he wants the boy dead. She hopes that the bearded man with the scar on his eyelid will have reappeared, but at the same time dreads to find him back at that table beside the door, playing cards with the others. If he knows Alexei followed him, she reasons as the tram bumps and rattles over the points, then surely he'll keep away? But *oh* – the thought recurs, chilling her anew like a bucket of cold water – if he knows about Alexei, then of course he'll want to kill him too.

Descending from the tram at the closest stop to the Mission, she wishes very much that the comforting reassurance she gave to Felix last night was true, and that right now she was heading off for the Limehouse Basin to find the master of *The Dawning of the Day* and enlist his help. But it was a falsehood – all right, a lie, she corrects the thought irritably – and told with the sole intention of stopping Felix nagging at her to let him go with her. Although she knows Tamáz is not far away – she's not sure how she knows, only that she does – for now she is on her own.

And I will manage, she tells herself as she strides up the steps to the wide doors.

She had feared that Alexei might have gone to ground after last night – and really wouldn't have blamed him if he had – but even as she sets off along the passage to the day room where she first spoke to the passengers from the *Oude Maas*, she hears a hiss from a narrow little passage off to the right and Alexei's voice whispers, 'Here, Miss Lady!'

Swiftly checking that nobody can see her, she hurries into the dark corridor. It ends in two doors made of cheap and flimsy wood that is already warping, and Alexei has gone back behind the one on the left. She can smell chloride of lime, the rough, rasping aroma of scouring powder and the stench of wet cloths that haven't been spread out to dry but left in a bundle to moulder. Her left foot kicks against a bucket, and she can make out several brooms propped in a corner. Alexei's hiding place is a cupboard for cleaning equipment.

He drags her inside and pulls the door to.

'Better to speak here,' he says, keeping his voice down. 'Not good if we are seen each with the other.'

'No, quite right,' she agrees. Before he can say anything else, she asks: 'Alexei, last night you told me the man you followed was big and had a dark beard, and I'm sure he also had a scar on his eyelid, because I recognized the description and I've seen this man in the day room.' Alexei nods, his face sombre. 'And you said another man joined him by the canal. Was this one slighter, younger and fair-haired?' She's almost certain he will say yes, for this is her memory of the younger man sitting beside the man with the scar, the one who smiled at her.

But slowly Alexei shakes his head.

'No. Other man was big like first man, man with scar, and maybe bigger. And . . .' He stops, then, apparently unable to find the word, mimes cowering away, his hands up to defend his face.

'He was frightened?' she asks, surprised.

Briefly Alexei grins, and all at once looks like the boy on the edge of manhood that he is. 'No, not *frightened*,' he says carefully. 'He *frightens*.'

'He – oh, I see! He scared you.'

'I think he scare everyone,' Alexei mutters.

'Have you seen him here, this other man?' she asks.

Alexei shakes his head. 'No. Not today, not ever here in this place. He—' He thinks for a moment. 'He wait out in dark passage for scar man. Keep himself hidden, I think.'

She nods. 'And the bearded man, has he turned up?' Alexei frowns and she amends, 'Has he come back here?'

'Not – not early, when I leave this morning. Now – cannot say.'

Lily wants to go and check in the day room herself, but she is wary. What if the big man with the scar *is* sitting there and sees her?

Castigating herself for her lack of courage, she ponders the wisdom of asking Alexei to look. He is meant to be here, she reasons, he's in and out all the time, and his presence is far less likely to arouse the attention of anyone watching. So she asks him, and has further cause to berate herself when instantly he agrees and dashes off before she can change her mind.

He is gone for some time; more than long enough for her to be sure he's been grabbed and even now is being bundled away out of a dark back entrance, and—

He's back. He's shaking his head. 'No man here, not man with scar, not big man who scares.'

Lily nods, her mind racing. Two men, then. One – or perhaps both – followed her. First one and then both followed a boy they thought was Yakov. Killed him, and presumably found out only after they had done so that he wasn't the boy they sought.

But who are they? What do they want with Yakov, one thin, hungry, dirty boy among so many fleeing danger and death?

She should be out on the streets again, she thinks. She has no idea where to look for Yakov, but he's not here and her job is to find him. She leans over to murmur her intentions to Alexei, but before she can do so he says, 'Please, Miss Lady, someone want to speak to you.' His tone is urgent, and she realizes that, perceptive lad that he is, he saw that she was deep in thought and waited to make his announcement until she had finished.

'I'm sorry, Alexei. Of course – who is it?'

But instead of answering he takes hold of her sleeve and leads the way through the spider's web of passages to the dark little yard that smells of drains. And there, just as she was three days ago, is Serafima.

Even as Lily crosses the yard to join her, she is already talking, in a rapid, whispered mutter of which Lily doesn't understand a word. Alexei says something to her, she nods and falls silent.

'This morning I tell her about boy like Yakov who was

killed,' he says to Lily. 'She very, very upset. Just then when I look to see if men are in room, she call to me, she say she must tell you more.'

Lily looks into Serafima's pale face. Her large eyes are almost black, and there are dark semicircles underneath them which, rather than marring her beauty, somehow enhance it. Amid all her concerns, Lily is struck by a sudden thought: *How intolerable it is, for a lovely young woman with a small child to be forced into this awful, uncertain, frightening existence, a stranger in another country, purely because someone else has decided she is no longer welcome in her homeland.*

Serafima has begun to speak again, in a low undertone, leaning close to Alexei and talking into his ear. What she has to say appears to be very urgent: so much so that she's reluctant to stop and let him translate.

'She say family of Yelisaveta very rich,' he says when at last she stops. 'But do not live like rich people, live so nobody notices them. Husband of Yelisaveta is Abram and he is teacher, teach languages, and house is not big, not with many beautiful objects, and Yelisaveta wear good garments but not fine cloth. But everyone knows there is wealth from behind?' He frowns, clearly not sure he has the right word.

'From before?' Lily suggests. 'Inherited wealth, from Abram's or Yelisaveta's parents?'

His face clears. 'Yes! Before family of Abram have much learning, many books, libraries, live in big house, this is what neighbours always believe, and—'

Serafima is talking again, eagerly, impatiently, and he breaks off to listen. Then, once again having a job to stop her, he turns to Lily.

'Others try to be friend with Yelisaveta on journey, to give comfort when daughter and her baby perish, but she will not . . .' He clicks his fingers, searching for the word to express what Serafima said.

'Unbend?'

'Unbend, yes. So she is unpopular on journey, holds herself apart like always back in Odessa, and this is not new way to behave but began long ago, at home and before they all fled and terrible journey begin.'

Serafima is off again, glancing repeatedly at Lily. It seems, she thinks, that there was much that Serafima held back when they spoke before, and she is fairly sure that it's the murder of the youth mistaken for Yakov that has made her open up. She speaks for some time, and Alexei is frowning as he turns to translate to Lily.

'She tell me son of Abram and Yelisaveta is Yefrem, is only son, very cared-for, like little prince in family, but when Yefrem still young boy is taken away, and Abram will not say where but Yelisaveta very sad, cry, become thin and white. But after many years Yefrem return, and is nearly a man, and soon he marry Rachel and then four years after Yakov is born. But family have trouble, much anger, try to hide away but neighbours hear loud words, father, son, many . . .' He snaps his fingers, impatient again for the word.

'Many rows? Many arguments?' Lily supplies.

'Yes, yes, rows. And—' He stops, because Serafima is speaking again.

Turning back to her, Alexei says, 'Serafima say people think family have treasure. Gold, diamonds, valuable jewels, precious stones, and that Abram and Yefrem argue so bad because Yefrem want money from father and father say no.' Once again he pauses for a great flow of words from Serafima. Translating, Alexei says, 'Rumour spreads on journey, on train journey north from Odessa, that Yelisaveta have family treasure hidden away under garments, that Abram, Yelisaveta, Yefrem and Rachel all carry treasure with them when they flee house. *She*' – he indicates Serafima – 'say Semyon and others speak quietly together and all say, where is treasure now?'

Lily tries to visualize how the valuables might have been carried: pouch? Purse? Drawstring bag in soft suede? Perhaps the precious items were divided between the four adults and each carried a share, which was passed to one of the others with each successive death until only Yelisaveta was left and took charge of the whole lot . . .

Serafima's voice breaks in on her thoughts. She sounds short, irritated, as if she's explaining something that doesn't need explaining. Nodding, starting to translate before she's finished, Alexei says, 'She say not possible that Yelisaveta had treasure when arrive in hospital. All have same treatment, all who come off boats, sick people going to nice clean hospital more than others, and are stripped, washed, clad in clean gown.' Serafima sounds really angry now, and Alexei puts a hand on her arm. 'Not good, women do not like because not dignity, but is necessary because trains filthy, boats too, and nobody can wash, everyone have lice.' At last Serafima stops speaking. 'She say all know what will be done when arrive on quay. Yelisaveta too, even when she sick and not clear in her head, she know.'

Yes, she would know, Lily thinks. She'd been told what to expect. She would be received into the care of the nurses, washed and put into a gown, because that was the hospital's custom; it is the same everywhere, and Lily performed the same tasks for so many incoming patients in her nursing past. Yelisaveta would know that, probably unconscious, naked as they washed her, there would be absolutely no possibility of hiding a bag of treasures.

And she can almost *see* what must have happened: before Yelisaveta was carried off the boat and onto the quayside for onward transmission to the London Hospital, she gave that precious bag to Yakov.

If I can work it out, she thinks wildly, then so can others. It seems that many people were aware of the rumours of Hadzibazy wealth, many of Yelisaveta's fellow passengers believed, perhaps, that it was to protect this hidden wealth that she was so determined to keep herself and her grandson apart from the rest.

So is this the reason why Yakov has fled, and why these terrible, violent, ruthless men are chasing him? Did they spot a boy who bore a passing resemblance to him, follow him, brutally hunt him down and cut away his garments because they were searching the body for the mythical treasure?

'But they followed the wrong boy,' she whispers softly. 'He wasn't Yakov, he had no treasure on him and he was murdered for nothing.'

She looks up to see Serafima's intense dark eyes staring at her. Abruptly Serafima turns to Alexei and whispers something, but Lily, naturally, wouldn't understand even if she could make out the words. The only one she does hear sounds like *ochre*. At this Alexei instantly shushes Serafima, shaking his head, panicky expression on his face, finger to his lips.

Serafima turns her sorrowful eyes back to Lily. And she knows that precisely the same emotion – deep pity for a young man murdered for nothing – is filling Serafima's mind.

She spends the day with Alexei, treading the towpaths along the canals, following the cuts, searching everywhere and asking, when they come across someone they feel they can trust – which is quite a rare occurrence – if they've seen a lad of twelve fitting Yakov's description.

Nobody has.

They visit the Limehouse Basin, but Tamáz is not there.

Finally, as the afternoon turns towards evening and at last the heat of the day begins to wane, she sees Alexei back to the Mission and, with very firm instructions not to go following any big, violent men again, heads for home.

On the tram, the relief to be off her feet and no longer walking is huge. For some time she lets her mind relax along with her tired body, closing her eyes and letting her head bump gently against the window beside her. It is very pleasant, and a couple of times she drops into a very brief sleep.

Then all at once she is wide awake.

Would those two men, the one with the scar and his frightening companion, really act that way? Even assuming there actually was treasure, and that somehow they'd found out, or guessed, that Yelisaveta had handed it into Yakov's keeping, would they murder someone who happened to look like the boy solely on the off chance that the rumours were correct?

Lily is not naive enough to believe that every person arriving in England to make a new life is pure and good and entirely without criminal intent. But really, knowing what would happen to them if they were caught, aware that, wanted for murder, they'd have to go on the run in a land where they had just arrived, possibly with no friends to hide them, no contacts to give advice, would the two men have acted as they did?

For the rumour of gold, diamonds and precious jewels?

They're so poor, she reasoned. They have nothing. The temptation would be too great.

Perhaps, answers the other half of her brain.

But still, the thought persists and will not subside: surely there has to be more to it than this.

By the time she is on the final tram that will take her along the King's Road to where World's End Passage branches off, she has made up her mind. The brief rest has restored her; besides, the intense hunger of her curiosity will not allow her to leave it alone.

There is far too much that she does not know. Accordingly, she alights from the tram many stops before her own and sets off into the network of residential streets between Royal Hospital Road and the King's Road, making a couple of wrong turns before finally finding Kinver Street. She stops in front of a tall, narrow old house. It is more than a little run down but full of charm, with high-ceilinged rooms, cornices and mouldings, an elaborately elegant staircase and black and white tiles in the entrance hall.

She hasn't actually been inside, but she knows what to expect because Felix has described it to her. It's where he lives; he shares the apartment on the first floor with his good friend Marm Smithers. Felix, of course, isn't there now. But Lily very much hopes that Marm is, for it is he who she has come to see.

'Sit there, in Felix's chair,' Marm says a few minutes later.

He is indeed at home, and in answer to Lily's ring at the bell, came down to open the door with an enquiring expression that instantly changed to a wide smile of welcome when he saw who it was.

She sits down. The chair is very comfortable: she must make sure to keep awake and not relax too much.

'Do you drink whisky?' Marm is saying, holding up a rather beautiful cut-glass decanter. 'I am not one of those men,' he adds, 'who believes a lady is less of a lady because she enjoys the occasional glass of spirits.'

Lily hadn't imagined he was; Marm Smithers is far too

much a champion of the female sex to subscribe to something so unfair and unreasonable.

'Well, a very small glass,' she replies.

He nods approvingly and hands her quite a generous measure in a glass that matches the decanter. He pours a measure for himself, raises his glass to her in a silent toast, and she takes a sip. She feels it slide down her throat, and it does her even more good than the brief nap on the tram.

Still holding his eyes, she says, 'I have come to ask for your advice.'

The eyebrows go up above the world-weary blue eyes. The eyes are full of intelligence and are now looking benevolently at his guest.

'Have you, Miss Raynor? I can't imagine what advice you could require of me, but ask away and I shall be glad to provide it if I can.'

'It's information that I want, really,' she says.

And she explains, as succinctly as she can, about Yelisaveta, Yakov, the flight from Odessa, the possibility of treasure, and her firm conviction that there is more to this than anyone thinks.

When she has finished, Marm is silent for several moments. Then he says, 'I believe you are quite right. All my journalistic instincts inform me that there is indeed a deeper tale here. There is much that I can tell you concerning the background to the dreadful events in Russia,' he goes on before she can respond, 'but it will take time, for I always like to give as full a picture as I can.' Now he smiles at her. He is in his late thirties but looks older, and the skin of his face is yellowish, tired and full of broken veins. But his expression is full of kindness, and there is a sort of glow about him, Lily thinks.

'A little while before you rang the bell my thoughts had turned towards my supper,' he says, 'and I decided that a hot steak pie and a baked potato cut open and filled with grated cheese and butter would fit the bill nicely. I dare say you can smell the pie, warming in the oven?'

She can. It's been making her mouth water because she's very hungry, and she's had to give an unconvincing cough a couple of times to mask the sound of her stomach rumbling. She swallows and says, 'Yes, yes I can.'

'Happily it was a very large potato – I remembered to stick a skewer through the middle to hasten the cooking time – and it is also a generously sized pie. I suggest, dear Miss Raynor, that we eat together, have another shot of whisky, and when we have finished, I will tell you everything that is relevant to your search.'

Although she is aware that it is totally inadequate, Lily mutters, 'Thank you, Mr Smithers. I should very much like to accept.'

THIRTEEN

Felix feels soiled as he strides back down Claypit Lane towards the middle of the village. He is certain now that Bert Quittenden's suggestion of George Croucher as Effie's murderer was no more than malice, and he regrets having listened to the old man, even more having acted on his gossipy, dirty-minded accusation.

As he strides across the green the church clock strikes the half: twelve-thirty. Glancing over towards the Leopard's Head, he sees Ezra Sleech standing on his doorstep, chest thrown out, hands on his hips, big white apron gleaming in the sunshine. Spotting Felix, he hails him: 'Just tapped a new barrel, if you've a mind to try a pint?' and all at once there is nothing Felix wants more.

'Now then, Mr Wilbraham, how's the investigation going along?' Ezra asks as Felix takes the top off his pint.

Investigation. The word gives Felix a jolt. Has Ezra guessed why he's really here, then? Has he discovered that the London journalist pose is all pretence?

Wisely he doesn't answer but waits for Ezra to elaborate: 'I hear you've been getting around a bit, asking your questions. Anyone come up with anything interesting for your article, or is it all just gossip, rumour and the settling of old scores?'

Felix makes a rueful face. 'Very much the latter, I fear,' he says. He thinks briefly, then, seeing no harm in it, tells Ezra about Bert Quittenden accusing George Croucher.

Ezra calls Bert a name that Felix is sure would not pass his lips if there were ladies present.

Felix sups his beer. Ezra comes and goes, and when he is absent, Felix guesses he must be in the kitchen, talking to Peg: at one point she raises her voice, although her words are not sufficiently distinct for Felix to make out, and Ezra murmurs soothingly to her.

This time when he returns to the bar, he makes a face at Felix; the sort of expression that says, *Women, eh!*

Felix grins. 'Mrs Sleech works hard,' he observes.

Ezra's expression softens. 'She does that,' he agrees. He hesitates, then leans across the bar towards Felix and, lowering his voice, says, 'Like I believe I told you, her back troubles her, and I'm ever trying to encourage her to take it a bit easier, put her feet up over a cup of tea now and then, but she's *driven*, can't seem to stop herself, and, when all's said and done, there's always work needing doing, and I admit I'm not as quick as I ought to be to carry out the heavier jobs when she asks.' He pauses, the handsome face creased in a sorrowful frown.

'She must be a great asset in a place like this,' Felix offers, filling the brief silence.

'Oh, she is, she is!' Ezra agrees. 'And capable? I'll say she is, turns her hand to anything, and even when she's caught up with every single task inside the pub, out she goes to her garden, digging, weeding, planting, and can I get her to have a rest now and again? Can I buggery!'

Felix murmurs soothingly, and almost straight away Ezra says, 'Sorry. Shouldn't curse like that, and anyhow it's not as if I don't know how lucky I am to have a wife like old Peg because I do.'

'Yes, so I can see,' Felix says. He is rather hoping the landlord's sudden burst of confidences will peter out before it becomes embarrassing, but Ezra, it appears, is only just getting into his stride.

'I've had my share of pretty women, Mr Wilbraham, or I should say I *used* to, before Peg and I became man and wife,' he says, and he gives Felix a very suggestive wink. 'But what I always say is that a pretty woman is a flighty woman, and often as not too full of the notion that it's up to her husband to go on spoiling her and flattering her, just like he did when they were courting, and constantly holding over him the threat of withholding her *intimate favours*' – the knowing wink again – 'if he doesn't comply. What I say is, choose a woman who's not too sure of herself, who's maybe somewhat scared of the world, and she'll be too grateful for the ring on her finger to entertain any such rubbish.' He nods once or twice. Then, surprising both Felix and also himself, if his expression is anything to go by, he adds softly, 'It was a good day's work when I married old Peg, even if what modest appeal the dear girl had faded pretty quickly, and I reckon I'd not manage without her.'

Before Felix can reply – he is in any case at a loss to think what on earth he might say – Ezra leaps up and disappears behind the door into the kitchen.

Not long afterwards, Felix gets up to go. The new barrel must have been somewhat stronger than those he has previously sampled, because he feels slightly light-headed as he walks towards the door.

He turns to say goodbye to Ezra, back in his accustomed place behind the bar, but just then the door to the rear quarters is flung open and Peg Sleech comes through it.

'Ezra, you've forgotten!' she says in an irritated undertone. 'I must have reminded you a dozen times, yet here you are seeing Mr Wilbraham go off about his business and that letter's still on the dresser!' As she says the last words – they emerge in a hiss like an angry goose – she pokes her head on its long, skinny neck towards her husband, who recoils slightly; an instinctive gesture, Felix thinks, looking compassionately at Peg, that does not go unnoticed . . .

Ezra slaps a hand to his head. 'Now what a fool I am!' he beams. 'You're quite right, my dear, you did indeed remind me, several times. Still, no harm done, eh? Just you wait a moment, Mr Wilbraham, and I'll run and fetch it, I know just where I put it and—'

Silently his wife holds up a cream vellum envelope. She gives him a look, nods at Felix, and disappears behind the door.

'Here you are,' Ezra says, handing it to him. 'His nibs up at the Old Abbey House left it for you.' He stares at Felix, curiosity written all over him. 'Now I wonder what he thinks he's doing, writing to you?'

Felix already has the door open and is heading out of it. Turning to give Ezra a grin, he says, 'I'm about to find out. Goodbye, Mr Sleech, and that's a very fine barrel – I commend you!'

Felix crosses the green and goes under the lychgate into the shade of the churchyard. He is still preoccupied with the Sleeches; with a man who apparently cares deeply for his plain wife while not finding her physically attractive, and with a hard-working, driven woman who takes on the care of a rather beautiful flower and vegetable garden in addition to all her other work.

Shaking his head to dismiss these thoughts, he makes his way through the overgrown graveyard to a corner out of sight of the road, where he finds a very old tombstone beneath an even older yew tree. He sits down, breaks the red wax seal and opens the envelope. It is heavy, of very good quality, and the cream vellum is lined with a thin layer of pale grey tissue paper. He extracts the single sheet of writing paper – also heavy cream vellum – and stares down at it.

The sheet is about five inches by nine, and there is a crest at the top that depicts a leopard and a unicorn (the latter has a spectacularly long horn, surely far too long for the creature to entertain much hope of holding its head up). Underneath is engraved in gold, in writing so heavily decorated with swirls and loops as to make it almost illegible, *Old Abbey House.*

Wilbraham (the handwritten message begins uncompromisingly.)

It has been reported to me by those concerning themselfs with my affaires that you are here in the village (*my* has been crossed out and replaced by *the*, both words half-obliterated by a large blot of ink) *interviewing my tenants concerning matters pertianing to the unfortunate events that came to pass almost a year ago this season of late summer and the witch are much regreted by all and would very much like to be forgoten and I would accord it a servise if yourself would deign to call on me to discus same at a time of mutual benefit and convenience I am at home habitualy in the early afternoons mostly and shall expect to be called on by you*

> *Yours*
> *Alderidge Cely Leverell*

Felix lowers the page, a broad smile on his face. He has already got over the peremptory nature of the summons: how can you allow yourself to be irritated or insulted, he thinks, chuckling, by a self-important oaf who can't spell, has not the least notion of the use of correct punctuation and whose handwriting would shame a six-year-old with his first copybook?

Besides, the one man in the village whom he particularly wants to meet is Alderidge Cely Leverell, and until now he has been unable to come up with a plausible reason for calling. Now he needn't bother, for his entry ticket is in his hand.

He makes his careful way out of the graveyard, pausing to brush a cleaver off his trouser leg, and notices absently that there is a fresh posy on the grave over by the far hedge. More pink, and again that blob of orange, against the green foliage. Then he is through the gate and out on the road. With a spring in his step, he sets off up Earlyleas Lane towards Old Abbey House.

He realizes soon after having taken the wrong turn that it is a mistake. He has gone up the track on the right that he thought led to Old Abbey House, but presently he sees that in fact it takes him to the ruins of the old abbey; he can see the house about a quarter of a mile ahead.

Alderidge Cely Leverell may have summoned him, but that is no reason not to pause for a look around. The remains of the abbey that once stood here – before Henry VIII allowed himself to be led by the codpiece and abandon the Church of Rome in order to marry Anne Boleyn – are all around him. Broken walls; impossibly low doorways built for much smaller men; the long, straight nave, paved now with nothing but grass; an imposing trio of high, pointed arches standing alone. The place has a haunting beauty. Its former inhabitants – dead these three centuries and more – seem to move closer, and his steps are led to what appears once to have been a walled garden. There is a wildly overgrown green shrub that shoves its way through a gap in the wall, the tight foliage on the long, slim branches emitting a scent . . . He's back in France again with Solange, eating a gut-busting meal and the wonderful aromas of roast lamb, garlic and rosemary – yes, of course, he knows now, that smell is rosemary – in his nose.

And, standing looking down at the vigorous plant, he understands why he failed to recognize it when he saw it in All Saints' Churchyard, on the grave beside the far hedge: rosemary is usually a tamed plant, neatly clipped, well behaved, and not this riot of leaf and far too evocative scent . . .

He wanders on. On the other side of the wall there is a little hollow, concealed by the old stones and the rosemary plant, sheltered by the tumbled remains of another unidentifiable structure. It is lined with soft grass, shaded from the sun, and totally private: Felix has only stumbled upon it by chance.

He stands absolutely still.

Perhaps it is his very fond and decidedly erotic memories of Solange; perhaps it is some echo that lingers in this secret place. But he knows – *knows*, doesn't just consider the possibility – that this place has been the refuge of lovers.

And his eyes are drawn to the base of the ruined wall of the building, where someone has taken a penknife and carved a simple heart in the sandstone. The heart is entwined with foliage, and inside it is the letter M. On the grass beneath there is a tiny posy of flowers tied with an old and faded piece of ribbon.

Felix stands a few moments longer. Then with a sigh and a silent blessing for whatever man or boy once etched his beloved's initial here, walks away.

It is time to go on to Old Abbey House.

Even as he strides up the drive, Felix can see that this house has been designed to impress. It is vast: that, he reflects, is pretty much the only plus point. It is a big, ugly rectangle dumped onto the landscape, the wide central section flanked on either side by two square towers with crenellated tops. Drawing nearer, he can see the huge carriage porch; surely big enough for a pair of vehicles standing side by side. There are elaborate stone columns holding up its roof, decorated inside with a design of nymphs in clouds.

He steps up to the vast oak door, raises the brass knocker and lets it fall. The sound echoes from within like an angry sea in a cave. He is about to repeat the gesture, but the door is opened and a tall man dressed in black stands there, white gloves on his hands, one of which grips the edge of the door so tightly that it gives the impression the black-clad man fears Felix will charge in without permission if he lets go.

'My name is Wilbraham,' Felix says pleasantly. 'Mr Cely Leverell has invited me to call upon him.'

After what seems at least a minute but surely can't be, the tall man gives the tiniest of nods and says, 'I will enquire as to whether the Master is at home.' He clearly wants to close the door in Felix's face while he goes off to do this enquiring, but Felix has his foot in the gap.

There is another long pause, then the footman opens the door a little further and says, as if it is a great concession, 'You may wait here in the vestibule.'

Felix listens to the sound of his heavy, measured tread striding away. He has not the least intention of waiting in the vestibule, nor in the wide black-and-white-flagged hall beyond, despite the latter's rather beautiful old oak furniture and the glorious scent of roses emanating from three large cut-glass vases set at regular intervals around the space. He glances across at the staircase – twin flights to the right and left of the hall which meet halfway up to proceed to the upper landing in a single, monumental display of carved wood – and then along the passages that lead towards the back of the house.

Along the left-hand one, light flows out through an open door. Listening intently, he can just hear soft humming: someone with an ear for a tune is halfway through 'Jeannie with the Light Brown Hair'.

He walks quietly down the passage.

He comes to a halt at the open doorway, blinks in the sudden sunshine after the dimly lit corridor, and peers into the light-filled room beyond.

Wide windows face green lawns edged with flowerbeds that

are a blaze of colour. A huge fireplace on the left-hand wall has the dark, cavernous gape of its hearth and chimney filled with an arrangement of delphiniums and early chrysanthemums. There is a sofa drawn up in front of it, angled so that it faces out across the garden. The sofa, like the matching chairs dotted around the room, is upholstered in pale blue. There is a small rosewood writing desk on the right-hand wall, either side of which are carefully fitted pale oak bookshelves crammed with books. The curtains are a paler blue than the upholstery, and lining them, lifting and dancing in the breeze from the open window, are light hangings of cream muslin.

It is one of the most appealing rooms Felix has ever seen, and, despite the lack of pie-crust tables, what-nots, side tables, frilled shelves, fringed throws, pouffes and an abundance of embroidered cushions, it is very plain that it is a woman's room.

And, sitting on the sofa, pale blonde head bent over a piece of sewing, is the woman whose room he presumes this must be.

He doesn't think he has made a sound, but somehow she knows he is there. Even as she begins to turn her head, slowly rising to her feet, the shock of surprise is racing through him.

He last saw her dressed in a coarse cream blouse, a thick skirt and stout shoes, one of which she was putting on her foot as she held his cousin Noah's shoulder for balance.

She is not dressed like that now.

She wears a gown of pale sea-green in the finest silk, its square neck edged in thick ruffles of ecru lace and low enough to show a little of the translucent skin of the throat and the ridges of the collar bones. The skirt is ruched all down its front panel and flares out into gathers at the back, and there are deep flounces at the hem. The waist is narrow, the bodice close-fitting, the flesh creamy-white and smooth above it. The woman's feet are encased in fine kid shoes with pretty little heels, and the glimpse of her ankles reveal them to be clad in fine white silk stockings. Her smooth fair hair is drawn back from her beautiful face and wound into an elaborate knot at the back of her head.

His first, absurd thought is, what is Dollie Turton doing

here in Alderidge Cely Leverell's great house? She can't
have come down in advance of the other hop-pickers to prepare
the sheds like she's doing at Ted Chauncey's farm because
there *are* no hops here . . .

And then there is the sense of displaced air being pushed
against his back, and the loud, heavy tread of some large body
striding along the passage towards him. He turns, in time to
watch as the master of the house advances, puffing and
sweating with exertion, chest thrown out, fleshy red broken-
veined face wearing the beginning of an angry frown.

But then, observing just where it is that Felix is standing
and what he has so obviously been looking at, the expression
turns to a wide beam and he extends his right hand. Closing
in on Felix, exuding self-satisfied pride as if the woman's
elegant beauty is the highest of compliments to himself,
Alderidge Cely Leverell booms out, 'Dawkins told me someone
had called, Wilbraham, and I see you have already seen the
great treasure of my house! May I present my wife, Mariah?
Mariah, my dear, this is the London fella here asking about
poor little Effie.'

And Felix understands his mistake.

Noah's lover is not Dollie Turton from the East End. She's
Mariah Cely Leverell, and she's the wife of the lord of the
manor.

'Come along to my study,' Alderidge is saying in his loud
bellow of a voice. 'No need to trouble my wife's pretty little
head with man talk, what?'

Following him down the passage, Felix watches the vast,
undulating backside of the master of Old Abbey House,
suppressing a smile as he wonders how the man would react
if Felix were to say, *I've seen you before, in your elegant linen
jacket as you tried to assault the auburn-haired Amazon who
works for Ted Chauncey.*

And even while his mind is busily assimilating this huge,
ostentatious house, correcting his erroneous belief that the
woman he saw with Noah was Dollie Turton and trying to
analyse what else, besides the business with the auburn-haired
woman, has caused his instant and powerful dislike of

Alderidge Cely Leverell, he is also trying to suppress laughter. Alderidge's face bears the clear mark of the auburn woman's fist, the nose swollen and a painful-looking cut on the wet and protuberant lower lip.

Alderidge ushers him into a room with a big desk, several cabinets for papers and a wall of bookshelves – most of them empty – and half-heartedly pulls forward a chair for him, taking the large leather swivel chair on the other side of the desk himself. Even as he lowers his ample backside into it, there is a tap on the door, which opens to reveal another black-clad man. This one is quite short, but of the sort of compact build that suggests strength. He has dark brown hair and light-coloured eyes, and he manages to maintain a total lack of any sort of expression.

'I wondered if I might bring refreshments for you and your guest, sir?' he asks in a low monotone.

'Certainly not, Beardsley,' Alderidge says bluntly.

That puts me in my place, Felix thinks. Once again, he's struggling not to laugh.

Alderidge looks up at him. 'Oh, sit, sit!' he says.

Felix does so. Studying the florid face opposite, he can't resist the temptation. 'Oh, dear, sir, what on earth happened to your poor nose? I expect you rode into a tree or something,' he goes on, 'I know you country types are rarely out of the saddle, out in all weathers all through the year!'

An unbecoming flush has spread up Alderidge's flabby cheeks, and he puts up a hand to cover his lower face. 'Yes, yes, that's it, damned fool of a horse, heavy branch right across the path and you'd think the wretched animal would have seen it, it was big enough, ha, ha, ha!' The forced laugh makes him wheeze and then cough. The coughing goes on for some time, and Felix watches as the red cheeks first go pale and then turn purplish.

Noticing a carafe and a glass on a brass tray on top of one of the cabinets, he says, already on his feet, 'Let me pour you some water, sir,' and hurries to do so.

Alderidge sips, sips again, the coughing subsides and he wipes away the tears. He grunts his thanks, glaring at Felix over the rim of the glass.

Felix guesses that he is angry at having been observed in his moment of weakness. As Alderidge makes some comment about having a bit of a summer cold, gone to his chest, what, Felix reflects that what ails the master of this house is of longer duration and much greater severity than a summer cold.

Abruptly Alderidge changes tack. 'Now I sent for you,' he says sternly, 'because I'm told by my tenants you've been asking questions about the Effie Quittenden murder.'

'Yes, so you said in your – er, your little note,' Felix replies calmly. He cannot bring himself to dignify the missive with the word *letter*. Alderidge draws breath to reply, which brings on another, milder fit of coughing, and Felix takes advantage of his host's indisposition to add, 'There was the distinct implication in what you wrote, sir, that the inhabitants of Crooked Green would infinitely prefer to put the murder, and presumably the subsequent hanging of Abel Cartwright, firmly in the past; to summon the benign spirit of Lethe, shall we say, to draw her veil of oblivion so that they may resume their life of bucolic idyll in peace and harmony.' Alderidge is watching him suspiciously, his mouth hanging open, and Felix would have bet fifty pounds that he has never heard of Lethe, and that quite a few of the polysyllabic words he has deliberately chosen have also hitherto passed him by.

'I'm telling you to—'

'If I may finish, sir,' Felix interrupts with smooth politeness, 'I was going to say that what you imply is certainly not my impression, for, on the contrary, once I hint that I am interested in poor Effie's death, my difficulty has not been to encourage the villagers to talk but to make them stop.'

It is an exaggeration, but Alderidge isn't to know.

He glares across the wide desk at Felix, working his jaws as if chewing his words until they are fit to utter. Courteously waiting, Felix observes that the desk top is entirely innocent of a single piece of paper, and that the ink in the two little inkwells on either side of the pen tray seems to have dried out to leave no more than a cracked residue. The work of the estate, he reflects, must be done elsewhere, and, with any luck, by someone a great deal more capable than the fat fool sitting before him; the underpaid estate manager that Noah mentioned, presumably.

'Well, that's as maybe,' Alderidge blurts out. 'Men will talk, I dare say, after a pint or two, and I hear you've become a fixture in the Leopard's Head, seducing my good honest villagers with your money on the bar!'

Felix pretends to think, then says mildly, 'In fact, sir, I don't believe I have bought a pint of ale for anybody but the land-lord, and that, as I'm sure you would agree, is plain good manners.'

Alderidge stares at him, mouth working again. Absentmindedly he begins worrying at the split lip and soon it is bleeding again, although not to the extent that it did last night.

'I don't want you here,' he shouts suddenly, and a dribble of blood runs down his chin. 'I want you out of my village, before you—'

Suddenly he frowns and puts a hand to his chin.

'You're bleeding, sir,' Felix says helpfully. 'That cut on your lip, I believe.' Again he gets up and goes to the carafe, this time pouring water on his own clean handkerchief and, feigning solicitousness in every move, bends over in a half-bow and presents it to Alderidge. 'There, press that firmly to your mouth, – like this, yes, that's it – and I'm sure it will soon stop.'

Alderidge, effectively silenced by Felix's handkerchief pressed hard against his mouth by Felix's right hand, swivels his eyes to stare up at him. He is the sort of man, Felix observes whose thoughts are as easy to read as words on a page, and what is obviously going through his little brain right now is *I was about to give this cocky London upstart his marching orders but then I opened up my blasted lip again and it hurts like the devil and so does my bloody nose and how can you bawl out a feller who's just given you his handkerchief and is even now ministering to you to stop you bleeding?*

Felix returns to his seat, sits down and crosses his legs. 'I am not planning to leave the area just yet, sir,' he says. 'I shall be here for a while longer.' He suppresses a smile. 'Shall we have another little chat in a day or so? I could report the progress I've made and summarize my thoughts on the events of last year, if you like?'

Alderidge is looking pale again now. He puts a hand to his throat, pulling at his collar. Then he sits up straight, throws down the bloody handkerchief and says, 'No. Be about your business, quick as you can, and then go. I don't want to see you again,' he adds, then, like the bad-tempered child he still is, mutters something that sounds very like *I don't like you.*

Striding away down the long curve of the drive, Felix is still chuckling. But then, stopping suddenly, he says aloud, 'Now why, I wonder, is the silly sod so keen for me to leave?'

And the thought sneaks into his mind that perhaps Noah is wrong about Alderidge Cely Leverell and his predilection for mature, earthy women of the world.

Perhaps the wretched man is hiding something he'd very much rather Felix didn't uncover . . .

FOURTEEN

'How much do you know about the situation in Russia as it pertains to your Yelisaveta and her missing grandson?' Marm asks. He and Lily have finished the food – plain, well-cooked, savoury and exactly what she needed – and are now back in the chairs either side of the fire with their whisky glasses replenished.

'Only a little,' she replies. 'It was the Reverend Mr Jellicote of St Cyprian's, over the river, who engaged the World's End Bureau on Yelisaveta's behalf, and he told us about the pogroms, and explained that the rise of antipathy towards the Jews was because people said they were behind the assassination of the Tsar, and—'

'Rather more than antipathy,' Marm interrupts. 'People driven from their homes, their houses looted and burned, and the target for unspeakable violence as they try to flee. People are dying, Miss Raynor!'

'I know,' she says quietly. 'My Yelisaveta, as you call her, lost her husband and her son, and also her daughter-in-law and the baby she was carrying. Even if those last two poor souls did not perish directly by violence, the pogroms were to blame because they wouldn't have been on a filthy train when Rachel went into labour had it not been because of the danger from which they were forced to flee.'

'What have you learned about the family's life in Odessa?' Marm asks after a short silence.

She relates what Serafima has told her. About Abram the language-teacher and his wife, their son Yefrem, his wife Rachel and the boy Yakov. It doesn't sound much.

Marm is starting to say something about language skills being useful to Yelisaveta, and even more to Yakov, in this new life when something occurs to her.

'She said – sorry to interrupt, Mr Smithers – Serafima said Yefrem disappeared for several years, only returning when he was on the brink of manhood. His father refused to say where he had gone, and Yelisaveta grew thin with the pain of missing him.'

Marm is looking at her, his eyes intent. 'When would this have been? Do you know?'

Lily calculates in her head. 'Yakov is twelve, and Yefrem married Rachel four years or so prior to his birth, according to Serafima, so that would be roughly 1865, and Yefrem wasn't yet a man when he returned to Odessa, so let's take another six years off that, so we arrive at 1859. Or thereabouts.'

Marm is nodding, apparently agreeing with her assumptions and her arithmetic. '1859,' he repeats. 'Of course, it was meant to have been abolished by then, but it's highly unlikely that every single school closed and sent the boys home the instant the law was passed, and many may have taken a year or two to get home . . .'

'Home from where?' Lily demands. Marm has an inward look, as if he's diving into his vast library of mental files, and she fears that if he goes too deep it'll be a job to pull him out again.

But before she has to prompt him his eyes spring back into focus and he replies, 'I refer to the Cantonist Schools. The system was instigated by Tsar Peter the Great early in the eighteenth century, and under it every regiment in the Russian Imperial Army had to have a school in which to educate and train fifty boys, who would go on to serve in the army. Then about a century later – in 1827, if memory serves – the schools began to take Jewish boys, who were drafted at the age of twelve for a term of six years, although it's said many were younger when they were selected.'

'Selected?' Lily asks warily.

Marm meets her eyes. 'Yes,' he murmurs, 'there's the rub. Each Jewish community had to offer four boys per every thousand of the population, and naturally the wealthy, those with position, the educated, the sophisticated, found ways to make the pointing finger pass them by.' He narrows his eyes. 'You said that the boy's father was a teacher? A man of culture and education, I would have assumed?'

'Yes, that's right. But . . .' She pauses, thinking. 'Serafima

– the woman at the Mission – said the family were unpopular because they held themselves apart, and I imagine people resented them giving themselves airs and trying to conceal their wealth. So perhaps Abram tried to plead for exemption for his only son, and the rest of the community out-argued him?'

Marm nods. 'Plausible,' he says. Then he goes on, 'Of course, from the point of view of the Jewish recruits, perhaps the worst thing they had to face – worse than the rigid discipline, the endless hours of hard work, the punishments, the icy barracks and the terrible food – was that they came under powerful and constant pressure to renounce their faith and convert to the state religion of Orthodox Christianity.'

'Why?' Lily asks. 'To what purpose?'

And Marm simply shrugs.

'As I was saying,' he resumes, 'the system was abandoned in the 1850s – 1856? – by Tsar Alexander II. The appallingly outdated state of the Imperial Russian Army had recently been demonstrated in the course of the Crimean War, and the good man had the sense to see that the day of the Cantonist Schools had passed. If they had ever indeed *had* a day,' he adds.

Lily is thinking rapidly. 'So if that was where Yefrem went, it could well be that he came back to Odessa in the late 1850s, just as we calculated,' she says.

'Indeed, and one might imagine that he brought home with him a powerful resentment of the system that had taken away so many precious years of his boyhood, so that—'

A memory hurls itself to the forefront of Lily's attention. 'Mr Smithers, does the word *ochre* mean anything to you, in the context of what we've been talking about?'

Now the look he gives her feels rather like a rapier aimed between her eyes. 'Where did you come across it?' he asks. He seems to be holding his breath.

'Oh . . . Serafima was whispering to Alexei about the two men who followed the boy they believed was Yakov, and she said the word, and Alexei very quickly shushed her, and he looked panic-stricken.' She pauses. 'You *do* recognize it.'

'I do indeed,' Marm says heavily. 'That is – could it have

been slightly different? Could Serafima have said not ochre but Okhrana?'

Briefly Lily closes her eyes and goes back to the little courtyard. Opening them again, she says, 'Yes. That could have been the word. What does it mean?'

Marm rubs his hands over his face. Then he says, 'The Okhrana are the secret police of the Tsarist regime. One of their chief functions is to search for, isolate, suppress and destroy all anti-Tsarist activity. And before you say what on earth could be the connection to a quietly living teacher of languages and his family, hear what I have to tell you, dear Miss Raynor, and then together we shall try to puzzle it out.'

'Very well.'

'Many in Russia have grown to resent the wealth and the absolute power of the tsars,' he begins. Lily notices that he has adopted another position in his armchair: leaning forward, elbows on the arms, hands clasped with the two forefingers pointing upwards. There is a definite frown creasing his brows, as if in demonstration of how deeply he is concentrating. 'Over the last ten or twenty years,' he goes on, 'reports have emerged from that vast country that there exists a group of men who spread the word that there is another way, a fairer way, under which all the wealth of the land is not concentrated within such a tiny proportion of its population. They point out the need for a proper wage for the enormous army of workers, for enough food, for decent housing, even – and what an extraordinary ideal this is! – for the education of the young, and they have the courage and the certainty to broadcast their socialist and revolutionary ideas among the working classes. In the 1870s, a mass movement began that was called Going to the People, under which the educated young left their city lives and went out to work in the villages – they were trained as teachers, doctors, clerks, and many had manual skills such as carpentry, and others still offered themselves as farm labourers. The aim, of course, was to spread their beliefs and encourage everyone to join them in the formation of a truly widespread movement. But in their well-intentioned naivety, the young men were not subtle enough, and it was an easy matter for the state police to uncover them and neutralize them.

Also – and perhaps it was out of fear of the Okhrana, perhaps because the traditional rural way of life has very deep roots – they met with very little success in their attempts to recruit others to the cause. The young intellectuals learned very quickly, however, and, understanding that they must go under-ground, became considerably better at keeping secrets and operating under cover.'

'Did they not fear for their own safety?' Lily demands.

'Of course they did! But they were young, and idealistic, and, as all young people should, they believed they could change the world for the better.'

'What happened next?'

'Well, broadly speaking, they became more aggressive and more stealthy, and as I'm sure you are about to say, the one was pretty much a consequence of the other. Late in 1874 an organization called Land and Liberty was founded in St Petersburg – in Russian it is *Zemlya i Volya* – which was no more and no less than a political party, and its chief characteristic was extreme secrecy. Whether it was this group or not I do not know, but in December 1879 there was an attempt to assassinate the Tsar, which of course was not successful.'

'But I thought the tsar – Tsar Alexander II – had been assassinated?'

'Yes, he was, but it was later. Patience, Miss Raynor, I'm coming to that. A new organization was founded late in 1879 called *Narodnaya Volya* – broadly meaning people's freedom, or perhaps people's will – and it had branches in many cities, including, interestingly enough, Odessa, where your people lived. Another attempt on the Tsar's life was made in February 1880, when a bomb went off in a palace dining room, but once again it was unsuccessful. Then, as you just pointed out, came March of this year, and the assassination attempt that succeeded.' He pauses. Then, with a sigh, says, 'It's ironic, really, that a man such as Alexander II should have died such a brutal, agonizing death, because he was not as unrea-sonable a man as his forebears and, indeed, his successor, and many believe he would have made reforms, given time. There are . . .' he pauses, clearly thinking – 'there were definite signs, for those with the eyes to see, that his mind was not set quite so firmly in the rigid stone of tradition as those of his forebears. Or indeed,' he adds, more to himself than to Lily, 'as that of the son who has succeeded him.'

After some time, Lily says, 'Ochre. Okhrana. I'm sure you're right, Mr Smithers, and it was the latter word that Serafima whispered.' She pauses, for the thought is almost too dreadful to put into words. 'Do you believe Serafima fears these agents of the Okhrana are here in London?' she says in a voice not much above a whisper, as if even now big, frightening men in dark clothing with glittering eyes and knives in their hands are crouched outside on Marm's landing. '*Could* they be in the East End, in the places where the Russian Jews have arrived and are trying to make lives for themselves? Is that the sort of thing these men would do? Disguise themselves as refugees, mingle with real refugees and spy on them in case any of them are secretly muttering against the State?'

'Dear Miss Raynor, so many questions,' Marm says with a kindly smile. 'I am by no means an expert on such matters but I would have said it's highly likely that agents of the Okhrana could be here in London if there was someone in particular who had for some reason aroused their interest. As to whether they would take on the guise of refugees, yes, I imagine that is precisely what they would do.' And, once again in that undertone, he murmurs, 'What it seems they *are* doing.'

'But surely if people have fled Russia – people like Yelisaveta and Yakov – then it doesn't matter what they think, what they say, because they've left?'

And Marm, looking at her sadly, says, 'That is not the way a vast, autocratic, not very well organized and perpetually frightened state such as Russia thinks, I'm afraid.'

She nods, prepared to believe him. Still thinking, she says, 'If those men *are* from the Russian state – the big man with the scar through his eyelid, the man with him who was even bigger and who so frightened Alexei – then why are they so desperate to find one young boy? Yes, admittedly everyone seems to think that Yelisaveta's family had wealth they kept quiet about, so let's say for the sake of argument that the pouch Yelisaveta passed into Yakov's keeping on the quay was stuffed with gold and diamonds. But even if that pouch's precious contents are worth thousands of pounds, tens of thousands, would these State agents really be going to such lengths to get hold of it?'

Marm looks at her, his expression unreadable. He doesn't speak for some moments. Finally he says very softly, 'If you're right – I'm not saying you are, mind, but *if* you are – then we have to ask ourselves what else it is that little boy may be carrying.' He pauses, then adds, 'And how many other boys and young men these utterly single-minded men may murder in their relentless determination to acquire whatever it is that his grandmother entrusted to him.'

Meeting his grave eyes, she is sure he is experiencing the same shiver of dread that she is.

Into the silence a clock strikes: it is eleven o'clock. Time has slipped by and neither of them has noticed. Embarrassed – although Marm tries gallantly to say it's as much his fault as hers – Lily leaps to her feet, picks up her bag, gabbles out her thanks for the meal and the whisky and even as she's speaking is heading for the door.

Marm insists on walking with her up to the King's Road and is all for boarding the tram so that he can come with her and see her safely to her door, but she is very firm and manages to dissuade him.

It is very important to do so, because after one stop, she gets off again and crosses the road to wait on the opposite side for another tram going west to east. She's not going home, she's going back to the maze of streets around the Mission and she's going to resume the search for Yakov. And, now that she and Marm have reached the very worrying conclusion that Yakov may well be in even graver danger than she'd imagined, how much more urgent the search will be. This urgency seems to have spread throughout her body; she realizes that she's sitting on the wooden seat with her fingers drumming against her leg, her foot tapping and her teeth clenched so tight it's giving her a headache.

It takes considerable effort to relax, and even then it doesn't last.

She has reached her destination. She watches the tram

trundle away, clutching her little bag tightly against her side. Despite the late hour, the roads, squares and courts of the area around the Whitechapel Road and the Commercial Road are heaving with people. It is still so busy: there are lights and sounds of activity behind the high fence of *Smith and Sons, Fine Quality Scrap Metal Every Need Served*, as there are in most of the other business premises. And it is so noisy: drunkenness, wild laughter, a brief and violent bout of fisticuffs as a sudden fight breaks out outside a music hall, all add their distinctive racket.

Lily walks briskly along to the Mission. She remembers being told long ago by her solicitous grandfather that if she was ever called upon to walk in less than law-abiding places after dark, she should always look purposeful, always give the impression that she knows exactly where she is going, and has every confidence that very soon she will safely reach her destination. She works so hard at the purposeful, determined stride that by the time she arrives at the Mission she is hot and out of breath. But Grandfather Abraham's advice has proved sound: nobody has even come near to accosting her.

She runs up the steps and goes inside, hurrying down the corridor to the day room. Although it is night now, it is still half-full; briefly she wonders where everyone else is, and concludes that they have probably retired to the segregated dormitories, wherever they are. She pauses, glancing quickly around the big room, but there is no sign of anyone who could be Yakov among the children still up and sitting yawning beside their parents. She does, however, spot Alexei, crouching opposite an older man over a chess board. She backs out again, pulling the door closed behind her, but she hasn't been quick enough to evade Alexei's notice. As she hurries out through the Mission doors, he catches up with her.

She stops at the foot of the steps. 'Alexei, I must hasten the pace of the search for Yakov, and I can't wait. He's carrying something that someone wants very badly, and having whatever it is in his keeping means he's in very grave danger.'

Alexei looks at her. 'We know that before, Miss Lady,' he says softly. 'I am too knowing of it, for I see that boy they killed when he was still alive and also I see what they do to him.'

'You did,' she agrees quietly. *I am too knowing of it*. Not grammatically correct, but what a powerful way to express it. Poor Alexei, she thinks.

'Men not here,' he adds. 'Man with scar, big brute who goes with him, they not come back. They are out, hunting, maybe even now finding Yakov and coming out of dark corner to pursue him, and—'

'*Don't*,' she whispers vehemently. 'Please, Alexei, don't make pictures in my mind.'

'In my mind too, and cannot stop,' he mutters.

All at once the full peril of being here dawns on her, and she quakes beneath the weight of responsibility: for Yakov, of course, and also for Alexei, who can't be many years older than the boy she is being paid to find. *But Alexei isn't being paid*, she hears a voice say in her head.

'Go back inside,' she says very firmly. 'This search is not for you, and the danger is too great.'

'You are taking danger,' he points out.

'I am a professional enquiry agent,' she replies sharply. 'It is my *job*, Alexei. Now please, do as I command.'

He stands quite still. Then he says, 'I am here alone. Nobody to care, nobody to care for, nobody I have responsible for.'

'Responsibility,' she corrects absently.

He smiles, very briefly. Then he says, 'I decide for myself, and I decide you no go alone.'

Something in his set expression tells her he's not going to change his mind. He'll follow her if she sets off alone, and they're wasting time standing on the pavement.

They set off together to find Yakov.

FIFTEEN

In the late afternoon, Felix walks up the track leading to Nightingale Farm. It is perhaps a matter of no significance – and undoubtedly he'd be better concentrating on other, more important matters – but he has an urgent need to satisfy his curiosity concerning the auburn-haired woman who works for Ted Chauncey.

He knows who he *thinks* she is: because he believed the pale-haired woman he has just left in Old Abbey House to be Dollie Turton, it has never crossed his mind that this name might belong to the auburn goddess. Now that he's been set straight on the cool, pale blonde's identity, however, it seems obvious that it does. And he is irritated with himself for his mistake; Noah told him that this Dollie had come down from London ahead of the other hop-pickers to earn extra money preparing the huts, and the very first person he'd seen when he walked into Crooked Green was a woman busy with a broom in Ted Chauncey's farmyard. Admittedly she wasn't actually cleaning the huts at that moment, but he's not going to let himself get away with that feeble excuse.

As he approaches the farmhouse, a lean-faced man in his fifties emerges. He has a large black dog at his heels. He stands staring at Felix, thumbs in his waistcoat pockets, eyes narrowed beneath the brim of his hat. In answer to Felix's smile and polite 'Mr Chauncey, is it?' he gives the faintest of nods, then waits for Felix to explain himself.

'I wonder if I might have a word with Mrs Turton?' is the best Felix can come up with, although it presupposes that the auburn goddess is indeed Dollie. The farmer continues to stare for what seems like at least another minute, finally jerking his head towards the rear of the house, the farmyard and the fields beyond, grunting, 'Back there.'

Felix hurries away before he can have second thoughts.

She's sitting under a hedge that borders the hop garden,

leaning back against the grassy bank, and she has her eyes closed. It is a beautiful spot, and the deep shade is very welcome. Felix flops down beside her, staring out at the wide acres of ripe hops that soar up into the blue sky and entirely cover the long, gentle south-facing slope leading down to the river in its valley. He is just reflecting that the widely varying greens of the hedgerow trees – birch, chestnut, yew, hazel, holly – contrast pleasingly with the brilliant green of the hops, when a sleepy voice beside him says, 'Well, if it isn't my knight on a big white horse.'

He turns, but she has her eyes closed again.

'I believe you must be Dollie Turton,' he says.

'I might be,' she says with a grin.

'Are you?' As he stares into her handsome face, her eyes flutter open. They are very pale, golden brown. Like clear honey, he thinks.

'Oh, all right, then. Yes.' She is staring hard at him now, fully alert. 'You're that bloke from London, who's asking about the Effie Quittenden murder.'

He's relieved she didn't repeat the fiction that he was a journalist as it means he won't have to pretend something that's not true.

'I am,' he agrees. 'Felix Wilbraham.'

She nods, still staring. 'What do you want? I knew Effie,' she goes on before he can answer, 'saw her about the village when I was down last year. Abel Spokewright never killed her,' she adds, with utter conviction. 'His family and mine all know each other and everyone's agreed they hanged the wrong man.'

'I think so too,' Felix says softly. 'You've come down early, or so I'm told, to prepare Mr Chauncey's huts for the pickers, and—'

'That I have,' she says, getting up, 'and I must be getting on, or I shan't be ready in time.' She glances up at the sun, frowns, and sets off for the line of huts at a fast walk.

'Is he a hard taskmaster, then?' Felix asks, keeping pace beside her.

'Ted?' She gives a shout of laughter. 'No. Ted's a lovely man. He and I are friends, good friends, Mr Wilbraham, and that's all, so don't go listening to any old Leopard's Head gossip.'

'I won't,' he says.

'He was kind to me at a time I needed kindness,' she adds quietly. 'I was in a right state this time last year, newly widowed – not that I was sorry about *that* – but I was dead worried over how I was going to manage, and that was when he offered me the extra work here. I helped out last year, and it put a few coins in the pot just when I was in greatest want. So naturally, when he said to come early this year too, course I said I would. Left the kids with my mother, and she's bringing them down with her when they all turn up.' She gives a soft exclamation, increasing her pace again.

'Do you mean they're—' Felix begins.

'Look, sorry, mister, but I've got to go to work,' she says, flashing him a grin. 'I'll talk to you another time, all right?'

And with that she leaps ahead, slips through a gap in the paling fence behind the huts and disappears round the end of the row.

Felix emerges onto Upper Road, stopping in a field gateway to take out his notebook and write a few brief lines about Dollie Turton. Then, arms resting on the top bar of the gate, he gazes out across the hop garden and down to the river, hidden in its bosky setting. Something is tweaking at his memory, but he can't bring it into focus. Eventually he gives up and walks on into the village.

Passing the Leopard's Head a short time later, he spots the Reverend Peter Tewks standing outside.

'Contemplating a pint, your reverence?' Felix asks with a smile, approaching him.

The vicar raises his old straw hat, his expression lightening. 'Indeed I am, and I was very much hoping I would encounter you in the bar.'

Intrigued, Felix edges past him towards the door, pushing it open and standing back. 'Shall we go inside, then?'

'By all means,' says Peter Tewks with alacrity.

The public bar already has a few early patrons. Five old men sit in a solemn line on the bench under the window, and their quiet voices form a sort of *basso continuo* to the laughter and the lively chatter from the bar. A trio of young men Felix doesn't recognize stand diffidently just inside the door, and the vicar mutters, 'Ah, so the hop-pickers have started arriving, then.' Ezra Sleech is pulling rapid pints like a man with four hands, keeping up a ribald exchange with Ted Chauncey, Mick Marchant and a trio of young men – boys, really – who appear to be with them. Even as Felix and the vicar approach the bar and await their turn to be served, the door to the rear quarters opens and Dollie Turton emerges, carrying a tray of clean glasses. Slipping into the role of barmaid with an ease that suggests this is by no means the first time, she jerks her head at the lads shuffling their feet behind Ted Chauncey and Mick Marchant and says cheerily, 'What'll it be?'

Felix, getting over his surprise at seeing her there, reflects that she merely said she had to go to work; she didn't specify where. She is working for Ted Chauncey to earn extra money for her young family, so it's logical she would take on any other work available, and it's quite clear that with the new arrivals from the East End, Ezra is going to need help in the pub. And of course, Felix thinks with a stab of sorrow, little Effie Quittenden with her dimples and her kind word for everyone, isn't here any more . . .

He watches Dollie Turton as she pulls pints and chats with the customers, moving nimbly around Ezra as if she's been doing it for years. He watches her with the landlord. It's clear that they like each other; Ezra looks at her with very obvious admiration in his eyes. Several times as they work side by side she leans across and mutters something in his ear, and each remark sets him chuckling, the big belly vibrating behind the clean white apron.

The door to the rear quarters opens and Peg Sleech passes out trays of pork pies, meat and potato pasties and hunks of bread with big slabs of cheese and pickled onions. She makes a slightly awkward third to the pas-de-deux being performed by Ezra and Dollie, Felix muses, memories of the Little Ballerina briefly flowing across his thoughts, like a new member of the company who isn't quite familiar with the routine. Which is odd, when it's Ezra and Peg who are the established couple and Dollie who is in fact the newcomer.

When at last it is his turn to be served, Dollie greets him with a smile. 'Ted's not the only good-hearted fellow in this village,' she murmurs, jerking her head in Ezra's direction.

Waiting while she draws his and the vicar's pints, Felix can't help wondering if Ted Chauncey and Ezra Sleech would have been so swift to offer employment – and the much-needed extra income – to a woman who was old, plain and didn't have a smile like Dollie Turton's.

'Now, why did you want to see me?' Felix asks Peter Tewks when they are installed behind a table in the corner and have sampled their beer.

'I hear that you have visited several households and I've been wondering if you've learned anything that might help prove Abel's innocence and clear—' he begins.

But he doesn't have the chance to finish the sentence.

There is the sound of rapid footfalls coming up the path, the door is flung open and Alderidge Cely Leverell's butler stands there. Although he has just been running he shows no obvious signs of it; he doesn't even appear to be out of breath. A fit man, that Beardsley, Felix thinks.

'I need the assistance of three strong men,' Beardsley announces, wincing and pressing his hand to his side in just the spot where the pain of a stitch strikes. Human after all, then, Felix amends.

'What has happened?' It is the Reverend Tewks, on his feet, already moving towards the door, hat in his hand and beer forgotten.

The Old Abbey House butler looks dubiously at him, then says with quiet courtesy, 'I would be grateful for your presence, your reverence, but the task in question involves some heavy lifting.'

'I'll come,' Felix says, leaping up to stand beside the vicar. Ted Chauncey and Mick Marchant put their pint mugs down and join them. They exchange glances, but all of them, it seems, recognize an emergency and nobody wastes time asking questions.

Beardsley leads the way at a fast walk, now and again breaking into a trot. Everyone keeps up, even the vicar, despite being the eldest by a couple of decades. They hurry straight across the green and onto Earlyleas Lane, after perhaps a quarter of a mile turning off in the direction of the abbey ruins. Over a field, along a track that follows a stream, under a stand of hazels and chestnuts, and Beardsley comes to an abrupt halt on the bank of the deep, steep-sided ditch through which the stream now runs.

There is someone lying at the bottom of the ditch, face down, the lower part of the large body in the water.

The vicar leaps down the bank, not appearing to mind or even notice that his well-polished black shoes and the cuffs of his dark grey flannel trousers are in the water. He has his hand on the fleshy neck, his brows clenched in a worried frown. Next he turns the head slightly and puts his cheek against the open mouth. He waits for what seems like an age then, straightening, says, 'I'm afraid he is dead. God have mercy on his soul.'

And from the bank there is a chorus of muttered *Amen*s.

Beardsley has gone pale. 'I feared it was so,' he murmurs. 'I too tried to feel a pulse, but I couldn't find it either.' Squaring his shoulders, he says in a different tone, 'I've told the lad who raised the alarm to find a hurdle to serve as a stretcher.' He looks around, his face anguished. 'Now where's he got to? He should be here by now, I can't think what's taking him so long.'

And they all turn as the sound of panting reaches them from upstream, and a boy of about twelve appears, dragging behind him what looks like the battered and very heavy door of some outbuilding.

'Didn't know what you meant by a hurdle,' he says, addressing Beardsley. 'Her in the kitchen said as to fetch a door instead, and hurry up about it.'

He throws the door down at the butler's feet with evident relief and barely disguised resentment at having been made to bring it. He starts to slope away, but the vicar calls out, 'Wait a minute, if you please, Albert. We shall want to speak to you presently.'

And Beardsley, Felix, Ted and Mick each take a corner of

the door and manoeuvre it down into the ditch. They have to put it in the water – the bank is too steep – and Ted shoves one corner into the earth to stop the current taking it away. With difficulty, two men to the shoulders, two to the ankles, they manage to raise the body sufficiently to place it on the improvised stretcher, but the dead weight of Alderidge Cely Leverell is too much for them, and it is only with the help of the vicar and the lad Albert – the distaste on his face saying as loudly as words that he really wishes he was somewhere else – that they make any progress at all.

As they struggle to raise the heavy load up the bank, all at once there is another man beside Felix, his strong arms and back instantly making the burden easier. 'You'd just left when I got to the Leopard,' Noah mutters to Felix. 'Thought you might need a hand.'

And you knew, or guessed, who we would be trying to help, Felix thinks. As soon as Ezra said it was Alderidge's butler who'd come racing to the pub, you knew. No wonder you came straight here.

Noah's strength makes the difference, and very soon the body is lying at the top of the bank, five panting men and a boy standing around it getting their breath back.

They walk in sombre procession to Old Abbey House.

Beardsley and the Reverend Tewks are at the front, Felix and Noah at the rear. Albert has melted away, Ted Chauncey and Mick Matthews have been dismissed and are heading back to the village. Watching the two men striding off, Felix reckons they'll be keen to return to their pints and the avid curiosity of everyone in the Leopard's Head, falling over themselves with eagerness to hear every last detail of what's just happened.

The vicar was resolute in his insistence on taking Mick Marchant's place as stretcher-bearer. 'I must be there in any case to support poor Mrs Cely Leverell when the terrible news is broken to her!' he said as they raised the stretcher and its burden, although nobody was questioning his decision.

Felix hopes it is only he who notices the brief look of anguish that crosses Noah's face.

And breaking through his preoccupation with what is happening comes a sudden blinding realization: M for Mariah.

And Noah always carries a knife.

Turning away from his cousin's distress, Felix thinks he knows the identity of the lovers whose secret little hideaway he found among the abbey ruins.

Someone, it appears, has been sent to fetch the doctor. As the small procession reaches the house and the men struggle to pass through the outer door, the porch, the inner door, the vestibule and into the hall, a man in tweeds carrying a leather Gladstone bag steps out of the shadows to meet them.

'Dr Scott, good to see you,' the vicar says. He frowns briefly. 'I regret that I cannot shake your hand,' he adds, 'but . . .' He glances down at the stretcher and its burden.

The doctor grunts a brief reply. 'In there, I thought best,' he says quietly, indicating the open door of a wood-panelled dining room. The room has been darkened by having the shutters closed and candlelight flickers within. 'A pair of trestles have been set up ready.'

Felix and his companions bear their heavy load for the last few paces and, with very evident relief, at last set it down.

The vicar is speaking quietly with the doctor, who nods, grunts again and then, escorted by Beardsley, steps up to the trestle. He stares down at the body for a few silent moments, then turns to the men standing watching.

'I don't know why I'm here,' he says, his tone terse. 'It'll have been a heart attack, no doubt about it. I've long been prescribing medication for his heart, *and* told him many more times than I care to recall that if he did not take steps to lead a healthier life, then I would not be answerable for the consequences.' The doctor glares out at them, scowling angrily, as if he takes Alderidge Cely Leverell's death as a personal insult. 'However, here I am, and here *he* is.' Once again he glances at the corpse, and this time the disdain – the dislike? – is clear in his expression. 'I suppose I must get on with it. Beardsley, I need more light,' he adds tersely. 'Bring some lanterns. The rest of you, thank you and goodbye.'

And, as Beardsley hurries off to fetch the lanterns, the doctor

ushers Felix, Noah and the Reverent Tewks out of the room
and very firmly closes the door.

'I shall go and find poor Mrs Cely Leverell,' Peter Tewks
says quietly to Felix, and he hurries away.

Felix looks at Noah, who is staring after the vicar. Now the
longing is naked in Noah's face, and, indeed, in his body, for
he stands, hands clenched, shoulders tensed, like a man about
to leap forward into some violent, desperate action.

I'm not meant to know, Felix tells himself. I can't possibly
commiserate. I can't say as I so much want to, *Yes, I understand, it's the vicar who's with her now, closeted with her in
some pretty sitting room, comforting her, giving her the support
and the kindness you long with every part of you to be giving.
But it's you she'll seek out, the moment she can.*

He gives his cousin a few moments, then says with patently
artificial brightness, 'I want to speak to that lad Albert. There
are questions I need to ask him. Coming?' he adds casually.

And Noah mutters gruffly, 'Yes.'

They find the boy in the yard behind the kitchen. The cook
told them where to look, and as they corner him he is cram-
ming the first generous bite of a large currant bun into his
mouth.

Felix and Noah move to stand either side of the lad.

'Now then, Albert, we're told it was you who ran to Old
Abbey House to raise the alarm?' Felix says. Albert looks
questioningly at Noah, who he obviously knows, and Noah
nods.

'Yep,' the lad agrees, turning a sulky face back to Felix.

'Did you see what happened?'

'No.' Albert stares down at the ground.

'So how did you know he was down there?'

'Heard the splashing, didn't I? Went to look.'

Felix says, 'What did you think had happened?'

Albert shoots him a glance, as swiftly looking back
down at the ground. 'I reckoned he'd probably fallen off his
horse again. He was just lying there, belly in the water, trying
to hold his head up, and I was scared because his face was
purple and his lips all blue.'

'I'm not surprised you were scared,' Felix says, 'it was a sight to—'

'He could still gather breath to yell at me,' Arthur interrupts angrily. 'Told me to go and fetch help and be quick about it, for all that he knows full well I'm no great shakes as a runner, and when I set off, doing my best like, he starts shouting at me, saying, *Hurry up, you lazy bloody blockheaded peasant!*, only the yelling makes him cough, and then he splutters, then he doesn't shout any more but there's a sort of moan, and a splutter, then a whimper, like something's amiss or he has a pain.'

Felix meets Noah's eyes. He guesses Noah is having the same thought: the tumble and the shock of falling in water was too much for Alderidge's already labouring heart.

Although Felix doubts that his cousin is contemplating the accompanying question, but then he isn't a private investigator.

Because what is clamouring for attention is, did Alderidge fall into that deep ditch or did someone shove him in?

He says, thinking carefully, 'Did you notice anyone else around?'

'No.' A pause, then Albert ventures, 'He weren't on his horse like what I thought at first. Can't have been 'cos he had his fancy clothes on, and shoes not riding boots.'

Felix's attention sharpens. 'Fancy clothes?'

'Yeah. That pale jacket of his. *Linen.*' He makes a scoffing sound. 'No jacket for a countryman, that ain't.'

Felix falls silent. He hadn't recognize the jacket, soaked and muddy as it was, but now that Albert has described it, he is sure he has seen Alderidge in that jacket before.

They leave Albert to his bun.

Noah has moved out through the kitchen yard gate into the field beyond. Felix follows him, still deep in thought.

'I'm off,' Noah says shortly, breaking in on his reflections. 'I can't be—' He stops. 'Getting late. Got things to do,' he says instead.

Felix looks at him. 'Very well,' he says. There is nothing else to add.

He watches as Noah strides away.

'What a business, eh?' says a woman's voice from right behind him.

Spinning round, he sees the cook, leaning her elbows on the top of the kitchen garden wall. She is a comfortable sort of woman, well into middle age, plump and with an air of calm. She also looks singularly un-grief-stricken.

'It is,' Felix agrees.

'Not every day the master sets out for a walk with a spring in his step and comes home dead on a barn door,' she goes on.

'No indeed. What a shock for you all,' Felix replies.

'Shock?' She considers the word. 'Well, yes,' she allows, 'although he's been told often enough he's too fat and too fond of his cigars, his good roast beef and his fine cognac.'

'Now he's paid the price,' Felix murmurs. It seems poignant that nobody seems to mourn the late master, although of course he can only guess at what is going on at the vicar's audience with the mistress of the house . . .

'I thought even when young Albert comes running up to my door that something bad had happened,' the cook goes on, as eager to tell her tale as anyone else on the fringes of a sudden death that doesn't engage their emotions.

'Did you?' Felix prompts.

'I did! He comes running up, that Albert, like I say, pounds up the path and bangs on the door, scarlet in the face, badly out of breath, gasping for air. Not much of a runner, isn't Albert, but it was clear he'd done his best, no question of it, and it was quite right what Dawkins did when he gave him a florin for his quick response.'

But Felix is thinking.

Alderidge's body was cold: even taking into account the fact that half of him was under water, he'd been dead some time.

For a lad – even a lad who wasn't much of a runner – to run to Old Abbey House, a distance of under a quarter of a mile, would take perhaps five minutes. For Beardsley to race to his master's aid, another fifteen minutes, and for him to pound on down the gentle slope to the Leopard's Head, another ten. Say fifteen for the rescue party to get back to the ditch, and it came to a total of not much under an hour.

But not only had Alderidge Cely Leverell been stone cold when they clambered down to him, he'd also been starting to go stiff.

So where had this extra time been used up?

Felix manages to extricate himself from the cook and hurries away to find Albert, who after brief reflection is the most likely candidate for the time-wasting. He hasn't gone far, but is mooching about under the willow trees beside the stream. He looks up unenthusiastically as Felix approaches.

'You again.'

'Me again. It took you a long time to cover the quarter-mile from the ditch to Old Abbey House,' Felix says. 'And it must have done, I know full well it did, because you said Mr Cely Leverell was alive and yelling at you when you left him, yet when we arrived to try to save him, he was stone cold and going stiff. I can account for all of the time,' he adds softly, 'except for the considerable amount between you finding the master and reporting it.'

'Like I said, I'm not much of a runner,' Albert says truculently.

'But the cook said you were scarlet in the face, sweating and gasping for breath when you banged on the kitchen door,' Felix says quietly.

Albert shoots him an assessing look through narrowed eyes, but his only response is a shrug.

Felix says, 'Now I noticed that just before the track you'd have taken reaches the house, it climbs a steep little slope, which is hidden from sight from Old Abbey House's windows by a stretch of woodland.' Albert starts to say something, but Felix talks over him. 'What I'm thinking is that someone dawdling his way to the house who wanted to give the impression he'd been running as hard as he could had only to hurry up that cruel little hill double-quick a few times, making sure he made himself red in the face and sweaty and was gasping for breath, for the pretence to be absolutely convincing.'

Albert is still looking at him, but now his face has taken

on an expression of open-mouthed dumb ignorance and a total lack of understanding. To complete the image of near-idiocy, he says, 'Uh?'

'I don't believe you hurried at all, Albert. I have a suspicion that you didn't like Mr Cely Leverell. That you were furious that he'd yelled at you and called you a lazy bloody block-headed peasant – I can't say I blame you – and that you asked yourself why you should put yourself out to go to the aid of someone so odious. Nevertheless, you wanted it to *seem* that you'd run for your life—' Albert mutters something that sounds like 'Run for *his* life, more like' – 'and so you made sure to look as if you'd been doing so before you banged on the door. Who knows,' he adds, 'perhaps you were even thinking that there might be a monetary reward for your quick action.'

He is probably imagining it, but he has an idea Albert flushes slightly. The lad risks a quick look up at Felix. 'What you going to do about it?' he demands.

'Nothing,' Felix replies. 'What could I do? It's only a suspicion, as I said, and to prove or disprove it would have necessitated someone with medical knowledge inspecting Mr Cely Leverell's body, providing a rough estimate of what time he died – notoriously difficult to determine, I'm told – and doing the same calculation that I did.' It is his turn to shrug. 'It's too late, and who's going to listen to me, anyway? The man is dead, the doctor said even before he examined the corpse that it would undoubtedly have been a heart attack, and I can't imagine anybody's going to contest the doctor's word. It seems to me nobody's very sorry he's dead,' he adds softly, 'so I can only conclude nobody liked him much.'

'I didn't like him at all,' Albert says fiercely.

'I thought as much,' Felix remarks. 'Care to tell me why, or was it just the comment about being a block-headed bloody peasant?'

Albert stares at him. It's clear he's thinking, and that the impulse to keep silent is warring with the urge to get whatever is troubling him off his chest.

'You meant it when you said about it's too late?'

Felix nods.

Almost instantly the words burst out of the lad, and they carry anger, deep resentment and also profound pain.

'Bloody old bastard shot my ferret.'

He is already walking away when Albert calls him back.

He returns. 'What is it?' he asks, although he has a worrying feeling that he already knows.

'Got something to tell you,' Albert mutters. 'Told you I never thought he'd fallen off his horse, didn't I? Cause of his fancy jacket?'

'You did.'

'Well, yelling out for me to help him and calling me a block-headed peasant wasn't all he said.' He looks enquiringly up at Felix, and resignedly Felix gives him a coin.

Leaning forward so that he can speak very softly, Albert tells him that he knows why the old man was beside himself with rage. And he told Albert that someone had shoved him in the water.

Into Felix's head the image of Dollie Turton waxes and solidifies. It was there already, because the last time Felix saw that pale fawn linen jacket was when Alderidge was trying to seduce her. Now as well as seeing her he can hear her powerful voice in his mind: *Stay away from me or face the consequences.*

It looks as if Alderidge didn't stay away.

And now he's dead.

Without another word to Albert, who is open-mouthed in surprise, he spins round and races away.

He is trying to calculate as he runs. He found her under the hedge beside the hop garden, apparently asleep, but what was to say she hadn't just hurried there from the stream close to Old Abbey House? If she did give Alderidge a shove, making him suffer the fall that led to the fatal heart attack, then that might well lay her open to a charge of murder, or at least manslaughter. He needs to tell her. Needs to warn her.

He looks inside the Leopard's Head, but he's not expecting her to be there and she isn't.

He runs on to Nightingale Farm, sweating and panting for breath by now. She's not there either.

Some of the hop-pickers have started arriving and are noisily settling in. He asks a few people but nobody has seen Dollie Turton.

She's fled, Felix thinks. She knows the danger she's in and she's run away, back home to the East End. He has to find her, has to talk to her. Has to tell her it's highly probable the doctor will say Alderidge Cely Leverell died of a heart attack.

Which station would she go to, Binhurst or Elm Green? He asks one of the new arrivals and he says they all use Elm Green, it's a much prettier walk and after dark you can hear the foxes and the owls.

He heads out of Nightingale Farm, crosses Upper Road and sets off at a run up Badgers' Bank to catch her.

SIXTEEN

The weight of responsibility for the young man beside her who she just can't seem to shake off is weighing heavily on Lily as, pretending a confidence she is far from feeling, she leads the way up the Commercial Road and away from the Mission. Half the trouble is that she doesn't want to shake Alexei off, because he's resourceful, eager, intelligent and brave. Moreover he speaks Russian, which has already been invaluable on the occasions that she needed to hear what Serafima had to tell her, and will prove so again if – *when*, she corrects herself firmly – they find Yakov. Her conscience, however, is wagging its disapproving finger at her and telling her in no uncertain terms that none of this constitutes a reason for her to take Alexei into danger. *I tried*, she silently shouts at this increasingly irritating and persistent part of her mind. *I did my best, but short of locking him in a cupboard, I do not see a way of stopping him. So will you kindly BE QUIET.*

'I did not say anything!' Alexei protests, and she realizes she must have been muttering audibly.

'No, sorry, Alexei, I was thinking out loud.'

She hears him whisper *Thinking out loud* under his breath as he commits this new phrase to memory, and briefly it makes her smile.

It is only when the smell of the river becomes too strong to ignore that Lily realizes where they are going: without conscious thought, her feet have led them all the way up Commercial Road East until they are almost level with Limehouse Basin, over to the right. Alexei has realized too; she senses him draw closer to her, and she detects incredulity in his voice as he mutters, 'We come back *here*? To where boy who look like Yakov *killed*?'

She stops dead, and he bumps into her. 'I have a friend here, Alexei,' she says. 'Also, there is good reason, isn't there, to believe that Yakov may be in the vicinity?'

He looks unconvinced.

'For one thing,' she explains swiftly, 'his grandmother told me he was always drawn to boats, to water, to canals and rivers. And also we know that the men who we believe are hunting for him came here, because, as you just reminded me, this was where they killed the young man they mistook for him. So—'

'So *they* think Yakov come here,' he interrupts, his expression brightening as he understands, 'maybe saw him come this way, follow him, then make mistake and follow boy like him instead?'

'Well, it's possible,' she agrees. And in all honesty, she adds silently, we have nothing else to guide us.

They are nearing the water when the noise reaches them. Emerging onto a quay from the end of a narrow alleyway, they see a scene of confusion and violence. A large group of men surround something lying on the ground, and two heavily built dock workers hold on to an undersized, middle-aged man with a thin, rodent-like face who is struggling hard, shouting out a long stream of obscenities. He already has a rapidly swelling black eye, and even as Lily and Alexei stand on the corner trying to understand what is going on, another man shoves them out of the way as he dashes past, yelling, 'We need a constable! That slimy bastard's just killed a young lad, and torn off his breeches and all!'

The thought flashes into Lily's head: *If the victim really is dead, then it wasn't that little struggling man who killed him.* She looks at Alexei. He nods once, and murmurs something in his own language. Then, for of course she doesn't understand, he says, 'You make right guess, Miss Lady. They are here. Not little fellow with fat eye but *our* men. They kill again.'

And, side by side, they creep back into the shadowy alleyway before anyone else notices their presence.

The thin boy in the ragged clothes and the broken shoes is agonizingly conflicted.

He can see the woman, and he has just watched her slip away towards the next alleyway along from the one he is hiding in. He has been offering a deep and fervent prayer of thanks that she is here. That, by some miracle, although he managed to lose her yesterday when she jumped onto a tram, the benevolence of whatever power has been looking after him so far has allowed him to find her again. Or, he corrects himself, allowed *her* to find *him*. For there she is, disappearing into the mouth of the alley, not twenty paces away, and she has the same young man with her who was with her before and who seems to be staying at the big building on the corner with the steps and the important doors where he knows that many people off the *Oude Maas* have gone.

The woman is his link to those people. To his past; to the life from which he was so violently torn away. He is all but sure now that she is searching for him. That she has been sent to find him.

But he can't bear to think about that for very long. Because imagining all those people he travelled with somewhere safe while he is out here alone and so frightened brings him very close to despair.

He watches the woman.

He wants more than anything to run over to her.

But outweighing even that almost irresistible desire is his terror.

Because *they* are lurking. He knows all three of them now, although it took some time to unmask the third one. They haunt him throughout the endlessly long waking hours, and in the short spells when exhaustion overcomes him and he crawls into some dark and filthy corner to sleep briefly, they crash into his dreams and he wakes sweating and shaking, and, once, actually crying out his fear.

One is the broad-shouldered, bearded man in the smart black coat with the scar through his eyelid.

The second is the very big man who wears a scowl and walks with his hands in fists.

The third is—

But the third one is the most terrifying of all, and the thin boy's mind shies away from even thinking about him. The third one is the truly vicious one: the one who wields the knife so expertly and with as little regard for the life he is putting to an end as a man cutting the throat of his old exhausted ewe.

The boy is safe in this secret hiding place. He knows this is so because it has been tested. Once – on that night he can't bear to remember but which refuses to be forgotten – once they were right behind him, one of them even calling out his name – *and how do they know what it is?* – but not near enough to grasp him, and then he was praying praying *praying* with all his heart and soul and his prayers were answered and his racing flying steps were guided here into this narrow alley and this tiny space so small that he can only fit into it scrunched up and because he is so thin and he held his breath and they pounded past and they were running after someone else and calling, *Yakov Yakov stop Yakov*, at another boy the same size as him and dressed like him in good clothes long gone filthy and ragged and they drove him into the cut and then they—

He must not think about that.

And now the woman he so badly wants to run to for safety is standing there, and he almost *almost* left his secret place and flew to her side, but he didn't and once again he is saying soundless prayers of fervent gratitude because now the crowds are starting to clear and he can see that another boy like him lies dead on the stone quay and his blood too is forming into a dark pool and drip drip dripping into the canal, and he knows what this means and it means the men are here and they still want to kill him as much as they ever did . . .

What can I do? he asks silently.

He puts his hands on the body belt fastened securely around his waist. He has to keep tightening the leather strap; he hasn't eaten anything to speak of for days and his belly has shrunk. He can feel the heavy circles of the gold coins within the pouch, feel the hard edges of the diamonds that are going to buy his future, or that is what his grandmother told him.

But these treasures, almost unbelievably valuable though they may be, are not the contents that really matter, for that is something else. Something that is disgusting and distasteful and unclean. Something that stank so badly the one time his curiosity overcame him and he unfastened the little oiled cloth bag to have a look that he retched and would have vomited, had there been anything inside him to bring up. Something so repellent that it was only out of fear of what his grandmother would do to him when she found out that he didn't hurl the bag and its horrible contents into the dark canal there and then.

He doesn't know what it is inside the bag. Has no idea, for all that he's thought and thought about it, why it matters so much. He only knows that it does.

He can still see his grandmother's face as she lay on the deck of the *Oude Maas*. The big boat was gradually coming to rest as the sailors and the dock hands wound the heavy ropes round the bollards on the quay, and even though his grandmother was so ill, coming in and out of consciousness, raving and rambling in delirium, somehow she understood where she was and what was about to happen, and under her heavy black shawl that was wrapped around her like a blanket she grabbed his wrist in her surprisingly strong hand and uncurled his fingers, closing them around the strap of the body belt. The strap and the pouch were still warm from her fever-hot body, the soft leather damp with her sweat, and he wanted to pull his hand away. Wanted to run from her, not have to be with her any more. But she held him fast, then dragged him down so that she could mutter hot-foul-breath right in his ear, telling him to guard the body belt with his *life* because what was inside included not only all that remained of the family wealth but in addition something more precious than jewels and gold that would change the entire future and it must not, *must not* – she shook him quite violently as she repeated the words – fall into other hands.

He had begun to ask questions, to demand answers, but she put her stinky hand over his mouth and stopped the words, hissing, 'Be quiet and do as I tell you! There is no other option, for I am very sick and in the hospital they will tend me and the body belt cannot, *must not* be found on me, and very soon they will be *here*!'

She was right, and the first of the well-meaning people who had come to help them all were already hurrying up the gang-plank, and there was only just time for him to slip the belt

under his tattered garments and fasten the buckle before three
men gently put his grandmother on their stretcher and carefully
bore her away.

He is ashamed, now, when he thinks about that moment.
Because although she was so sick – and he knew he should
have insisted on going with her to look after her – as they
reached the quayside he saw her close her eyes and lapse into
unconsciousness and he took his chance. He slipped away,
lost himself in the crowds surging off the *Oude Maas*, and
when a man in uniform tried to grab him, he kicked out,
snapped his sharp teeth on warm flesh and fled.

And since then he has been alone, with three men who want
what he is carrying hard on his trail. He knows that they will
not be content with taking the body belt, for he has seen what
happens when they catch other boys who they mistake for
him, and the boys do not survive.

He wants to survive.

He really does.

For a time, when Father and Grandfather Abram were killed
and then on the train when Mother had her baby and they died
too, and it was only him and Grandmother left alive of the
whole family, there had seemed little to live for. But now
he is here in London, and even though he is running for his
life and starving hungry and *very very* afraid, something in
this vibrant place is calling out to him, and there are boats,
so many boats, drawn by big powerful horses, and a great
wide river, and canals, and men who live and work on
the boats, and he wants that too, and—

Oh no, no, *no*!

The woman is moving off, and the young man from the
Mission is going with her!

The boy leans the top half of his body right out of the secret
place, stretches his neck so he can peer along the quay and
see what is happening there. They have taken the body away,
the crowds are rapidly dispersing, and the woman has taken
her chance when nobody is looking and she is striding off
towards the wide basin beside the big river where the boats
collect.

He pauses, looks both ways perhaps a dozen times. Then

he gathers every bit of his remaining courage, slips out of the alley and runs after her.

Alexei has said at least twice that the dead boy who has just been borne away is not Yakov, and Lily desperately wants to believe him. 'How can you be so sure?' she demands. 'We could barely see him through the press of bodies, and you can only have caught a glimpse of him at best, so—'

'Look,' Alexei interrupts, and he points along the quay. 'Not Yakov, because someone know him, someone grieve for him.'

And Lily follows his outstretched finger to where a woman crouches in an agony of grief, her shawl over her head and her face, an older woman beside her trying to keep her on her feet as she leads her away.

Not Yakov, then, Lily thinks. Another boy, valued, loved, the heart of someone's existence, and now he is dead.

For a moment, her hatred for whoever these vicious, ruthless men are who are hunting for Yakov is so fierce that it burns up in her like fire and she seems to see only flame.

It abates as swiftly as it came, and she stands quite still, Alexei beside her, as gradually the people on the quay melt away.

When she leans over to speak quietly to Alexei, her voice is quite calm.

'These men are a grave danger not only to Yakov, but also, I believe, to any who are trying to help him, by which of course I mean you and me. It would be foolhardy to ignore this, and therefore, Alexei, I propose that we proceed immediately to try to find the friend I told you about, who I hope very much is on his boat in the Limehouse Basin and—'

'He help us?' Alexei demands urgently.

'He will,' she replies.

Slowly, not drawing attention to themselves by haste, they move off along the quay. To the left, to the right, over a little bridge, and the open water of the basin is just widening out before them when feet come pounding up behind, a small, thin body flings itself against her and a boy's high, terrified treble bursts into a stream of words in an alien tongue.

Alexei recovers seconds before Lily, and even as she begins

to understand he has grabbed hold of both her and the boy, dragging them off the path, back over the bridge and down a narrow, muddy slope that leads to a lower path running under the bridge. He pulls up short only when all three of them are beneath the very centre of the bridge, invisible from anyone passing above.

The thin boy now has his arms tight around her hips, his face buried against her breast. He says something else, and this time Alexei answers in the same language.

Lily waits. Then Alexei looks up at her and says softly, 'Here is Yakov. He is not harmed but he is very frightened.'

Gently Lily unwinds the skinny arms, pushing the boy away from her just far enough to enable her to look at him. It is dark under the bridge, but there is a gas lamp on the upper path and by its faint light she makes out a haggard face half obscured by filthy hair that looks black, and out of which a pair of dark eyes wide with fear stare up at her. The boy says something else, and as he speaks she catches sight of his teeth.

In her head she hears Yelisaveta: *Teeth are white, even, very fine, sharp, with . . . hole here.*

And now, gazing up at her, his expression naked with supplication, is a boy with well-cared-for but now very dirty teeth. The canines are distinctly pointed and there is a gap between the top incisors.

Yakov.

She says slowly and carefully, 'I have been searching for you, Yakov. Your grandmother is very worried about you, and she told me what you look like.'

She waits for Alexei to translate, but as he starts to speak, Yakov says, 'My grandmother?'

'Yes, she's—' Lily begins, then exclaims, 'You understand English! You speak it, too!'

'Little, not so good,' Yakov replies. 'My grandfather Abram, father of my father, he give lessons. Read from English book.' He pauses, frowning, then says slowly and carefully, 'Shar-les Die-kins, Day-vied Cop- Copper . . .' The attempt tails off.

'David Copperfield.' Suddenly Lily sees an image of this desperate little boy sitting with a calm, dignified old man, side by side in mutual regard and affection, together reading their

way through Charles Dickens. For a few moments she wants
to cry. Giving herself a mental shake – this is not the time or
the place for maudlin sentiment – she says briskly, 'Of course,
your grandfather was a teacher of languages,' and Yakov nods.

With her hands still resting on his shoulders, but only lightly
now, she says, 'I think you had better tell us what has been
going on, Yakov.'

He nods, a quick, almost impatient movement. 'I will,'
he says. His restless eyes skitter rapidly from side to side,
as if he's trying to see in every direction at once, and the
fear coming off his slight frame is palpable. Lily is about
to reassure him but Alexei speaks first, murmuring soft
words in Russian, one hand on the boy's arm. Yakov relaxes,
just a little.

'I tell him, I keep watch, you listen to him,' he says to Lily,
and soft-footed he moves to a spot from which he can look
out at the upper path.

Turning back to Yakov, Lily says, 'I know what happened
to you until the moment on the quayside when you fled,
because your grandmother related your story to me.'

'I have to run!' he exclaims. 'She – Grandmother – she tell
me—' He clamps his mouth shut on the words.

And Lily is quite sure he was about to say that he fled
because Yelisaveta told him to protect the object she gave him
at all costs, and he was afraid anyone who approached
him – especially men in uniform – were undoubtedly going
to wrest it from him.

You poor, poor boy, she thinks.

After a short pause she says quietly, 'I am very sorry about
the deaths of your parents and your grandfather.'

The boy nods but does not comment.

'You asked about her just now,' Lily continues. 'I saw her
in the hospital three days ago and she was already much better,
and the fever had gone.' She is speaking slowly, and Yakov's
curt little nods suggest he understands. 'The nursing sister in
charge told me that your grandmother would not be there very
much longer because they needed her bed for people who
were much more sick, and by now she may well have been
moved to the Mission.'

But he shakes his head firmly. 'Not there today morning,' he says.

She wonders how he knows, but she accepts that he does. Even after such brief acquaintance, she is starting to get the measure of Yakov Hadzibazy. 'We'll return to the hospital and I'll take you to her,' she says, 'unless of course she left later in the day, and—'

Once again he shakes his head, an even more violent gesture. 'No,' he says. Just the one word: *No*.

'But you must be returned to her care,' Lily says gently. 'You are only twelve years old, and a boy alone in an alien land.'

'Thirteen,' he says. 'My grandmother forgets. Always she treat me like little boy, always say I am small for my years, always takes off a year, sometimes two years.' He pauses, taking a shaky breath. 'Now it is only Grandmother Yelisaveta and me, she will *grasp* and never let go.' And he holds up his right hand, the fist so tightly closed that the knuckles are bone-white.

Indeed she will, Lily wants to agree.

But it really is not the time to enter into a discussion about Yakov's future. Besides, Yelisaveta has engaged her to find him and return him to her, and that is what she is going to do.

'Your grandmother gave you something just before you left the *Oude Maas*,' she says. 'A body belt, perhaps?'

He eyes her suspiciously. 'Ye-es,' he replies slowly.

'It contains gold and jewels?'

He nods.

'And, I believe, something else,' she goes on in a whisper.

His dark eyes narrow to slits. 'Something else?'

There is no option but to reveal what she and Marm suspect, and so she says in the same soft undertone, 'I overheard Serafima mention the Okhrana. Then I talked to a wise friend, and he told me about the people who struggle in your country, some supporting the old ways of the Tsar and the others fighting for change. If we have guessed right, and Serafima was really telling me that members of the Russian state police are hunting for you, then I think that what is in your body belt is far more important than gold and diamonds. Why else would they be going to so much trouble?'

He is watching her so intently that she can almost feel it. 'They kill boys who they think are me,' he says, so softly that she can barely hear. 'Older boy in little waterway off bigger canal. Tonight, boy over there.' He jerks his head in the direction they've just come from.

'I know,' Lily says. 'That's why we've been trying to find you.'

His face takes on a considering expression. 'Long way to hospital. Men watch, men find, men follow perhaps. And once at hospital Grandmother old woman, cannot fight, cannot protect,' he observes.

'No. You are right and all of that is quite true,' Lily agrees. 'If you are willing to trust me, Yakov, I will take you to the basin where the boats tie up. I have a friend there, and he has other friends, and together they will do rather better than one old woman.'

His expression changes again as she mentions the canal basin, and even before she finishes speaking he is already eagerly nodding.

Lily is aware that she's very weary; far beyond weary. The maze of alleys and passages is confusing, and now it's quite dark. She has two people with her, one a youth, one still a boy, and she knows it is up to her to get them to safety. Even concentrating so hard that it makes her head ache doesn't help much in finding the way back to the Limehouse Basin, and she makes the mistake of accepting Alexei's assurance that they must take a *right* turn when her own good sense of direction tells her it should be a *left*. And so after several minutes of walking faster and faster and finally running through totally unfamiliar passages, she pulls them to a halt and says, 'We're going the wrong way. It *was* left back there where the little alley turned off the bigger one. Come on, *hurry!*'

She does not know why she is suddenly so afraid, but now dread is like a fourth person keeping pace with them and she increases her pace, her stays cutting into her flesh as her ribs fight to expand and let her take a deep breath.

Then, straight ahead, a strange illusion materializes. The tight passage down which they are running seems to widen out like the bell of a trumpet, and this open end is lit by a soft glow. For a second she wonders if it's an illusion, brought about by her fatigue and the lack of oxygen – is she imagining some sort of celestial bliss, with angels and a beautiful golden light? – but then, cross with herself for being so slow, she understands: they are almost at the basin, and the glow is the combined effect of the lamps and the lanterns on the boats tied up for the night.

She wonders, as they steadily draw nearer, why she can't hear anything, for whenever she has stayed overnight with Tamáz she has always noticed the evening sounds: quiet conversations, laughter, the clatter of pans on stoves, children at play, even sometimes an impromptu musical performance on banjo and jaw harp, singing voices joining in . . .

Tonight, the assembled company of the boat people is silent.

Or perhaps her own desperate panting breath is making her deaf to all else.

There is a shallow S-bend in the passage, gently left then right, and at the point where left becomes right it happens: a confusion of rapid, violent movement, a man's deep voice muttering hoarse words in an alien language, and Lily watches in absolute horror as a broad-shouldered man grabs Alexei and a huge brute pounces on Yakov.

Perhaps men who work for the state don't expect women to be resourceful. Perhaps these two men, having already seen Lily, have dismissed her as an ineffectual female they don't have to include in their reckoning. If so, it is a mistake, for Lily's blood is wild with fury because she has got her two young companions *so close* to safety, only to be jumped on from the very last place of concealment before the passage emerges onto the quayside of the basin.

She doesn't even realize how loudly she's shouting, but a deafening howl of rage is pouring out of her wide-open mouth, and she is flailing round in tight circles, punching, kicking, and as a small amount of sense takes cool hold, forming her hands into claws tipped with her hard, sharp fingernails and raking at the faces of the two men. She lands a lucky hit on the man with the scar and her forefinger goes straight into his wounded eye, and as he screams and flings his hands up to his face, Alexei spins round and raises his knee into the man's crotch. He howls again, Alexei follows the first assault with a second, and the man is on the ground, his wounded eye forgotten in the overwhelming agony emanating from his testicles.

Lily throws herself on the brute, but he is already dragging Yakov backwards into the deep doorway under which the two men have surely been hiding, and she watches in horror as the light from the end of the passage catches the blade in his hand. She grabs at his knife arm, but it's like trying to take hold of a log, and she is raising her foot to kick at his shins when suddenly someone puts a hand on her shoulder and Tamáz's voice says, 'We will take care of him, Lily. Take Alexei on to the basin – others are waiting.'

She wants to protest, to say this is her fight and she won't give it up, but there are more men with Tamáz – two, three, maybe four, surging into the small space of the doorway – and they somehow pass her between them until she is in the passage, where Alexei is leaning against the wall.

She grabs his hand. 'Come on,' she says. 'We have done what we can. Let's get out of their way.'

She sees her own resentment in his face, but there's no sense in them staying here, they'll only be in the way, and she heads off along the last few yards of the passage and out into the basin.

They emerge and are faced with an extraordinary sight: the wide quay is blocked by a line of ten or a dozen men, all of them armed with cudgels, axes and in a couple of cases a firearm; perhaps, wonders Lily's exhausted brain, these are old weapons retained after the Indian Rebellion of thirty years ago, or another of the many conflicts of the Queen's long reign? The men are backed up by a second row and, she thinks, a third.

'What are you *doing*?' she yells.

She recognizes the big man in the middle of the first row: he is called Stone, she has met him a couple of times and he seems to be the unofficial leader of the boatmen. He gives her a savage grin. 'Waiting, miss,' he replies.

'*Waiting?*'

'We wanted them to return. Tamáz Edey said they would – he seemed to know what they were doing here. We heard you yelling – well, they probably heard you over in Shadwell, in St Katharine Docks and maybe even as far as the Tower, you were that loud – and straight away Ed Snell and his brother took off, and Tamáz and the Barton lads went with them.'

She shakes her head, not understanding why all these men should have been prepared to take on the killers.

Stone seems to perceive her confusion. He comes closer, all the time keeping his eyes on the end of the passage, and, bending down to her, says softly, 'The lad they murdered yesterday in the little cut was known to us. He wasn't a bad lad, and for sure he didn't deserve a death like that.' He pauses, and she knows what's coming. 'The boy they cut down earlier this evening was one of ours. He was Ed Snell's nephew – his sister's boy.'

Lily remembers the woman in the shawl, grief-stricken, crouching in agony, and the older woman trying to lead her away.

And now she understands.

They hear footsteps pounding up the passage, and one of the men who accompanied Tamáz appears. He looks at Stone. But he doesn't speak, merely nods.

All the men know what this means – Lily does too – and straight away the weapons start to disappear, the men disperse, and presently the uncanny silence begins to fill up with the normal sounds of night in the boat basin.

A surprisingly short time later, Lily, Alexei and Yakov are all on board *The Dawning of the Day*. Tamáz has lit the lamps and the kettle is on the stove, water coming to the boil for a pot of tea. Lily has been trying to look closely at Yakov without making it obvious, and as far as she can tell, he appears to be none the worse for this most recent of his experiences. There is a bruise on his left cheekbone, but she has the clear impression he's quite proud of it, and he has told her at least three times that he bit his attacker's hand very hard and made him cry out in pain.

Those sharp canine teeth again, Lily thinks.

Tamáz has sent his two crewmen off somewhere; the boat's interior isn't really big enough for six people. The doors are closed, the curtains drawn across the ports, and it is very cosy. When the tea is made, Tamáz sticks a pan on the stove, and presently Alexei and Yakov are wolfing down big bowls of stew accompanied by hunks of bread.

Sitting close to Tamáz, Lily says very softly, 'What of the two men?'

Tamáz glances at the boys and, seeing they are both intent on the food, makes a swift gesture of drawing his hand across his throat.

'Their bodies?' she breathes, even more softly.

'Waiting for the tide,' he says briefly.

The tide. She pictures it, that great swirl of power as the huge volume of water pauses, waits for a spell and then flows back the other way, towards the open sea, faster and faster, mighty and unstoppable, picking up anything in its path and bearing it far away. She knows the men had to be slain – there would have been no safety for Yakov otherwise, and probably not for Alexei or herself either – but still, it is a lonely way to end . . .

Tamáz seems to pick up her thoughts.

'Their deaths were swift,' he says quietly. And, meeting his eyes, she sees the hardness in them.

She knows they'll never speak of this again.

SEVENTEEN

F elix hurries up Badgers' Bank, expecting at any moment to see the silhouette of Dollie Turton ahead, striding out on her way to the station at Elm Green and the next train back to the East End.

He has no idea why he's so sure he's going to catch her up. The last time he saw her was in the Leopard's Head, when Beardsley came bursting in to fetch help for the fallen body of Alderidge Cely Leverell, and that must be getting on for a couple of hours ago now. He has been trying to reason out what she would have done: seeing Beardsley, she'd have realized why he was there and known that Alderidge had been found. Would she also realize that she would fall under suspicion?

Yes, she would, he suddenly thinks, because Alderidge wasn't dead then. And perhaps, knowing him to be alive and furious when he fell into the ditch – when she pushed him, it seems – can she have any notion that she's under suspicion of being involved in his death?

Perhaps she's not.

The thought stops him dead.

But if she's innocent, and knows perfectly well she's innocent, then why has she run away?

Perhaps she hasn't.

Almost without thinking, he is walking again, striding on up the lane. So deep in reflection is he that he forgets to peer ahead in the hope of spotting a solitary female figure walking ahead of him.

And he stumbles over something lying under the deep shadow of the trees on the bank.

He falls over, landing hard on his left shoulder, and his head bangs against the beaten earth of the lane's surface. For a few moments he sees bright stars and zigzags in front of his eyes and feels slightly sick, but it quickly passes.

He sits up, twists round and tries to make out what he tripped on.

It's a body. A woman's body, dressed in a flannel skirt and a calico blouse, a shawl splayed out beneath her. The long hair is escaping from its bun, dark against the pale background of the lane. She lies on her side, her head resting on her out-flung right arm, her left arm curled in front of her belly.

It's Dollie Turton.

He bends right down so that his face is close to hers.

The twine is still twisted around her neck, biting into the soft, creamy flesh. She was a tall, strong woman – he can visualize her in his mind as she was the first time he saw her, banging that broom against the wall, the dust flying – but not strong enough, for here she lies, dead in the lane.

Deep in him – in his heart, perhaps – he feels the pain of profound sorrow begin to wake up and slowly turn over.

Firmly he suppresses it; it's not the time to mourn her.

He glances up, looking round to assess the murder scene, almost relieved that this analytical part of his mind can be active even while he kneels here before this sudden horrific tragedy.

The bank rises steeply on the right of the lane just here, ascending to a sort of ledge about two feet up before the slope continues to the summit. Trees and shrubs grow quite thickly. The spot offers both concealment and a height advantage from which to attack . . .

Out of recent memory comes an image that he saw late one night before returning to his bed in the New Cock Inn: a man, bent over in grief, there and gone in a couple of blinks.

The man – the shadow, the ghost, whatever it was – had been standing just here.

Violently Felix shakes his head, dragging himself back to the present. He stands up and clambers up the bank, easily reaching the little ledge and finding it makes a good, firm place to stand. He is under the thickly leaved branches of the hazel and chestnut trees, in deep shadow; he would be hard to spot in the daytime, he thinks, and now, in the rapidly fading light of evening, even someone expecting him to be there could easily miss him.

It is clear that the killer was well prepared. He had checked the ground and chosen the spot carefully, attacking his victim from this spot beneath the trees. Where he stood before, a year ago? Felix can't seem to banish the thought, and the more it rests in his mind, the more he is sure that the same man killed both Effie Quittenden and Dollie Turton.

And, of course, if there remained any doubts about Abel Spokewright's guilt, they have now been demolished, for not only is this the same place but the same method has been used.

He jumps back down into the lane, dropping to his knees beside Dollie, gently lifting her by the shoulders and laying her head and upper body across his lap. He murmurs soft, reassuring words to her, and as he does so his fingers are busy feeling around her neck. It feels rigid, as if every muscle and sinew is tightly constricted. Slowly, so very carefully, he unfastens the stick that has been used to twist the twine tight, and, fraction by fraction, it begins to loosen. He knows it is a futile gesture, but he can't bear to see it there, deforming the beautiful throat.

When it is done, he takes the twine and the tensioning stick and hurls them away into the undergrowth. Then he cradles her against him, the fingers of his right hand gently stroking the fatally damaged throat, as if this tender touch could ease the rigid tension and ease the agony of her death. He rocks her gently, crooning a quiet lullaby, and her beautiful wild hair is soft against his lips.

He hears a sound, somewhere on the bank, quite near at hand.

He sits stock-still.

Nothing.

Then it comes again. He tries to look everywhere at once, but it is very dark here now at the foot of the bank, the trees obscuring the remaining light. The sound comes again, a more continuous sort of rustle this time, and it seems to be all around him . . .

Then there is a rush of sound, almost deafening after the silence, and some ten paces up the lane a dark shape breaks out of the cover of the trees and the undergrowth and hares off up the lane, something that looks like a black cloak streaming out from the shoulders so that it looks as if the man is flying.

Felix feels as if a burst of flame has just run through him, and every muscle goes tight as he prepares to launch into action.

But Dollie still lies propped against his breast.

He's in the very act of laying her body gently on the ground so that he can leap up and give chase when there is a very soft gasp.

It's coming from directly in front of him.

All thoughts of the fugitive, even now making his escape across the fields away to the left, flies out of his mind. Frantically he puts a hand on her breast. At first he can feel nothing, and a cry of anguish breaks out of him. But then, moving his fingers to the base of her throat, he detects a very faint, very erratic pulse.

She's not dead.

He wishes with all his heart that Lily was there. If she was, then he could leave Dollie with her and race off after whoever has just fled. And – far more importantly – Lily would know what to do for someone who has just been almost strangled to death, who is now starting to revive and making the most awful sounds that are a cross between a gasp and a deep, chest-wrenching cough. Lily used to be a nurse, she knows about giving aid to victims of violence, she—

She's not here. You are, says that calm voice in his head.

So he does what comes naturally. He sits up straight, legs out in front of him, and turns Dollie so that she is sitting in the apex of his thighs, his body supporting her as if he was an arm chair. Gently he draws her shoulders back, having some vague idea that the ribs need to be open in order for the lungs to expand. The thought flashes across his mind that he hopes her corset is not laced too tightly and wouldn't it be good if he could cut the tapes and loosen it?

And then from out of memory he hears a conversation with Lily, and Lily is saying that often even a deeply unconscious patient can hear you if you speak to them . . .

'Dollie, I'm here, it's Felix,' he says softly, his lips against her ear. 'I found you in the lane and you'd been attacked, and there was a length of twine around your neck and I thought you were dead' – he chokes – 'but I took it off and I don't think you are dead because I can hear you trying so hard to breathe, so please, *please*, dear lovely Dollie, try, try as hard as you can, and I'll be here with you, I promise I won't leave you, and if he comes back I'll have him, I won't let him hurt you again, but oh, Dollie, you must *breathe!*'

After a moment Dollie gasps again and, as if she has heard and is trying her best to do what he is begging her to do, it does indeed seem to be a deeper breath this time. Then abruptly she breaks out into a paroxysm of coughing.

It is too soon to shout out a prayer of thanks that she isn't dead. So Felix simply holds her.

After quite some time, she whispers in a voice that is so cracked and hoarse that it sounds nothing like hers, 'My throat's on fire.'

And he has not so much as a drop of water with which to comfort her.

Because there is nothing else he can do unless he abandons her there – which he has just promised not to do – he wraps his arms round her and holds her until her breathing slowly begins to improve.

Presently – he knows he's going to sound callous but he can't hold back the question any longer – he says gently, 'Who did this, Dollie? Who jumped on you and tried to kill you?'

There is a long pause. Dollie shudders – at the horror of remembering that awful moment? – and he holds her closer.

But he knows what she's going to say before she speaks, for he can feel her shaking her head.

'Knew you'd ask,' she manages, her voice rasping and the effort making her cough again. 'Didn't see. He leapt' – she raises a feeble arm and indicates the slope of the bank – 'on my back.'

'Big? Small? Strong?' Oh, God, Felix wants to shout, surely you noticed *something*?

But Dollie gives a sob, and he's in no doubt now that she's reliving the terror.

'Sorry, sorry,' he murmurs, dropping a kiss on her wild hair.

'I shouldn't have pressed you, I should have realized you were too busy fighting for your life to take any details of the man trying to kill you.'

She leans into him, and he hopes she didn't hear.

'I thought you were running away,' he says to her some time later. They are still sitting in the same position, but he no longer fears she may still relapse and die. Her whole body seems more relaxed now, and at last she is breathing without every other intake of air making her cough, splutter and spit.

She mutters a single word which he interprets as 'Why?'

'Because you were in the Leopard's Head when Beardsley came running for help and I thought that meant you'd realize Alderidge had been found and that you'd be accused of having been responsible, because you'd shoved him in the ditch to stop him molesting you yet again.'

He feels the faint movement as she shakes her head.

'You weren't running away?'

Again the shake of her head.

'You didn't push him in the ditch?'

This time the movement is stronger, and she whispers, 'Nowhere near. At farm, then pub,' the six words making her cough again.

'Yes, yes, I understand!' he says hastily. 'You weren't anywhere near Old Abbey House, Alderidge or his ditch, you were at Nightingale Farm and then you went straight to the Leopard's Head for an evening of work there.'

This time the head movement is a nod.

'So why were you setting out for the station at Elm Green?' he asks. '*Were* you going there?'

She nods again, and says hoarsely, 'Train. People. Family.' She tries to add another word but it makes her cough, and swiftly he puts a hand on her shoulder and says, 'Don't talk, *I* will and you can just nod or shake your head. Yes?'

A nod.

He thinks he knows.

Noah said, *One of the Londoners has arrived already. Been here a week or so.* He went on to describe a woman who used to come regularly when she was a child, in the company of her family. A woman whose violent husband stopped her going, until his fatal tumble into the Thames left her free to make her own decisions, upon which she resumed the visits. A woman who, according to Noah, the other women had tenderly cared for last year, when she still carried the scars of her dead husband's brutality.

Yes. Dollie came on ahead, but now the rest of them have begun to arrive.

'Your friends are arriving tonight,' he says. 'Your friends and your family.'

She nods, one quick, firm movement.

'And because you are very much looking forward to seeing them, you were heading off to Elm Green station to meet their train.'

This time, if a nod can be said to be joyful, he thinks with a smile, then Dollie's is.

He can hear footsteps. So can Dollie: he can sense her straining to look up the lane. But they're not coming from that direction, they're coming from the village. Now he feels her fear and very quickly he leans down and says, 'Don't worry, I will protect you, he's not going to attack you with me here.' *And anyway*, he adds silently, *I just saw him run off in the other direction.*

He very much hopes he is right.

The footsteps are rapidly coming nearer, and he thinks he can make out a big shape, a darker outline in the shadows. Suddenly feeling very vulnerable, he yells, 'Who's there? She's no longer alone, you coward, you can't overpower her this time!'

A man appears, stopping in the spot where no trees extend over the lane to cast it into shadow.

It's Noah.

Relief floods through Felix. Before Noah can say a word, he bursts out, 'It's Dollie. She was going to Elm Green to meet her family and friends off the train, and someone tried to strangle her – I would put money on it being the same man who murdered Effie, because—'

'This is exactly where Effie's body was found,' Noah says softly, coming to crouch beside Felix and Dollie. 'Dollie my love? Are you all right?'

She gives him a brave little smile and nods.

'She can't really talk,' Felix says, 'her throat is very painful and I have nothing to give her to drink, and I didn't dare leave her to fetch help in case—' But he doesn't think there is any need to explain. 'For the same reason,' he adds, 'I couldn't follow her attacker when he broke cover and hared off over the fields.'

'No, I do see that,' Noah says absently. He is reaching into an inside pocket in his waistcoat. He extracts a flask, unstoppers it and hands it to Felix. 'You do it,' he says. 'She will try to drink too quickly, and that won't help.'

'What is it?' Felix sniffs at the flask, expecting the powerful vapours of brandy or some other strong spirit.

Noah grins and says, 'It's cold tea. More refreshing than alcohol when you're working outdoors in hot weather, more reviving than water.'

Felix holds the lip of the flask to Dollie's mouth. She tries to tip his hand to pour more, but he is expecting this and holds on firmly. He and Noah watch her drink, sip by slow sip. After quite a long time, she says, 'Thank you. Better.' And she looks up at Noah with a smile.

'That's good, our Dollie,' Noah replies. 'We're only just getting to know each other, I wouldn't want to lose you before we've had the chance to do so.'

Our Dollie . . .

Getting to know each other . . .

Family coming from the East End . . .

A suspicion is dawning in Felix's mind. Is he right? Can he have guessed correctly?

He glares at Noah. 'What was her name before it was Turton?' he demands.

But it's not Noah who answers, it's Dollie. 'Smith,' she says. And, surely risking her raw and painful throat, she chuckles.

'You should have told me!' Felix shouts, hurling the words at Noah. 'Why didn't you?'

Because, of course, if Dollie is related to Noah, then she's also related to Felix.

Noah shrugs. 'Didn't see the need,' he says off-handedly.

But Dollie says, the words slow and clearly still hurting, despite the cold tea, 'Because, like all my kin, Noah's got into the habit of protecting me,' she says. 'Last year, we barely spoke.' She looks up at Noah, and the echo of past pain is in her face. 'Mind you, I was in a bad way, I barely saw anyone outside my immediate family and a couple of very old friends, and they looked after me as if I was a little child.' She nods towards the flask, and Felix gives her more sips of tea. In the brief pause, he remembers what Noah said: *The other women seemed to be protective of her. Word was she'd been given a hell of a beating from which she was only just recovering.*

And now here she is again, a strong and vibrant woman, fully engaged in her life once more and not cowering, afraid, because of what happened to her in the past. Which makes it all the more terrible, Felix reflects, that someone has just tried to kill her.

Will she recover from this new assault, as she has evidently done from her late husband's violence?

As if Noah is thinking the same thing, he says gently, 'She's tough, our Dollie, aren't you, my lass?' He reaches for her hand. 'The Smiths breed strong women.'

'Who are you?' Felix asks her. 'How do you relate to Noah and me?'

But she doesn't answer, instead jerking her head at Noah.

'She's Frank Smith's great-great-granddaughter,' he says. 'Frank Smith who was your grandfather Derek's father, and father to *my* father, Noah Smith I. The two of them are Dollie's great-grand-uncles.'

Felix lost the thread with *your grandfather's father*, but he doesn't really think it matters. What is important is that this brave, strong and very lovely woman is his blood relation, and he couldn't be more proud to claim her as such had she been blue-blooded royalty. In fact – he smiles to himself – he'd far rather have Dollie than any number of pale, chinless, pop-eyed and overprotected princesses.

After quite a long and thoughtful pause – Felix suspects all three of them are thinking about much the same thing – he says to Noah, 'What were you doing heading up Badgers' Bank just now?'

He grins. 'Same mission as Dollie,' he replies. 'Going to welcome the Smith clan to Crooked Green.'

With a start, he jerks up his head and stares into the sky, then takes out his watch from the little pocket in his waistcoat.

'What is it?' Felix asks.

'Roger – that's my cousin Roger, married to Adelaide—'

'My uncle,' Felix interrupts. 'My mother's younger brother.'

'Yes, him. He said they were aiming to catch a late train last night, but we're past last night now, it's not long till dawn. I reckon they'll be on a train in the small hours of this morning.'

'Do they always travel at night?'

Now Noah and Dollie exchange a grin, and Noah laughs briefly. 'Of course,' he says. 'There's a great many of them, including a crowd of children, and all those fares take a big slice out of what they'll make hop-picking.' He must have seen Felix's puzzled frown, because he adds, 'Fewer guards on the platforms and the train during the night, see.' He makes a short sound of impatience. 'They don't pay for all the children! The little ones get passed over the fence and smuggled onto the train, and then they keep watch and when a guard does turn up, they stick the children under the seat behind their mother's skirts.'

Now Felix is grinning too.

Dollie is moving, and he thinks she is trying to sit up. 'Careful,' he warns, 'are you sure you're ready?'

She glances at him. 'Can't lie here all night,' she replies. She puts her hand up to her throat. 'Does it – can you see anything?'

Both Felix and Noah peer at her, trying to see in the faint light as the beginnings of dawn begin to touch in the eastern sky. There is enough light to see a deep, dark wheal. They exchange a glance, then Felix says, 'Yes.'

She is still feeling round her neck. 'There's a – a *dent!*' she whispers. Now, for the first time since she regained consciousness, she looks alarmed; frightened.

Noah says, 'It will fade, Dollie.'

And Felix adds, 'We will look after you.'

'I want to go back to the farm,' she says, and now it is clear to them both that she's determined to get up. 'I want to—'

They don't find out what she wants to do, because just then, from up the lane in the direction of Elm Green, comes the sound of striding feet in boots, voices and laughter.

The first hop-pickers of the new day have arrived and are making their way to Crooked Green.

EIGHTEEN

'These boys must go back to the Mission, and before that I must take Yakov to see his grandmother,' Lily says firmly.

The food has been eaten, Tamáz has cleared up, Alexei has loosened his waistband and Yakov's eyelids are drooping. At Lily's words, however, his eyes spring open and he says, 'No.'

'No?' Lily frowns. 'I realize you're exhausted and have been through a very distressing time, but your grandmother is old, she's recovering from a serious illness, she's been extremely worried about you and seeing you alive and well will do more to make her better than any medicine, so—'

'She more worried that I lose what she gave to me for look after,' Yakov interrupts. Before Lily can protest that she's sure this is not so (and in fact on reflection she's not sure at all), Yakov ploughs on. 'Grandmother plan life for me, and this I know because she tell me all – every . . .' He snaps his fingers impatiently.

'Every detail?' suggests Tamáz.

'Every detail.' Yakov gives him a nod of thanks. 'Lessons, study, must live close with her in tiny room, save money, always save, save, save, and I must work so hard and do good work, find . . .'

He looks at Tamáz.

'A good job? A profession?'

'Yes. This way I make much money and care for her, always, for ever, and she want this very much and talk, talk of it always, but me, no, *no*, not for me.' His dark eyes are narrowed in anger now.

'But you're still a child, Yakov,' Lily protests, 'you're only twelve and—'

'NOT twelve,' he says furiously, his thin face flushing, 'I tell you, you forget, I am *thirteen*, soon be fourteen, and here in this place I see boys of age like me, already working, doing job like man on boats, and me, I want that too!'

Tamáz catches her eye. 'He's quite right,' he says. 'I was doing a man's work when I was younger than him.'

'But you come from a long line of boat people!' she exclaims. 'You belong here, you understand the life, and . . .' She trails off. She's not quite sure why she's objecting so vehemently; if she was in Yakov's position, she'd feel exactly the same.

'Lily, I know of other men and boys – some even younger than Yakov here – recently arrived from Russia who have quietly slipped away and made a new life on the water,' Tamáz says, 'and I'd be willing to take Yakov to meet them.'

Yakov springs up. '*Now?* You take right now?' His eyes are alight with excitement and hope.

'No, that's quite impossible!' Lily exclaims.

And Tamáz says calmly, 'I won't even think about it until you've seen your grandmother, Yakov, and she agrees.'

The boy looks absolutely livid. 'But she will *not*! You take now, *right now*!' he repeats, and this time he's shouting, on his feet, fists clenched.

'Sit down and shut your mouth,' Tamáz says in the sort of tone that carries far more weight than shouting, 'or I'll take back the offer.'

There is a brief battle of wills which Yakov loses, and he subsides onto the bunk.

'You will go to see your grandmother in the morning,' Tamáz says, 'and stay with her until she has moved into the Mission, if she is not there already. You will make sure she is settled into whatever accommodation she eventually finds, and ensure that she has people around her who will befriend her, for as I need not remind you, like you she has lost her family.' He pauses, and now he looks at the boy with understanding and pity. 'Then, if you persuade her that a life working on the boats is what you want and she stops trying to turn you into someone you are not, seek me out and I will help you.'

'Will you?' Yakov's voice trembles.

'I will. In the meantime – until that happens,' he amends, seeing that Yakov has not understood – 'I will look out for countrymen of yours and speak to them, tell them that I may have someone who will be joining them in time.' He pauses. 'I do not wish to see anybody forced to live a life that does not fit.'

Out of the past a memory floats into Lily's head of Tamáz doing this same profoundly compassionate service for someone else; a young woman called Maeve – a girl, really – whose baby Lily delivered one night aboard *The Dawning of the Day*; a baby that died. For all the baby was not his and although Maeve was only a distant relation who he had never before met, Tamáz helped her to find a better life with a chance of happiness.[4]

She thinks Tamáz is remembering, too. It was the first time they met, and he had come knocking on the door of 3, Hob's Court because he thought her apothecary grandparents and aunt still lived and carried out their life's work there. He turns to her, and the smile he gives her suggests he can picture that night as well as she can.

Yakov seems to be thinking very hard, if the intense frown creasing his forehead is any guide. Eventually he gives a deep, gusty sigh and says, 'I will go to find my grandmother. In hospital, in Mission. Do like he say.' He shoots a glance at Tamáz. 'He come with me.' He jerks his head at Alexei.

If anybody expects him to be grateful for Tamáz's offer of help, Lily reflects, they're going to be disappointed. The boy has thrown himself down on the bunk, pulled a blanket over himself and turned his back on the rest of them, the very set of his thin shoulders eloquent of resentment and disappointment.

After a short and not very comfortable silence, Lily gets up. 'I will go to see Yelisaveta now,' she says.

'Lily, it's the middle of the night!' Tamáz protests.

'It's not, it'll be dawn soon.' She pulls aside one of the curtains. 'Look. The sky's definitely lightening.'

He grins. 'If you say so.'

He is right; the sky is still uniformly dark.

'Besides,' she goes on, 'there are always nursing staff on duty, day and night. And Yelisaveta has waited long enough.'

[4] See *The Woman Who Spoke to Spirits*.

He gets up too. 'You should not go alone.'

'You cannot leave Yakov,' she says sternly, leaning towards him and lowering her voice. 'Yes, I know the men hunting him are – are no longer a threat, but left alone, he may well run off again. And,' she reminds him, 'you have promised to help him.'

It is stretching the truth a little, but Tamáz acknowledges that, in essence, this is exactly what he did.

Alexei says quietly, 'I will stay here, Miss Lady. Yakov will sleep, perhaps' – he glances at the still form – 'and I will keep watch.'

She is halfway up the little ladder leading up to the deck when she remembers, and straight away she wonders how on earth she forgot; it can only be because she's so tired. Turning, she bumps into Tamáz, right behind her.

'There is something we have to do,' she says, and, jumping down into the cabin, she shakes Yakov gently by the shoulder. 'Yakov?'

He turns round immediately. 'What?'

She says simply, 'The body belt.'

And, with a sigh, he reaches inside his ragged garments and unfastens it, holding it out to her.

'Do you want me to open the pouch?' she asks. He nods, his eyes on hers shooting briefly to the belt, a look of revulsion crossing his face.

She sinks down beside Tamáz, opens the pouch and tips the contents out on the blanket.

Gold coins, a great many of them. A series of small leather bags with drawstring tops, some containing sapphires, some rubies, but most of them diamonds. One of the diamonds is huge – as big as her little fingernail – and another is only slightly smaller.

She glances at Yakov, but his face is closed up, without any expression.

There is something else: a small oilskin bag, about three or four inches square. There is something inside it; something stiff. She opens the bag and a deeply unpleasant stench emerges. It smells of rotten things; of putrefaction.

She does not want to touch it. It is as if a cloud of darkness has issued from the bag, and with it a sense of deep and ancient evil . . .

'What is *that*?' Tamáz murmurs. Alexei is staring at it, eyes wide, looking slightly sick, but Yakov has turned his head away.

'Cloth, I think,' Lily replies. 'Good wool cloth. Dark in colour. There are places at one edge where you can see it properly.' She pauses, suddenly finding it hard to draw a breath. 'But most of it is soaked in blood, and there are fragments of human flesh adhering to it.'

'But what *is* it?' Alexei echoes Tamáz.

She has closed the oilskin bag. 'I don't know. But it's malign. It is giving off evil.' She looks up, meeting Tamáz's eyes, then Alexei's. 'Isn't it? You must feel it too?'

And both of them nod.

Without a word Tamáz stands up. He opens the stove, digs in a small shovel, and when he extracts it once more there is a heap of glowing embers balanced upon it, red-hot fragments of wood and some small pieces of coal. With a glance at Lily – who nods, understanding – he goes up the steps, across the deck and down onto the quay, and she follows, the oilskin bag in her hand. She senses the presence of Alexei and Yakov behind her, but they are keeping well back.

Tamáz crouches down and places the shovel on the quayside. He blows the embers until they flare up, and she drops the bag right into the flames. At first it dampens them down, but after a few moments their power surges up again, and the bag and its contents begin to smoulder, then to burn.

A deeply foul stench fills the air, and with a gasp, Tamáz grabs her and pulls her back just as a cloud of oily black smoke rises from the pyre. The stench is appalling; instantly Lily begins to feel dizzy, and she has the strange illusion that, beyond the veil of smoke, she is looking at a different world. Gazing into it, quite unable to look away – even as she tells herself this is absolutely impossible and cannot be happening – she thinks for a moment she sees the face of a big man, mouth wide open in a howl of agony, and as he rises swiftly up into the night sky, she makes out a heavily built body whose legs trail away to nothing. For the blink of an eye there are other images . . . an even larger man writhing on a beautifully dressed bed; another man with a deeply haggard face with a pale boy on his lap . . .

Then they are gone.

Tamáz comes as far as the hospital with her.

'You must go back!' she says to him as they stop on the steps. 'I don't trust Yakov not to run, and it's asking a lot of Alexei to prevent him. I *said* you shouldn't have come,' she reminds him.

'I remember,' he replies. She thinks he looks worried, and she is about to reassure him that in fact Yakov was probably exhausted, and would have fallen asleep soon after they left. But then he says, 'That boy, Yakov, there was something he was holding back. I don't think you need worry about him running off; not tonight, anyway. I don't believe there is any chance that he'll leave the safety of my boat. And I don't know why,' he adds, frowning, 'when he knows that the men who were trying to kill him are themselves dead.'

'He's probably just exhausted,' she says, but it doesn't sound very convincing.

She doesn't think Tamáz heard her.

'There is something . . . I sense something amiss in the air,' he says quietly. 'It may be the residue of that – that *thing* that we destroyed.' He shakes his head. 'I'm not sure.'

'We did right,' she says firmly. 'And how wise you were not to burn it on board *The Dawning of the Day*, because—'

Because it emitted something dreadful as it burned, she almost says. Some terrifying substance holding the power to make me see things that weren't there.

But she finds she really doesn't want the reminder.

'I must go in,' she says instead. 'Thank you, Tamáz.'

He smiles. 'No need to thank me.' She is about to head off up the steps but he catches hold of her hand. His face intent now, he says, 'Be careful, cushla.'

He only calls her that occasionally.

She wants to ask what he means, what he senses that she must be careful about, but he tips his hat and turns away.

*   *   *

As Lily predicted, there are nurses on duty despite the hour, although it is a different sister this time who leads her to Yelisaveta's ward. The old woman is awake, fully dressed, sitting on her bed. Her expression is unreadable.

She looks up at Lily.

'You have found him.'

She knows, Lily thinks. 'I have.'

Now the lined old face is alight with joy. 'He is here?' she breathes.

'No. But he is safe. The men who were hunting him are dead.' She reaches under her jacket. 'He sent this for you.'

Yelisaveta grabs the body belt. With flying, fumbling hands she opens the pouch, fingering through the contents. There is a flash as the soft light catches a large diamond.

Then she looks up and hisses at Lily, '*Where is it?*'

'It is no more. Destroyed. Burned.'

Yelisaveta lets out a low wail. '*No!*'

'It was a rotten, foul thing, and two young men have recently been murdered because of it!' Lily whispers. Then, for she can't stop herself: 'Whatever *was* it?'

Slowly Yelisaveta shakes her head. 'I do not know. My son, he bring it home, shut himself away with Abram my husband, much muttering behind closed door, and Abram, he say not for woman to know but this thing is powerful, so very powerful, must be guarded, must be kept safe.' She stops. For a moment her face is haggard with the memory of all that she has lost. 'And I obey,' she concludes softly.

'Your obedience almost cost your grandson his life,' Lily says neutrally.

Yelisaveta looks up. 'He is angry with me?'

'Yes.' Lily hesitates, but it is surely better to tell this sad old woman straight away that the future she is hoping for – expecting – will not happen. 'Yakov has solemnly promised to come to see you,' she says, 'but you should know that he does not want the life of education, long study and lucrative employment that you have in mind for him. Instead he is determined to seek work on the canal boats. It is a good living,' she hurries on, 'and I have a friend who has undertaken to make sure a suitable position is found for the boy.'

She watches as several expressions flash across the old face. Then, with a deep sigh, Yelisaveta says with sad resignation, 'I told you he always like best canals and boats, did I not?'

Lily leaves.

She's exhausted. The early trams are running but as yet they are not very frequent. She starts walking, heading roughly westwards. She finds herself in the Commercial Road, not entirely sure how she got there, when suddenly she's aware of someone right behind her.

And a voice says in accented English, 'Miss Raynor, you have something that does not belong to you. Something I want you to give me.'

Before she can reply, or run, or even turn round, she feels his right arm go around her waist and she looks down to see the glint of a blade, pressed against her belly. With his free hand he reaches down to take hold of her left hand, and he hurries her off the street and into a side alley. He pushes her face-forward against a doorless, windowless expanse of wall and says, 'You have slain my two hunters.'

'Your *hunters*—' She struggles, trying to wrest herself round to look at him, but he is far too strong.

'Did you imagine they were acting alone?' he goes on, speaking right into her ear. 'The man with the scar through the eyelid, the big one with the strength of body but not of brain?'

And now she thinks, no, of course they weren't.

One of the first things Alexei told her about the man with the scar was that he returned to the Mission on the night the first youth was killed: not to fetch his knife, as Alexei thought – which she had always wondered at for surely he would have had it with him already – but to report back to someone else and take fresh instruction.

There were *three* of them lurking around the Mission. The man with the scar and the brute were both the underlings of a third, senior and far more efficient and ruthless man.

She closes her eyes, remembering.

And she thinks she knows who the leader must be.

As if he can pick up her thoughts, the man holding her relaxes his grip a little.

She turns round.

She is staring into the face of the slight young man who, when she first saw him in the Mission, was shuffling the cards. Despite the circumstances he is smiling the same cheerful grin – and this is perhaps the most chilling, terrifying thing about him – and the long fair hair still flops over his forehead.

The fact that he is not what he pretends to be – that he is no amiable, friendly soul but a ruthless killer – is frightening Lily so much that her heart is thumping far too fast and she can hardly breathe.

And he has just demanded she give to him something she does not have in her possession and never did. Something that no longer exists.

Her fear ratchets up until she has to lean against the wall for support. 'What is it that belongs to you that you think I have and should give you?' Lily asks, hoping her assailant won't hear the tremble in her voice.

But he does, because he laughs – and it's not at all a nice laugh – then says, 'Oh, you do have it, and let us not hear any *should* give it to me, as if there was doubt, because I can smell and taste your terror and you will obey me.'

And, hopelessly, Lily thinks, *I can't.*

'You know what it is,' he goes on, leaning over her, the quiet voice breathy in her ear. 'It was in the pouch which the old woman had, which she gave to the little boy, and every instinct informs me that he gave it to you and you will keep it until the old woman is recovered and can keep it safe.'

'There were a quantity of gold coins and jewels in the pouch,' she says. 'Most of the stones were diamonds, and one or two were very large and fine.'

Suddenly his grip tightens, and he sounds like the embodiment of evil as he hisses, 'Do not try to make a fool of me! Every second that you insist on this pretence of ignorance is merely serving to ensure your death will be the harder. *What else was in the pouch?*'

She gasps aloud – she can't help it – because his left hand is on her throat and he has just dug two long, sharp fingernails deep in her flesh. 'Very well!' she cries. 'There *was* something else, but Yakov didn't tell us what it was, even if he knew –

he was disgusted by it – and there was no way of identifying its source, although it had an evil feel to it and—'

She stops. From close behind her he emits a long sigh of satisfaction, and she doesn't think he has even noticed that she's stopped speaking.

'Shall I tell you what it is, Miss Raynor?' he croons in a sing-song voice. 'Would you like to know why my companions and I followed this wretched family right across Russia, over the sea and into the filthy depths of the East End of London?'

He is still holding her throat and she can't speak, so she nods.

'Then let me tell you a story,' he says. 'It took place in the beautiful city of St Petersburg in March of this year, and it concerns a foul band of disobedient, undisciplined rats who had the effrontery to pass a sentence of death on their revered Tsar. It was not the first time they had tried to murder him, but possibly they learned from their past mistakes, and this time they had made more careful preparations. Our beloved Alexander was travelling home in his carriage when a bomb was thrown beneath it. Bystanders were injured, a mounted soldier in attendance on the Tsar later died, but the Tsar was not hurt. Despite being implored not to, such was the quality of the man that he insisted on alighting from the safety of his bulletproof carriage to see what damage had been done and to address the wounded.' There is a sudden pause, and then in a voice that breaks with emotion, the man says, 'He said – Alexander said, bless him, "Thank God, I am untouched," but even as the words left his lips a second bomb was thrown, and both the Tsar and the devil who had thrown it fell mortally wounded to the ground. The beloved man who had ruled our country so well and so fairly lost both of his legs, torn away from him from the knee downwards, and his belly was laid open, ripped by fragments of metal.' Another pause, and Lily hears what sounds like a sob. 'He was taken back to the Palace and he died shortly afterwards.'

'I am sorry for his death,' Lily manages to whisper.

Her assailant gives her a rough shake. 'So you should be, so should everybody!' he says in a suppressed scream.

There is silence for a moment, then, his voice resuming its

narrator's tone, he says, 'Unbeknownst to all those guarding and tending the Tsar, there were other revolutionary rats among the throng. As the crowd milled around, one of these devils spotted something that had been overlooked. It was a piece of heavy woollen fabric, soaked in blood and with pieces of flesh adhering to it, and it was a fragment of the dead Tsar's trousers.'

Lily thinks, *So that is what it was.*

She struggles against the sudden urge to vomit.

'A mythology quickly grew up around this piece of material,' her captor continues, 'and it is believed to have a power of its own.'

Perhaps it does, Lily thinks. *After all, each of us sensed evil.*

'I told you, did I not, that the assassin was mortally injured?'

'Yes,' she whispers.

'As was his co-conspirator who found the fragment of cloth. His name was Vladimir Grovt, may the Devil torment him, and after the blast he was taken away and crudely patched up so that he could later be tortured into revealing the names of his co-conspirators. But he held out, he refused to give them up, and he tore off the bandages and re-opened his wounds so that he bled to death only days after the Tsar was murdered.'

Lily sends up a silent prayer for the killer and the victim, her heart aching with pity for both of them.

'Vladimir Grovt died in torment,' her assailant goes on, telling his dreadful take in a calm, level tone, 'but he clutched the piece of cloth until the end. With his last breaths, holding the bloody fragment in his right hand against his heart, he screamed out a curse. Shall I tell you what he said?'

Lily nods.

'He screamed, "We have killed the Tsar and now the curse is laid on those destined to rule after him, that every one shall end his days before his time and by fatal sickness or bloody violence."' His face suddenly right up against her cheek again, he says urgently, 'Do you see? Do you see what this means, why this relic is so vitally important?' Before she can answer he pushes on. 'The curse that has been bound up within it spells ruin to our precious Alexander's descendants, condemning as it does each successive Tsar to die prematurely and in agony, just like the one who has so recently been killed.'

He has almost managed to convince her; such is the power of his words that she has very nearly been swept up in his story; very nearly believes him.

But a nagging little thought won't leave her alone.

She says – and now she sounds as calm as he did – 'I can very well understand why the revolutionaries were so intent on keeping this relic safe.' It had come to Yelisaveta as the last surviving adult, she realizes: Yefrem had it in his keeping, or perhaps he shared the guarding of it with his father Abram, and at some point one of them tucked it away in the body belt's pouch with the gold and the jewels. In this way it passed to Rachel after their deaths, and to Yelisaveta after hers. The two men had kept the macabre contents of the oilskin bag from their womenfolk – it is, Lily reflects, just the sort of thing men do – but Yelisaveta sensed it had great power, even if she didn't know what it was.

Then, finally, Yelisaveta gave it to Yakov.

She swallows and, sensing his growing impatience, continues. 'They guarded it because of the curse, and it is for precisely the same reason that you and your companions have so ruthlessly sought it. But I cannot accept,' she says – and now her voice grows firmer, harder – 'that men like you believe in cursed relics! You are servants of the state, agents of the Tsarist regime, not superstitious peasants!'

There is what seems like a long pause.

Then he gives a horrible chuckle. And says, 'Clever, Miss Raynor. No, you are quite right, and, speaking for myself, I have no faith in curses and the power of bloodstained relics.' Swooping right up close again, he adds, 'But the Russian people do, you see, and such an item carrying such a charge has the potential to do so much harm.' He takes a breath. 'And so, now I would like you to give it into my keeping, if you would be so kind.'

She can't. It's gone. Tamáz would not destroy it aboard *The Dawning of the Day* by burning it on the stove because it carried evil. Instead he took it out onto the solid stone of the quay and got a good blaze going before laying the piece of heavy fabric, stiff with the blood and the flesh of the dead Tsar Alexander II, on the top. And they had all watched, Yakov, Alexei, Tamáz and Lily, while it burned away to nothing.

And if any of the others also saw what Lily saw – for all that she told herself very firmly it was her imagination – they had the sense not to admit it.

For herself, she knows it will be a long time before she forgets the dark cloud that rose up from the fire; the cloud that seemed incredibly to mould itself into the shape of a tall man writhing in agony whose long legs no longer had feet . . .

Her assailant has released his very tight hold and she turns to face him.

She says, 'I have to reach beneath my garments to get my hands to where I have hidden the body belt. I can't imagine you will have the decency to turn your back, but you must at least give me some room.'

He steps back. As she had thought, his eyes remain fixed on her.

She bends right over, runs her hands up the inside of her left boot and grasps the leather-bound brass hilt of the long, fine, very sharp boning knife that once belonged to her grandmother. Pretending to fumble, intent on giving herself time, she mutters, 'The buckle is stiff, I—'

And even as he grunts with furious impatience, she straightens up and thrusts the knife right in his face.

He is a trained agent of the state and his instincts are sharp and precise, and he backs out of the way of the lethal blade. But even the small movement away from her gives her space, and she pushes herself off from the wall and flees out of the passage and into the street.

The Commercial Road is busier now than when she last walked down it, and, dashing straight across it without looking, she very narrowly avoids a drayman's wagon being trundled along at some speed by a pair of huge greys. There is a shout, another shout that turns into a scream, and all at once there are people crowding all round her, pushing her, shoving at her, and a rough man's voice yells very loudly, 'Get out of the way, woman, damn and blast you, can't you see there's a man badly injured lying there in the road?'

Shaking, trembling, she turns round.

She managed to escape the enormous horses and the heavily laden wagon.

But the fair-haired, card-playing, brightly smiling agent of the Tsarist state police has not been so lucky. In the desperate urgency of his haste to catch her, he didn't look either. She does not know what hit him, a horse's hoof or a wagon wheel, but whichever it was has crushed his head and the fine blond hair is already stained red and cream with blood and brain matter.

She's near the place somewhere along the Commercial Road where there is a scrap-metal yard, and over the gates is a huge sign that reads *Smith and Sons, Fine Quality Scrap Metal Every Need Served.* She has passed it more than once in the course of the last days.

She remembers wondering if these Smiths are Felix's Smiths. If the Smith in *Smith and Sons* is Felix's grandfather Derek Smith. *Was* Derek Smith, she corrects herself, her shocked mind for some reason grasping this minor detail and thrusting it into much greater importance than it merits, since Felix's grandfather is dead.

She walks up to the high wall of the yard. There are signs of activity within, as there always appear to be, and she can hear voices, men's and women's, and the high-pitched, excited chatter of children. It sounds as if there is quite a gang of them . . .

The gates are shoved open and the people within appear, spilling out onto the street. They all carry bags, even the smallest children, and they are all talking, laughing, joking with each other. There is a holiday mood about them.

Lily is desperately aware that she needs to melt away before the police arrive to tend the dead man and start asking everyone in the vicinity what happened, what they saw, whether there was anyone with the man and if so where they are now because they must be questioned.

I was with him. The knowledge of this makes her tremble. *He accosted me, pulled me into the alley, I escaped and ran into the road and he followed.*

It is not all that likely – or at least she fervently hopes it isn't – that anyone actually saw her dart out just before the fair-haired man ran after her. But still she can't seem to stop herself imagining the over-helpful witness, flattered to have the full attention of a policeman, saying, *Oh, yes, I saw what happened! He was running after a woman, thirtyish, fair hair under a little hat, dark clothing, knife in her hand.*

With a gasp, for she is still clutching the boning knife, Lily slips into a doorway and puts it back in its place inside her boot.

It really isn't something to be seen with in these streets, even if she hasn't just escaped from a dead man trying to kill her.

The people from the scrap-metal yard are milling round her now, shoving and pushing on the pavement and spilling into the road. Not really pausing to think – she's not sure she is capable of thinking just now, not with any sort of rationality anyway – she falls into step among them. There are a few men, quite a lot of them well advanced in years, but the majority of the cheery group are women and children, ranging in age from adolescence to toddlers and even some babies in arms.

She seems to be preoccupied with whether or not they are Felix's Smiths, although quite *why* this is so important she can't just now work out . . .

One of the young women carries a very young baby on her breast in a cloth sling, and a weighty-looking canvas bag hangs off her shoulder. The bag keeps slipping, and the young woman is colourfully cursing it, making those around her laugh.

Lily says, 'Shall I carry the bag for you?'

The woman spins round to glare at her. 'Who are you?'

'Lily Raynor,' she replies.

'You going my way, then?'

'I don't know. Where are you going?'

'Station. Charing Cross station.' The baby begins to whimper, and the woman cups its downy head in a tender hand.

'Boy or girl?' Lily asks. They are still striding along, and the woman's canvas bag is still sliding off her shoulder.

'Girl.' The woman's strong face softens as she looks down at her daughter. 'Rose. Rosie, we call her.'

'Six weeks or so?'

'Seven.'

'She's hungry,' Lily says. 'She'll need feeding and changing, once you get to the station. I'll help, if you like. I used to be a nurse.'

The woman eyes her for what seems like rather a long time. Then, apparently approving what she sees, says, 'All right.'

Silently she hands the canvas bag to Lily.

'You going hopping and all?' she asks as they march on.

And now the confusing mist in Lily's head suddenly clears and she knows why she needed to know who these people are. They are heading for the hop fields, as some wise part of her brain seems already to have worked out, and if they are Felix's Smiths, then perhaps, just perhaps, they are bound for the hop-farming village where Noah Smith lives.

Where Felix is.

Something twists and tugs quite hard in Lily, and she realizes how much she needs Felix just now.

She says to the woman beside her, trying to sound as if it doesn't really matter, 'Are you Smiths? I bumped into you coming out of the yard,' she adds.

Again that hard, assessing look. But then the woman says, 'Yes. Going to the hop fields, like I said. Nice in the Kent countryside, it is. Go every year, big, extended family group of us.'

Lily hesitates for a moment, then says, 'I know someone who's a member of your family.'

The woman stares suspiciously at her. 'Who?' she demands.

'His name's Felix Wilbraham and Derek Smith was his grandfather.'

Lily hasn't noticed – she really isn't herself on this surreal night – but several of the men and women walking nearest to the woman with the baby have been listening. As Lily utters Felix's and Derek Smith's names, quite a few of the men react, and there are some exclamations and a lively exchange of remarks. It seems Felix's name is well known within his family, and several men say they know, or perhaps know of, Felix and that dear old Grandad Derek was very proud of him and never stopped talking about him. Lily tries not to take this lively chatter too seriously, for she has detected that the men are rather well oiled, one or two of them advancing on her in a decidedly flirtatious manner, and she reckons it's quite possible they'd claim anyone she cared to mention as a long-lost relation.

But all the same she asks, 'Where are you going?'

She knows they're going to say Crooked Green, and it's exactly what they do say.

'Felix is down there already,' she says before she can change her mind. 'Is it all right if I come with you?'

NINETEEN

L ily is sitting in a very crowded and not at all comfortable carriage on a very early train out of London heading for a place called Paddock Wood, where apparently there will be a second train to take them up a branch line to a small rural station called Elm Wood.

She spends a while wondering if trains always run down into Kent at this hour of the morning, or whether special ones are put on for the hop-pickers. Then she realizes that short of asking some guard or porter she is not likely to find out, and discovers she doesn't much care anyway.

It's that sort of a night. Or, she corrects, looking out of the window, very early morning. There is still that sense of unreality about everything that is happening, which she attributes in part to the fact that she has been up all night – and it's been a very eventful night too – and in part to having accepted a couple of slugs from the bottle of spirits that the man next to her has kept offering.

The Smiths have started singing now. She joins in, feeling her usual inhibitions about singing in public (unless it's in church) tumbling away.

Maybe it's been more than a couple of slugs of spirits . . .

The train taking the hop-pickers on from Paddock Wood is late arriving, and Lily joins the short queue purchasing mugs of tea on the platform. The tea is powerfully strong and someone has put sugar in it, but it is extremely reviving and she tells herself it is counteracting the effects of the spirits.

Nevertheless, on the little train that takes them into hopping country, she falls into a brief and very deep sleep, head bumping on the shoulder of the man sitting next to her, and when she wakes up – the sensation of the train braking and a loud shout of 'Elm Green! Elm Green' have combined to shake her out of her sleep – discovers she's been dribbling.

But her fellow passengers are preoccupied with gathering up bags, parcels, walking sticks, hats and children, and she doesn't think anybody has noticed.

They set off from the tiny station in a loose file, younger men at the front striding strongly, older men walking more sedately with the women, many of whom are encumbered by children who are rapidly becoming tired and argumentative. Lily is reunited with her new friend – whose name, she discovers, is Agnes, which she hates and so Lily is to call her Aggie – and she is still carrying the canvas bag. Now it feels so heavy on Lily's tired shoulder that she wonders if it's full of stones. Or bricks. Or an enormously weighty fruit cake, or several pounds of potatoes, or—

Someone is shouting up ahead.

'Now what's that all about?' Aggie demands, and she sounds cross. 'Bloody nearly at Crooked Green – it's only just down this lane and across the road, then Nightingale Farm will be in sight – so we don't want any problems now, not when the kids and the oldies are dead on their feet and . . .'

But Lily has heard a very familiar voice. Dumping Aggie's bag, she pushes through the people standing in front of her until she can see past the trio of Smiths who were walking the lead. They are now engaged in lively conversation with the two men standing on the track that winds beneath the overhanging trees on the bank rising to the left.

There is a woman standing between these two men, and it's quite clear they are holding her up.

One of the men bears a resemblance to Felix.

The other one *is* Felix.

He catches sight of her as she breaks out from behind the three Smiths. His face is like a book illustration of surprise: open mouth, wide eyes, hand up to his head.

'*Lily!* Good grief, what on earth are you doing here?' he cries.

She hurries up to him, and she has to battle the strong urge to hug him. 'I found Yakov,' she says. 'He's safe. But I ran into a little spot of trouble.' Oh, heavens, she thinks wildly, what a way to describe that fair-haired killer and that ghastly bloodstained relic he was demanding and that I couldn't give him! 'I'm quite all right,' she adds, although he hasn't actually asked and in fact still looks too shocked to speak. 'But I needed to get away quickly, I was right by your grandfather Derek's yard and these very kind people said I could travel down here with them. So here I am!' she concludes lamely.

The Smith clan have surrounded the woman who was being supported by Felix and the other man, the males being shoved out of the way by their wives, mothers and daughters, who seem to know her and are very clearly disturbed that she seems to have been injured. 'Oh, Dollie, dear old Dollie,' one woman exclaims, 'if anyone's going to get herself into bother, it's you!'

'What's happened? What's wrong with her?' Lily whispers to Felix as the woman – Dollie – is gathered up by the group.

'Tell you in a moment,' he whispers back.

Then, with an apologetic grin, he goes to stand beside the woman, has a brief conversation with her, nods a few times and then returns to Lily, the man who looks like him coming too. The three of them watch as the Smiths and the woman called Dollie head off down the road.

'They'll look after her,' Felix's companion says. 'They've done so before' – he darts a glance at Felix, who nods – 'and she said she wanted to go back to the farm, didn't she?'

'Yes,' Felix agrees. He's still gazing after the woman, who was, Lily reflects in hindsight, very lovely in a wild sort of way, full-figured and with gorgeous auburn hair.

She nudges Felix quite sharply in the ribs. 'What's happened?' she repeats.

He comes out of his reverie, turning to stare at her. 'Sorry, Lily, I just can't believe you're here,' he says vaguely. 'I'm very glad you are,' he adds hastily, 'it's just that I wasn't expecting you, and we've had quite a night.' *You've* had quite a night, she thinks. 'This is my cousin Noah,' he is saying. 'Noah, this is Lily Raynor, founder and proprietor of the World's End Enquiry Agency.'

Noah has been studying her closely. Now he smiles – a lopsided, attractive sort of a smile – and says, 'Delighted, Miss Raynor. You—'

But Felix interrupts. 'You asked what's wrong with Dollie,'

he says, and his voice is full of anger. 'Someone tried to strangle her, in all likelihood the same man who murdered Effie Quittenden.'

'Oh, God!' Lily exclaims. 'Is she in a fit state to walk? Do you want me to go and have a look at her, see if I can help? I used to be a nurse,' she adds, turning to Noah, in case he thinks she's some nosy woman who believes she's better than any man could be at looking after the seriously wounded.

'She'll be all right.' It is Noah who replies. 'She's a strong woman, and she's survived worse than some bugger trying to choke her with a length of twine.' The lopsided smile is back. 'She has Felix here to thank for her survival, however. He found her on the track and seemingly knew what to do.'

There is a short and fairly intense silence. Under cover of the dim morning light, Lily reaches out, finds Felix's hand and squeezes it. It is the best way she can think of to say, *Well done.*

'It was merely what anyone would have done,' Felix mutters. He is squeezing her hand in return.

'Well, I'm grateful to you,' Noah says, 'as everyone else in the family will be when they hear what happened.' Perhaps thinking some light-hearted remark is required to ease the solemn mood, he adds, 'I wasn't ready to put the lovely Dollie in the earth just yet, even in that pretty and peaceful spot up under the far boundary where poor little Effie's buried, so—'

His words have an extraordinary effect on Felix, who jumps as if he's put his hand on a bare electric wire. Spinning round to stare at Noah so fast that Lily is sure she hears his neck crack, he says, 'That's *Effie's* grave?'

'Up under the high hedge with the little wooden cross? Yes, we—'

But Felix's eyes have gone unfocused. He is gazing into the distance. 'I wonder?' he says musingly. 'Any of the locals who cared for her could have put the posies on her grave, but surely, *surely*, this means something?' He spins round to stare at Lily, his eyes narrowed and intent. 'Rosemary for remembrance,' he mutters, 'and there were those long strands of it that I failed to recognize.' Then he demands sharply, 'Flowers, what do they mean?'

Trying to follow his incoherent thoughts, she says, 'Are you referring to the language of flowers? Red roses for true love and that sort of—'

'*Yes*,' he interrupts, impatience making him shout. 'Sorry. Yes. Little pink carnations, marigolds?'

Sensing this is somehow very important, although she can't begin to think why, Lily taps her forehead quite hard to shake up her tired brain. Her beloved Aunt Eliza gave her a little book on flowers and their meanings when she was small and she memorized it . . . 'Pink carnations say, *I'll never forget you*, like rosemary for remembrance, which you just mentioned. Marigolds express profound grief. They are often used in wreaths for the dead, as is a plant called asphodel, which means, *My sorrow will always lie with you in the grave.* Asphodel has white flowers in spring and long, thin green leaves.'

Felix is nodding as she speaks. 'Yes. *Yes.* And now I know where the rosemary came from *because I've seen it growing*!' Suddenly his face lights up and he grabs her shoulders, pulling her towards him and bestowing a smacking kiss right on her lips. 'Oh Lily, my dear, lovely Lily, you're so *clever*!'

Then he is running away up the road, back the way she has just come.

'*Felix!*' The deafening yell comes from Noah, and his voice is powerful and authoritative enough to stop Felix in his tracks. 'Where are you going? What about Miss Raynor?'

'Oh – Lily, would you go back with Noah, please? I'm really sorry but I can't stop to explain now! He ran off, you see, up Badgers' Bank, up there' – he waves his arm – 'and if you go left at the top and take the little path that wiggles behind Newhouse Farm, eventually you can drop down onto Earlyleas Lane without having to go through the village. That's where he went – he *must* have done, because that's where he got the rosemary, and there's also the love-nest with the heart, and maybe I was wrong about M and perhaps he loved Effie and couldn't have her and M was somehow to do with that . . . *I don't know!*' The last three words are a shout of anguish. 'But I've got to go after him and see if he's still there.'

In the shocked silence he leaves behind him, after a moment Noah turns to Lily.

'Before you ask, Miss Raynor, I have no more idea what he's talking about than you have,' he says, and the attractive smile is back. 'However, you look as if you've had a rough few hours, so I suggest I do what Felix asked me to and take you back to my cottage. Cup of tea and a bite to eat, then I'll draw the curtains in my little second bedroom and you can get your head down for a while till Felix comes back and explains himself.'

Lily, drooping with fatigue, thinks that plan sounds like heaven. Noah heads off down the lane, she falls into step beside him. She badly wants to ask if this cottage of his is very far, but, thinking it might sound ungrateful, refrains.

He has picked up on her exhaustion, however. Presently his strong hand goes under her elbow, and soon she is leaning against him.

And eventually they arrive at his cottage.

Felix is running along the path that winds behind Newhouse Farm to emerge onto Earlyleas Lane. His feet pound out a rhythm and his thoughts bang around inside his head to the same beat.

Because he has suddenly understood that the person who killed Effie Quittenden must be full of profound regret. He has put posies on her grave, beneath the tall boundary hedge of the churchyard. His offerings featured rosemary, the plant of remembrance. And marigolds, for grief. And pink carnations and, for all he knows, leaves from that asphodel plant that Lily also mentioned.

The killer will believe that Dollie is dead too.

Will the regret be stirring already? Will he have run away to the abbey ruins to pick more strands of rosemary? To stand in the little secret place where perhaps he dreamed of bringing first Effie, then Dollie, the women he desired so powerfully but could not have?

But that initial M . . .

He is flagging, and with a huge effort forces his exhausted legs to run on.

Effie's real name was Euphemia.

Did her killer have some private pet name for her, one only known to himself? And *who is he*? Bert Quittenden? Harold Marchant? Mick Marchant? George Croucher? Ted Chauncey? Ezra Sleech? Alderidge Cely Leverell?

Such is Felix's state of mind that he forgets for a moment or two that at the time he found Dollie's inert body and the killer broke cover and fled, Alderidge was already dead.

Felix shakes his head, his mind too preoccupied and his urgency too frantic for reasoned thought.

The end of the track looms, he jumps down onto Earlyleas Lane, only to turn off it after a short distance and hurry the last hundred yards up to the abbey ruins.

Approaching the stately old remains, he slows to a trot, then to a walk. The sharp panting of his breath eases. He mops the sweat from his forehead.

Then he marches on through the skeleton of the abbey church, the cloister, the chapter house, refectory and dormitories until he is on the far side of the kitchen garden and beside the gap in the wall where the rosemary bush grows.

Very slowly now he edges forward until he can see over the wall and down into the secret little hollow beyond.

And just as he knew they would be, someone is sitting there, legs drawn up, arms hugging knees, head dropping down, back shaking with deep sobs.

But it isn't anybody that Felix has considered in the role of the killer.

Shock rockets through him, and he experiences a fleeting sense of unreality. *Surely not*, he thinks wildly, *this person is here for some perfectly innocent reason and everything I thought I knew is wrong . . .*

Why, then, demands the answering voice of reason, *the profound grief? The heartbroken sobs?*

And Felix gathers his courage – because he understands now that he's facing a very different sort of threat than the one he was expecting – and slips through the gap in the wall to join Peg Sleech in the secret hollow.

She raises her head as he sits down on the soft grass beside her. 'It's you,' she mutters. Then, leaning towards him slightly as if about to put her head on his shoulder, she says wistfully, 'I'm so tired. It's worn me out, see, the pain, the rage, the guilt.' And the thin body shudders with a vast sigh.

'It's over now, I think,' he says gently.

She nods. 'Yes. Thought you'd probably work it out in the end.'

'I didn't,' he admits. 'Oh, I guessed about the regrets and the grief.' He hesitates. Every instinct tells him she is ready – far more than ready – to confess. If he's wrong and she clams up or, worse, embarks on outraged denials, then he'll just have to face Lily's wrath.

He says quietly, 'You didn't want to kill them, did you?'

She sighs again, and he sees her lips working as she mutters to herself. There is a moment of very fine balance; he hardly dares breathe.

But then, in a surprisingly everyday sort of voice, Peg says, 'No, you're right there.' She shakes her head slowly. 'It just took me over, see, and before I could stop myself, there I was up on the ledge above Badgers' Bank, twine in my hands, and it was like I was outside myself watching as I wound it round those lovely necks.' She starts to sob again, and her head falls onto her raised knees. 'Oh, forgive, *forgive me*!' she wails.

He is afraid for her. Felix doesn't know much about mental illness but the rapid changes of mood are worrying, and he senses Peg is close to a total breakdown. He says gently, 'Why don't you tell me all about it?'

There is quite a lengthy silence. The sobs slowly stop, Peg gulps a few times, then in a very different voice says, 'I fell pregnant, see. Ezra and me had been courting a while, and I knew I shouldn't have let him but he was so handsome, so charming, treated me so *kindly*, and I loved him so much, I *wanted* him so much, I'll admit it, and in the end I just couldn't help myself.'

As she pauses, smiling gently, Felix recognizes two things.

The first is that the drastic change in Peg's voice is because she has somehow transported herself back to the joyful time when Ezra Sleech was courting her.

The second is that, recalling who she is and what her upbringing was like – for she is of course George Croucher's sister – the kindness with which Ezra treated her was undoubtedly the first she had ever received.

And, recalling what Mick Marchant had to say on the subject of George's – and Peg's – brutal father, he wonders what that violent man's reaction would have been to a daughter pregnant outside wedlock. Lust, that was the stark, ugly, brutal word he'd have used to describe Peg's tender love for Ezra. And Felix can't bear even to think about the punishment that would have been meted out to his sinful daughter by that terrible brute who terrorized his defeated wife and his two deeply damaged children in that mean, cold little cottage down at the bottom of Mill Lane . . .

'Ezra said he'd marry me,' Peg says now, breaking in on Felix's dark thoughts. 'Well, if you slip up like I did, you have to marry when you live in a village like Crooked Green. That or one or both of you go away. And Ezra and me, we both belonged here, our parents and their parents lived here, we were bound to the village by ties of kinship and long tradition. And he said he knew I'd be a good wife,' she adds with pathetic eagerness, 'said he'd seen for himself I was a hard worker, had a good head for figures and a green thumb to make the vegetable plot flourish, and he reckoned that the two of us running the Leopard's Head would work out just fine, and it did, it *has*!' She grabs his arm and shakes it quite hard, as if determined to convince him.

'Yes, I can see that,' he says kindly. 'But you said you were—'

He had been going to ask about the pregnancy, but she is talking again, quickly now, faster and faster as if there is a deadline looming.

'We married and settled down and I worked as hard as I could manage, and Ezra did too, and everything would have been all right except I had this crippling sickness, and it wouldn't stop, and then I started having this terrible cramping pain deep down in my belly and it got worse and then in the small hours one morning I woke up and there was blood, and I . . . and I . . .'

She can't go on.

And you went out to the privy in the yard, Felix finishes

for her, *and the contents of your inhospitable womb slipped quietly away.*

Despite what this woman has done, he is filled with profound pity for her.

'I never got pregnant again,' Peg whispers.

Briefly he touches her hand.

'Ezra, he's always liked a pretty face,' she goes on after a while. 'Loves to flirt, hug a slender waist, bestow a friendly pat on a rounded backside, but I always knew, I *knew*' – she repeats the word with such vehemence that Felix wonders if she's trying to convince herself – 'that it went no further, that he wouldn't risk anything more in a place like Crooked Green where eyes are always watching.' She pauses. 'I used to try to be what he wanted,' she says softly. 'I wanted to tell him, here I am, I'm longing for you, I lie here beside you every night just *yearning* for you to turn to me, but all you do is give me a peck of a kiss and a kindly word, tell me you're worn out and then turn away and go to sleep.'

Yes, Felix thinks sadly. I've seen.

And he pictures that moment of recoil, when Ezra leaned away from Peg's face poking out at him on the end of the long, thin neck . . .

'I knew he liked Effie,' she is saying now. 'Well, everyone liked Effie.' There is an ocean of sadness in Peg's tone, as if she can see what makes a young woman loveable and knows full well she hasn't got those elusive qualities. 'Knew too, if I'm honest with myself, that he wouldn't do anything about it other than a bit of flirting, and even that'd stop soon enough once Effie and Abel were wed.' The flat chest rises as Peg breathes in and emits a very deep sigh. 'But then, night of the cricket match, Effie's been there with us most of the day and working alongside Ezra in the bar, and she's just going and Ezra grasps her hand and he says, "Just one little kiss from my pretty, pretty barmaid before she slips away to her sweetheart!" and it's like something just breaks inside me.'

Felix has heard those words before; Peg clearly wasn't the only person in the Leopard's Head that night who remembered them.

'I thought you were looking after Noah Smith?' he says.

'Holding a cold compress to his head where the cricket ball struck him?'

'Oh, I was,' Peg agrees. 'I took good care of him, don't think I neglected my duty. But after a bit he fell deeply asleep, and I reckoned I'd have time enough before he needed tending again.'

'You knew where she would be?' Felix prompts.

'Ah, now then, there I was lucky,' Peg says with a smile. 'I knew she and Abel used to kiss and cuddle in the darkness under the trees up Badgers' Bank, and I ran all the way up there hoping to catch them and get Effie alone once Abel had gone back to Nightingale Farm. But I saw Abel coming towards me as I started up the track – singing, he was, happy as a dog with two tails, walking on air, I reckon – and I thought I was too late. But something made me hide as he went by, then go on beneath the trees till I came to where there's a little ledge, and I clambered up onto that. I sort of knew, somehow, that she – Effie – would be full of happiness too, and that she'd come back to enjoy it just a little longer before going home to that old sod of a grandfather of hers.'

And Effie did go back, Felix thinks, riven with sadness.

Tristram Cox's words sound in his head: *Was it for one more kiss, one more exchange of promises? One last reassurance that their plans would work out? Simply to live again those precious moments with the man she loved?*

If only you'd resisted, Effie, he says silently. If only you'd gone straight to your bed and snuggled down to dream of your beloved Abel.

But you didn't.

He comes out of his sad little reverie.

'And Dollie Turton?' he prompts. His pity for Peg is overshadowed by the memory of that vicious length of twine around the creamy flesh of Dollie's lovely neck. 'Did Ezra want one little kiss from her too?'

The change in Peg takes him totally by surprise. 'That slut! That whore of a woman, in my pub!' she screams. 'Seen off one husband, she has, and doubtless she's after another one, but she's not having mine, oh, no, not her, *not her, NOT HER!*'

The echoes of the wild howling slowly fade and die.

As Peg subsides again, something occurs to Felix.

'This is where you did your courting, wasn't it?' he says quietly. 'You and Ezra? It's how you came to know about the rosemary you put in the posies? Because it's always grown here.'

And Peg nods. 'Yes.' She stretches out her hand and with her forefinger outlines the heart. 'Look.'

'I'm looking,' Felix says. 'I've already seen it. But the initial is M.'

She turns to him, her eyes narrowed in a scathing stare. 'Of course it is,' she says with deliberate slowness, as if he's an idiot.

'But you're called Peg!'

'I wasn't christened Peg, you fool!' she cried harshly. 'What's Peg short for?'

And slowly, sadly, he says, 'Margaret.'

'I went out looking for her earlier,' Peg says. 'Thought she'd be out over Old Abbey House, carrying on with that bloody old Alderidge Cely Leverell.'

'She loathes him,' Felix protests, 'she—'

But he doesn't think Peg hears.

'Didn't find her,' she is saying. 'Saw him, though, all dressed up in his fancy jacket.' She chuckles. 'Wasn't so fancy once I'd pushed him in the ditch.'

And the creeping horror flows through Felix as the woman beside him, surely deranged, rocks herself to and fro as she crows with wild, violent laughter.

TWENTY

ily slowly comes awake.

She has been sleeping so deeply that it takes her several moments to orientate. She lies with her eyes half-open watching the breeze through the window blow the light curtains, then gazing round the little room. She is lying on a brass-framed bed, and someone – Noah presumably – has put a blanket over her. The window is in the opposite wall, the door is to her left. The walls are painted a soft green. Under the window is a very handsome wooden chest – oak, she thinks – and in the corner to the right of it is a wash stand with a bowl and a jug; there is a mirror on the wall above. Getting to her feet, she discovers the jug is full of warm water. She washes her face and hands, then – for there is still plenty of water and she feels grubby after a night in her clothes – she strips and has a more thorough wash. Once she has finished, and re-done her hair, she feels a great deal better and almost totally restored.

Taking a steadying breath, she opens the door to find herself on a tiny landing with another half-open door opposite, the steep stairs in between. Holding on to the banister, she goes down.

She enters what is clearly the main room of the cottage – range, sink, big table, chairs, a settle, a dresser – and the initial impression is that everything is of good quality and well cared-for. There is a bright rag rug on the stone flags and some very beautiful cushions: straight away Lily detects a woman's touch.

Noah has risen from his seat by the table, and she is discomfited that he has obviously seen her staring round his room. Meeting his slightly amused eyes, she says, 'What a very welcoming home,' and he smiles.

'You're thinking that since men never acquire cushions, never mind put them inside such extravagant covers, there must be a woman in residence,' he says.

Since it is precisely what she has been thinking, she feels herself blush.

Noah has turned away and is filling the kettle, sliding it onto the top of the range. Either he was about to make tea anyway, Lily thinks, or he is being supremely tactful.

'No woman in residence just now,' he says presently. He pours the boiling water into the pot. Turning back to face her – and she notices an expression on his handsome face that she hasn't seen before: as if he is filling with some private joy – he says, 'But I am confident now that there very soon will be.'

'You're to be married?' she says, thinking she understands. 'How wonderful, is she—'

But she doesn't finish the question, for the door bursts open and Felix falls into the room.

He pauses for a moment to catch his breath, then says, 'It's Peg. Peg Sleech.'

Just as Lily says, 'Who's Peg Sleech?' Noah says, 'What's Peg Sleech?'

And the pot of tea goes cold as Felix tells them.

After quite a long time – and the making and consumption of a fresh pot of tea – Lily says briskly, 'So she has confessed, she has been taken into custody, but already there is talk of her urgently seeing a doctor before she is questioned further. Have I understood aright?'

'You have,' Felix replies.

'How's Ezra?' Noah asks.

Felix sighs. 'You can imagine. He's racked with remorse because it seems to be his innocent flirting with Effie and Dollie that put them in such peril. That cost poor little Effie her life.' There is a short silence while they think about that. 'People are all telling him he's not to blame, not really, but I don't think he believes them.'

Lily, watching the two men, perceives that they both know a great deal more about this business than she does, but she does not think this is the moment to ask for a full explanation: there will be time for that when she and Felix are back at Hob's Court.

Remembering the auburn-haired woman someone – this Peg

Sleech, of course – had tried to strangle, she says, 'Is Dollie all right?'

'She's recovering,' Noah says. 'I went out to see her while you were asleep, Miss Raynor, and, I'll admit, to greet all the others of my extensive family who are arriving in the village. She's strong,' he says, just as he said out in the lane under the trees. 'Don't worry about our Dollie.' And he gives her that smile again.

And – possibly because it makes her realize again what an attractive man he is – it reminds her. 'You were about to reveal some very happy news, Mr Smith, when Felix burst in,' she says. 'Will you now share it with both of us?'

'Gladly.' That look of joy is back. Turning to Felix, he says, 'I'm to be married, Felix. You haven't met her but—'

'Oh yes I have,' Felix interrupts. He is looking at his cousin with deep affection and . . . yes, it has to be admitted, and a certain amount of envy. Or so it seems to Lily. 'I didn't tell you,' Felix continues, 'but I saw you with her, the first time I came here. I thought from what you said later that she was Dollie Turton, and I didn't realize my mistake until I was summoned to Old Abbey House by Alderidge Cely Leverell and met his beautiful wife.'

'If this is the woman you are to marry, Mr Smith' – even in her own ears Lily's tone sounds impossibly prim – 'how can this be if she already has a husband?'

Noah and Felix turn to her with identical grins. 'He's dead,' they chorus.

And she can't think why they both look so cheerful about it; something else, she tells herself, to ask Felix once they are back in the office.

'Mariah will own this cottage now, I suppose,' Felix is saying to Noah. 'How will that be, once you are man and wife?'

Noah is grinning. 'Spinfish Cottages haven't been a part of the Cely Leverell estate since my father bought them off Alderidge's father more than thirty years ago,' he says.

'Alderidge's father *sold* them?' Felix sounds incredulous. 'But—'

'He wasn't given much choice,' Noah says. 'Father had

become aware of . . . certain matters that old Percival Rowley Cely Leverell would much rather did not become commonly known. Oh, don't imagine Father blackmailed him or in any way cheated him,' he adds swiftly. 'He offered a fair price and old Percival Rowley recognized that it was in his interests to accept. So numbers 1 and 2 Spinfish Cottages became the property of the Smith family, and it now seems highly likely that's where they'll remain.'

Lily has been aware of light, hurrying footsteps approaching, and as Noah finishes speaking, the door opens again and a woman that she can only describe as radiant stands on the step. Oh, and beautiful: very beautiful, with pale hair, a creamy complexion and a strong-looking, fine figure. 'Noah, I'm quite sure several people in the village saw me but I don't care any more, I—' Belatedly she becomes aware that there are two more people in Noah's house. 'Mr Wilbraham,' she says politely, 'How nice to see you again.'

'And you too, madam,' Felix replies. 'May I present my colleague, Lily Raynor? Lily, this is Mrs Cely Leverell.'

'Mariah,' the woman corrects him rather firmly, stepping forward to shake Lily's hand. Then, turning back to Felix: 'Do I take it that your enquiries concerning Effie Quittenden were not in fact those of a journalist?'

'No,' Felix replies. 'Sorry. Lily is the proprietor of the World's End Enquiry Bureau in Chelsea, and the Bureau was engaged by Jared Spokewright to prove that his brother Abel was innocent of Effie's murder and wrongly hanged.' His voice grows stronger as he speaks, Lily notices, and, glancing at his expression, she thinks that this case has really touched him, and his emotions at having achieved what he set out to do affect him deeply.

She thinks no worse of her friend and colleague for this; in fact, she thinks a very great deal more.

Lily and Felix are back at 3, Hob's Court.

Before they left the Kent countryside, Felix visited the telegraph office in Binhurst to send word to Jared Spokewright. The message consisted of four words: *Innocence established. Full confession.*

As the day is ending, Jared arrives. He is out of breath, flushed and he smells rather powerfully of alcohol. Felix, who lets him in, suspects a celebratory drink or two have already been imbibed.

Jared stands in front of Lily's desk, cap in his hands, and, looking first at Felix and then at Lily, simply says, 'Thank you. You cannot know what this means to us.'

'I believe we can, Mr Spokewright,' Lily says. Felix notices that her eyes are glistening.

After a moment, Jared says, 'Who was it?' and Felix tells him.

He can't seem to take it in. He keeps shaking his head, repeating, 'Peg? Peg Sleech? *Peg?*'

Felix takes pity on him. 'We will send you a full report very soon, Mr Spokewright. It is a sorry story, and perhaps now is not the time to give you the full account.'

Jared turns to him, his face a picture of confusion. 'Yes,' he says, 'yes, I reckon that's for the best.' He smiles – a huge beam of a smile – and adds, 'Right now I'm that glad I don't know if I'm on my head or my heels, and even if you did tell me, I'd have to ask you to repeat it.' He tries unsuccessfully to stifle a beery burp.

'Go home,' Lily says kindly. 'Go and be with your mother and your family.' She stands up, moving round her desk and extending her arm to shake his hand. But the formality of a handshake won't do for Jared, who lurches towards her, enfolds her in his arms and gives her a very enthusiastic kiss, instantly letting her go and, blushing furiously, muttering his apologies.

He is still very red in the face as Felix sees him out. On the step he turns, and, eyes intent on Felix's, says, 'You'll have your payment directly, Mr Wilbraham.' Then he adds fervently, 'By God, you've earned it.'

Then with a salute he leaps down the steps and hurries away.

Over the weeks since their return from Crooked Green, Lily and Felix have found the time for each to tell the other the full story of their respective cases. Felix has been horrified

– again – that once more Lily has been in grave danger, and he can still be heard occasionally muttering that he doesn't want her risking her life in this way, it's just not right.

Since the chance that one's wellbeing might occasionally receive a temporary threat appears to Lily to be part and parcel of what she does for a living – which she loves more and more as cases such as that of the missing Yakov come her way and are successfully concluded – she is doing her best to ignore both Felix and the mutterings.

Tamáz understands, she reflects one morning when Felix has none too tactfully suggested they should vet their cases more carefully in future to ensure it is he and not Lily who runs into danger. Tamáz also fears for her safety – she knows because he's said so – but appears to appreciate that she won't stop doing what she does any more than he would abandon *The Dawning of the Day* and take work ashore.

The Bureau has a visit from Yelisaveta Hadzibazy, fully recovered and looking a great deal better than when Lily last saw her. She presents Lily with a cheque, and it is in a sum larger than Lily was expecting. 'You find grandson, my Yakov,' Yelisaveta says simply. 'No money can pay for this.' Then, disarmingly, she leans closer to Lily and confesses that the Bureau's fee was largely funded by the coffers of Lady Venetia Theobald's Mission to Limehouse, via the intervention of the Reverend James Jellicote.

(Yelisaveta, Lily reflects afterwards, is thus still in possession of almost all of those gold coins and precious jewels.)

She asks Yelisaveta about Yakov's future. With a dark scowl of disapproval, Yelisaveta replies that Yakov is diligently complying with all of Tamáz's conditions, that the lad is still in regular contact with him – Yelisaveta refers to him scornfully as 'That boatman' – and that, with Yelisaveta's grudging permission, Tamáz regularly takes the boy on trips aboard *The Dawning of the Day* when Yakov's other commitments allow.

Remembering Yakov – both the good and bad elements – Lily does not think she needs to worry about *his* future.

* * *

The Reverend Jellicote brings news of Alexei.

Lily's last sight of the young man was when she hurried away from *The Dawning of the Day* in the very early morning to find Yelisaveta and tell her Yakov had turned up, unharmed and, now, safe. She and Tamáz had left Yakov asleep, and Alexei was watching over him. Tamáz later reported that Alexei had left the next day, and for a disturbingly long time nobody had seen him. Lily had tried not to worry too much – all three of the men who might have done him harm were dead – but her last thoughts every night were for him, and often she breathed a short prayer for his safety.

But then James Jellicote arrives one day to say Alexei has turned up at the Mission. When asked where he had been, the young man simply said he'd been keeping out of the way; discussing this rather opaque statement, Lily and the vicar conclude that Alexei feared other agents of the state might well follow where the first three had led, and decided it was wise to remain out of anyone's sight for a spell.

'What is he doing now?' Lily asks.

James Jellicote smiles. 'For the moment, he is officially in the employ of Lady Venetia's Mission, being paid a wage for doing what he was already doing so efficiently and diligently, which is helping those newly arrived from his former homeland to find their way in their new lives. His command of the English language,' he adds, 'is improving all the time.'

'I'm so glad!' Lily exclaims. 'And he's living at the Mission, is he?'

James Jellicote's smile turns rueful. 'No, Miss Raynor. A room was offered, but Alexei declined, saying he already had somewhere.' Studying Lily's expression, he adds softly, 'I do not think we have to fear for young Alexei. He will be all right.'

And, thinking back later over all of her dealings with Alexei, Lily concludes that the vicar is quite right.

Peg Sleech is in custody. She has confessed to Effie Quittenden's murder and the attempted murder of Dollie Turton, but there is grave doubt whether she will face trial, for apparently she is now far down the path into mental darkness. Wherever she ends up, Felix and Lily agree, it is to be hoped she will be treated with kindness.

A month after their return to London, Felix and Lily treat themselves to a day out. They take a succession of trains deep into the Sussex countryside to a tiny village on the South Downs, so that Felix can honour his promise to tell the Reverend Tristram Cox the outcome of his enquiries in Crooked Green.

Tristram Cox has already heard the news, but nevertheless he is gratified that Felix has come to see him.

'I'm sorry it took so long,' Felix says. Lily can see he is embarrassed.

'I expect you have been busy,' the Reverend Cox replies magnanimously.

And – mystifyingly – asks Felix if he's had second thoughts about the choir.

In the months after the conclusion of the case, the official process of clearing Abel Spokewright's name grinds very slowly into motion, but it's not fast enough for Lily.

She remembers the very good turn that she did last year for the very important member of society. She recalls how when he left after their one brief late-night meeting, he said, 'This is not the first time that I have heard good things of the World's End Bureau, Miss Raynor, and I very much doubt it will be the last. Virtue is its own reward, they say, but if I can assist your fortunes in any way, I shall.'

Well, she is perfectly aware he has been assisting the Bureau's fortunes since – all those sordid society divorce cases – and she is grateful for the work. However, she has yet to ask a really big favour of him, and she reckons now is the time.

She sits down late one evening after Felix has gone home and writes a carefully worded letter. She sets out the facts – which are indisputable – and, playing down the Bureau's role (for she is quite sure he will check for himself), she describes poor Mrs Spokewright, her shame at having a hanged son and her enduring grief over there being no grave she can visit

and where she can lay flowers and sit in quiet communion
with her dead child. 'I understand that a posthumous pardon
is to be issued,' Lily's letter goes on, 'which is, of course,
Abel's due in the light of Peg Sleech's confession. However,
I believe that an even greater comfort would be given to his
mother by having the poor young man's body removed
from the prison graveyard and buried somewhere out in the
world, the location to be selected by Mrs Spokewright.'

She is tempted to say that if her illustrious correspondent
will grant this kindness, she will not trouble him again. She
resists: you never know when having the ear of the Prime
Minister might come in handy.

Before there is time for second thoughts, she signs off, blots
her letter, addresses the envelope and sticks on a stamp. Then
she slips out of 3, Hob's Court and puts the letter in the box
to await the early collection.

She doesn't expect a reply, which is just as well since he
doesn't send one. However, early in December she receives a
letter from Jared Spokewright in which he says that his
brother's body is no longer in an anonymous grave inside
Lewes Gaol. It is in a place chosen by the family, close enough
for Mrs Spokewright to visit regularly, and having her son
thus returned to her has brought her a measure of peace.

He sends his heartfelt thanks. And reveals where this place is.

It is a week before Christmas. Felix and Lily have come down
to Crooked Green for Noah and Mariah's wedding. It's
happening rather too soon after Alderidge's demise to accord
with convention, but for one thing Mariah is pregnant and
for another neither she nor Noah appears to give a fig for
convention.

Felix and Lily are deliberately early for the service. They
arrive at All Saints' Church before anyone else, with the
exception of a group of middle-aged and elderly villagers –
largely female – who have arrived even earlier to claim the
best viewpoint by the lychgate.

Felix leads the way across the churchyard to the grave over
on the far side under the boundary hedge. The little wooden

cross now lies on top of the grave, and it has been replaced at the head by a gravestone and right beside it – as close as two people lying in a double bed – is a new grave.

On it is written this:

Sacred to the memory of Euphemia Quittenden
"Effie"
of this village, 1862–1880
and to
Abel Spokewright
of East London, 1859–1880
They loved each other in life
And are together now in death.

Felix stares at it, and his mind fills with the two tragic young people interred beneath it. He never met either of them, but he has been deeply affected by the emotions of others towards them: all those men, led by Jared Spokewright, who proclaimed Abel's innocence so loudly and persistently; the people of Crooked Green, who all spoke so fondly of the sweet-natured girl with a dimpled smile and a kind word for everyone.

As he has thought so many times before, once again Felix thinks about the savage indifference of the world, that allows the ruthless, the cruel, the self-obsessed and the simply unkind to prosper and live to a ripe old age, while life is ripped away from people like Effie and Abel before they have had a chance to fulfil their promise. He feels his eyes fill with tears, but he does not brush them away.

Lily, beside him, seems to have noticed. She moves closer, takes hold of his hand. After a moment or two she passes him a delicate linen handkerchief that smells of lavender water.

'I understand,' she whispers, her voice full of compassion.

They stand in silence together for some time.

Then she nudges him. 'Felix, I don't want to break into your reflections, but I've just seen your cousin Noah striding under the lychgate wearing a very elegant suit, and I believe you told me you are to be his groomsman.'

It is so typically Lily, Felix thinks. The quiet sympathy,

then the practical kindness. He wipes his eyes and, turning to give her a smile to demonstrate to her that he's all right now, hurries away to where Noah is already looking round for him.

Lily lets them go on together into the church. She walks slowly over to the path, watching as the guests arrive and follow the groom and his groomsman inside. When the pews are almost full and the vicar in his starched white surplice is moving to stand before the altar, she goes in and sits down in the back row.

And as the organ begins a very familiar hymn, she turns to see the beautiful bride, radiant with happiness, start her walk up the aisle.

AUTHOR'S NOTE

Tsar Alexander II died aged sixty-two on 1 March 1881 in St Petersburg, his legs blown off by an assassin's bomb.

His successor Tsar Alexander III died aged forty-nine in November 1894, of terminal kidney disease which was said to be the result of blunt-trauma injury sustained by the Tsar in a train crash in 1888.

His successor Tsar Nicholas II died aged fifty on 17 July 1918, assassinated with his family at Ekaterinburg.

The boy who would have succeeded him, his son who had been the Tsarevich Alexei, died with him by the same means.